Impending Love and Lies

by

Laura Freeman

Impending Love Series

This is a work of fiction. Names, characters, places, and incidents are either the product of the author's imagination or are used fictitiously, and any resemblance to actual persons living or dead, business establishments, events, or locales, is entirely coincidental.

Impending Love and Lies

COPYRIGHT © 2016 by Laura Freeman

Cover Art by *Debbie Taylor*

The Wild Rose Press, Inc.
PO Box 708
Adams Basin, NY 14410-0708
Visit us at www.thewildrosepress.com

Publishing History
First American Rose Edition, 2016
Print ISBN 978-1-5092-1044-2
Digital ISBN 978-1-5092-1045-9

Impending Love Series
Published in the United States of America

Cole was different.

She had captured his imagination. She was seductive with every confident movement, but her reaction to his brazen invitation to share the bed had been outrage. He couldn't be the first to make a proposition to spare her a life of drudgery. "A beautiful woman like you shouldn't have to work."

Her hand remained on the rung, but she turned to face him. Her breasts rose with a tired sigh, straining the seams of her bodice. "Are you going to whisk me away to your castle, decorate me with jewels, and dress me in silk gowns? I've had my fill of romantic lies." Cole's voice cracked in a husky tremor of pain, and her eyes glistened. "You're missing a button from your coat, your sleeve needs mended, and your trousers have been patched. When I marry, and I said marry, it will be a man of wealth and prestige not a beggar who can't afford the fare for the train."

Blake stared as the fortune hunter escaped, her frayed hem swaying above her bare feet. She had high ambitions for a canal brat. She couldn't write her name, but she could count the coins in a man's purse. Beneath the disguise of his beggar's garb, she might have seen the heavy money bag thickening his middle.

Praise for Laura Freeman

"The scenes where Logan talks to young veterans of the First Battle of Bull Run, and Jem organizes the cleaning of the entire makeshift hospital ward in an afternoon, are powerful and convincing."

~Akron Beacon Journal

~*~

"The author obviously did a tremendous amount of research before tackling this book. Not only was I entertained, I learned quite a bit about the War Between the States."

~Dorothy Markulis, reporter

~*~

"I thoroughly enjoyed this book. Clever banter, strong characters, and a great detail to history pulled me in. I couldn't put the book down."

~Devon McKay

~*~

"Wow! What a rollercoaster ride!"

~GumboMom

~*~

"The author did a great job of weaving elements of humor into the scenes in the book with ease."

~Cocktails and Books

Dedication

To Civil War reenactors
who bring history to life.

Chapter One

Blake Ellsworth spotted the two mercenaries at the depot, searching the crowd, waiting for him to board the train so they could kill him. The Cassell brothers were stocky brutes armed with pistols and knives, eager to cut a man to shreds, slowly if time allowed. He'd escaped their clutches in Kentucky and Central Ohio, but like bloodhounds, they had dogged his trail. Confederate deserters turned opportunists, Buck and Clyde weren't going to forfeit the generous reward for retrieving the money strapped around his waist. Or if greed was their master, they would keep it all. But they would have to wrestle the belt from his lifeless body before he would willingly surrender his gold.

The train was the fastest way north, but he'd have to find an alternate mode of transportation to Cleveland. The sign on the depot read Akron, Ohio. He was in abolitionists' territory, the former home of John Brown, who had planted the seeds of war. Blake had followed the battle news religiously. After the defeat at Bull Run, President Abraham Lincoln called for three-year enlistments.

Battle lines were being drawn in 1862 with both sides testing for strengths and weaknesses.

Blake adjusted the pouch tied around his waist. The gold was heavy, but he didn't trust banks. Local bonds and currency could be counterfeit or not honored by other banks. His father had trusted a banker with his life savings only to have him empty all the customers' accounts and head for Europe.

An honorable man, Loren Ellsworth had worked to pay off his debts, but his death more than a year ago had left Blake in charge of his father's properties and bills.

Only twenty-three, Blake did his best to manage the family-owned hotels he had inherited. He had promised his father he would support his stepmother and spoiled stepsister. But his heart was elsewhere. Drawn by the beat of the drummer, Blake had wanted to enlist in the Union army, but his training at West Point had taught him duty and honor first. His own desires would have to wait.

In Southern territory, the Lucky Gambler hotel had been difficult to visit, but with victories at Memphis and Cumberland Gap earlier in the month, Blake had traveled to Tennessee to collect revenue from the neglected property.

Although The Lucky Gambler was no longer under enemy control, Blake jumped at the offer from J.P. Smith to buy the hotel. The payment in gold had made him wary, and his instincts proved correct. After Blake transferred the deed, a loyal servant warned him Smith had hired two men to attack him and steal the money once he was past the Union sentries.

The gold had belonged to the Confederacy and had been *misplaced* during the retreat. Both sides sought to recover the stolen coins, and the hotel was being watched by spies from the Union and Confederacy. Smith had been waiting for an inconspicuous carrier when Blake had arrived, served on a platter for his plan.

Sentries searched Blake's bag but didn't think to search the young gentleman dressed in a starched white shirt and dark wool suit. Beneath the frock coat and oversized vest, the money belt was carefully packed with cotton to silence any jingling of the coins.

Blake wasn't going to return the stolen gold to the Confederacy or donate it to Union coffers. As payment for the Lucky Gambler, no one was going to take it, especially the two men at the depot. The money would purchase a replacement hotel in Yankee territory, a safe investment, if he wasn't killed.

The train station was on the rise of a steep hillside sloping toward the center of town and its canal. Pulled by mules through a man-made ditch, the shallow boats were slow, but he'd be in Cleveland in two days. He'd buy Timothy Scroggs' inn on the shore of Lake Erie with the gold. Scroggs wouldn't ask why it was stamped with CSA. Gold was honored whether it belonged to the Union or Confederacy.

He walked west along the steep descent of Market Street. He'd been in Akron a couple summers ago with his father scouting properties, looking for investments, but nothing was familiar. The charred remains of former shops stood as reminders of how quickly fire could destroy wooden buildings. Large commercial structures, made from stone cut from nearby quarries and brick formed from the abundance of clay, offered rental space for shops and offices. Akron was benefiting from the war and bursting at its seams with goods to transport, whether by train or canal boat.

He reached Howard Street and followed the boats making their way through a series of closely-placed locks down the staircase of water to Lock Fifteen in

3

front of Mustill Store. The pilot, who had guided the long, narrow boats through the stack of locks, handed the rudder control to the boat's captain, collected his fee, and took another boat up the same locks.

Mustill Store was a two-story structure with a *Meat Market* sign on the far right of the roof line and *Groceries and Provisions* advertised in another sign along the front of the porch roof. Six square posts supported the roof. Double doors were flanked by twin windows that ran the height of the first floor. The store was well stocked with supplies and provisions like salt, coffee, and manufactured goods packaged for canal boat owners, the crew, and passengers.

After barely escaping the Cassell brothers the first time, he had replaced the clothes of a young gentleman with the garb of a common worker. A canal boat would provide the low profile he needed to avoid the two hired men. He could ask for help from the local sheriff, but he was a stranger, and the gold would attract unwanted questions. Instead, he'd slip away, quietly, and float to Cleveland. He purchased the local weekly paper, the *Summit County Beacon,* for two cents and read about the fashions and market news. Printed on Wednesday, June 25, 1862, it was a day old.

"That's Captain Michael Donovan." The storekeeper pointed toward an older man as he strutted through the door. "This man is seeking passage, Captain."

Michael removed his hat to reveal a full head of thick white hair. "I'm not takin' passengers on this trip," he said in a thick Irish brogue.

"I'll double your rate," Blake said.

Michael's blue eyes widened. He extended his

hand and gave a hearty handshake. "Welcome aboard, laddie."

Blake waited as Michael collected a hatchet, rope, fishing line, coffee, and a jar of Schumacher's oatmeal. The clerk loaded the supplies into a wooden box, and Michael added a bottle of whiskey and a dozen peppermint sticks. He paid with paper currency and received postage stamps in change. Blake carried the box and followed Michael from the cool interior to the bright sunshine.

The *Irish Rose* was docked north of Lock Fifteen in front of the store. The canal boat consisted of three separate cabins, the roofs connected by a catwalk. The stable cabin was in the center where three mules were stored inside to replace the three tied in tandem to the towline. A tall, thin boy with red hair and blue eyes checked the harness of the three mules on the towpath, ready to tow the boat along the canal.

"Where's the crew, Paddy?"

The boy pointed toward the boat. "Down below storing their gear."

"This is Blake Ellsworth. He's riding with us."

"Welcome aboard," Paddy said. "You're our first passenger of the season."

Blake nodded since his hands were full. "Paddy?"

"Short for Padrick," he said. "We Irish love nicknames."

"Put the box in the cargo hold." Michael pointed to the open area between the three cabins filled with barrels, crates, and seed sacks. It was too early in the season for the rich harvest of corn, wheat, and other crops grown on the farms in the county, but cheese, leather, and metal products filled the hold.

Blake had worked on a boat for a few summers when he was Paddy's age. Canal boats were standard size, no more than eighty feet long and fourteen feet wide, to fit through the locks. He secured the wooden box and stepped onto the gunwale running the perimeter of the boat. Above him at eye level was the deck, a single plank joining the three cabin roofs. A pair of shapely ankles below a short skirt floated along the catwalk, bare feet dancing along the narrow platform.

Blake scrambled up a series of footholds outside the cabin to reach the deck.

"We're ready, Captain."

Blake turned to the sensual melodic tone of the female voice. He had expected a weathered hag, worn out from long years of hard work. Instead a young woman pirouetted on the stern deck, her skirt flaring and falling with the motion. She wore no crinoline, and her corset wasn't stiff and unyielding but emphasized the curves of her breasts and waist. The floral dress had long full sleeves with cuffs, and a bodice opened at the neck that hinted at the fullness of her feminine attributes. Her face was shielded by a wide straw bonnet tied under her chin with a green ribbon. The color contrasted with the shock of ginger curls at the end of two thick braids framing a face that stole his breath when the morning light lit her delicate features.

"Cole, darlin', we have a passenger," Michael said. "Show him where to stow his bag."

She tilted her head, and his gaze locked onto dancing blue-green eyes. His previous estimate of her beauty had been inadequate. Not quite angelic, her earthy beauty could send a man to heaven with a smile or hell if she spurned him. He couldn't stop staring, studying every angle, curve, and lovely feature. "Who are you?"

What *was* his name? Blake shook his head to clear the spell he had fallen under. "Blake, Blake Ellsworth."

She slid open the hatch in the stern of the boat and descended. She turned her head, her hat tilted to reveal a portion of her face. Her full lips revealed straight white teeth when she spoke. "Coming?"

Blake searched his surroundings. White clouds floated in the blue summer sky, a gentle breeze rustled through the tall grass along the bank of the canal, and songbirds chirped in the treetops in between. He wasn't dreaming. She was real. He descended a ladder nailed to the wall and surveyed the small cabin. Two bunks were stacked on the far wall with storage beneath.

She opened a drawer and moved the folded clothing to the side. "You can place your belongings in here."

Blake dropped the leather bag with a few personal items and clean clothes in the drawer. His trunk had been left on the train, and he would collect it in Cleveland. The bunks were narrow with thin feather-filled mattresses over straw bags and rope supports. "Is this your bed?"

"That's Ethan's bunk, but he won't board until we reach Peninsula." She turned to climb the ladder. "Paddy has the top bunk."

Blake sat on the thicker mattress of the large bed built against the stern wall. "Will we be sharing this bed?"

She turned slowly, her fingers clenched into fists, and her face an angry blush. "That's the captain's bunk, but since you're a passenger, you can sleep there.

Alone. I'll be busy on deck."

He'd insulted the canal brat. She couldn't be an innocent. Too many men made it their purpose in life to seduce beautiful girls before they were aware of their power over ordinary men. He was terrified of the mysterious gender but eager to learn the secrets women possessed, especially this one. Blake had fumbled his first attempt at seduction and didn't want her to leave without making amends. "The captain called you Cole. That can't be your Christian name."

A secretive smile formed on her lips. "Colleen. Miss Colleen to you."

"How do you know the captain?"

"He's my grandfather."

An orphan. Was Paddy her brother? They had a family resemblance. Three beds in the stern were accounted for. "Where do you sleep?"

"In the bow cabin with Jess, Cass, and Jules."

Three more crew members, or was one of them something more? She wore no ring. "One of them your husband?"

She laughed as if he'd made a joke. No twittering parlor maid laugh that set his nerves on edge. The sound was hearty and ignited a sensual response. Cole stepped on the bottom rung, revealing a hint of a petticoat beneath the worn and faded fabric of her gown.

"Do you have to leave?"

"I have work to do."

Blake's father had believed in hard work and a strong moral character. Employees and guests of the hotel were not romantic partners. Nothing was more embarrassing than a pregnant maid or a female guest who expected her bill to be dismissed because her favors had been bestowed upon the owner. Older women trying to recapture their youth with brazen suggestions had never interested him, and the giggling girls with finishing school manners reminded him too much of his annoying stepsister.

Cole was different. She had captured his imagination. She was seductive with every confident movement, but her reaction to his brazen invitation to share the bed had been outrage. He couldn't be the first to make a proposition to spare her a life of drudgery. "A beautiful woman like you shouldn't have to work."

Her hand remained on the rung, but she turned to face him. Her breasts rose with a tired sigh, straining the seams of her bodice. "Are you going to whisk me away to your castle, decorate me with jewels, and dress me in silk gowns? I've had my fill of romantic lies." Cole's voice cracked in a husky tremor of pain, and her eyes glistened. "You're missing a button from your coat, your sleeve needs mended, and your trousers have been patched. When I marry, and I said marry, it will be a man of wealth and prestige not a beggar who can't afford the fare for the train."

Blake stared as the fortune hunter escaped, her frayed hem swaying above her bare feet. She had high ambitions for a canal brat. She couldn't write her name, but she could count the coins in a man's purse. Beneath the disguise of his beggar's garb, she might have seen the heavy money bag thickening his middle.

She had scoffed at his ability to clothe her in silk and decorate her lovely skin with jewels. Did he dare show her the gold in his pouch and buy her affection? Would she be impressed if he told her he owned the

Dutchman Hotel, a favorite lodging for the rich elite heading to New York City? What would the wealthy patrons think of his bonny Irish brat?

The men would wish they were bedding her, and the women would be envious of her beauty. He would spoil her with gifts, and they would have a fine time, enjoying the sights, lavish dinners, and exotic entertainment. She would be none the worse from the experience and would gain a bit of refinement to tempt the next man.

He removed his coat and examined the missing button and torn sleeve. She couldn't see the bruised ribs and shallow blade cut from the attack by the Cassell brothers he'd barely escaped the previous day. He had risked life and limb to keep his gold, but the sad smile of an Irish lass had tempted him to see what his money could buy besides a lakeside inn.

His father had taught him to respect women, even those who offered their bodies for coin, but Cole had vanquished any cautious approach. He was smitten, but he had blundered by insulting her. How did a man soothe the prickly emotions of a woman?

Blake put the coat on to hide the bulky bag and scrambled to the deck. He closed the trap door and surveyed the crew. Cole was giving orders to three younger girls. Although they each had different hair color, they had to be sisters. She called the tall slender blonde Jess, the brunette Cass, and the strawberry blonde Jules. Her bunk mates. No wonder she had laughed when he'd asked about a husband among the crew. The girls wore their hair in loose braids tied with ribbons beneath wide brimmed hats to protect their fair skin from the sun. Their dresses were faded and patched. What parents had created these beauties and condemned them to poverty and hard labor?

Another boat was ready to exit the lock and would pass them if the *Irish Rose* didn't push off and head downstream.

Cole put her hands on each side of her narrow waist and studied him. "Have you decided to earn your fare?"

He'd paid her grandfather, but he wouldn't mind showing off. Blake rubbed his hands together. "What needs done?"

Cole waltzed along the deck plank, and Blake followed at a cautious wobble. The single board had seemed wider as a boy. "Toss me the line!"

Paddy swung the towline in a high arc.

She snatched it from the air and attached the rope to a deadeye ring on the front cabin of the boat.

The other end of the rope was attached to the three mules where Jules waved a long switch in her hand. The pink ribbons tying her bonnet beneath her chin matched the gingham dress she wore. She was the only one wearing shoes, and they were boots instead of slippers. A practical choice considering the towpath was decorated with manure piles and buzzing flies.

Cole grabbed two eight-foot long wooden poles with metal tips and handed one to Blake. "Don't let go of the pike and try not to fall in." She reached toward the shore, stabbed the sharp stick into the ground, and shoved, moving the boat away from the edge. Blake followed her example, but as the boat left the shore, he pretended to lose his balance.

"Watch out!" She grabbed the back of his coat.

Blake stood with ease. "Did you think I was

11

falling?"

Her stormy features displayed her displeasure at his faked distress. "You should be in a sideshow." Cole handed him her pike. "Store these."

He'd meant to amuse her, gain a smile, but he'd angered her instead. When he turned to apologize, a soft smile played on her pouting lips. She wasn't as angry as she pretended. She had a sense of humor. A rare trait among the sophisticated young ladies in New York.

Cole pointed north. "Take us away, Jules."

Her sister tapped the lead mule with the switch, and the towline grew taut, tugging the canal boat through the still water. Paddy whistled as he walked behind the young girl.

Cole was an enigma. She didn't belong on a canal boat, yet she commanded the deck like a seasoned sailor. Blake scratched the short growth on his face, searching the fading streets of Akron for any sign of the Cassell brothers. He'd escaped them.

Chapter Two

Cole Beecher had been fooled by Blake Ellsworth. She had believed it when he had waved his arms and threatened to fall overboard. She should have shoved him into the muddy waters of the canal. Yet his school boy antic had made her smile. Her broken heart wasn't completely destroyed by Simon Blackwater's betrayal.

Cole studied the scruffy-looking stranger with eyes gray like an overcast sky. She didn't like men with beards even though Blake's black growth hardly qualified. The shadow of whiskers outlined his strong jaw and framed his well-formed mouth.

She wasn't sure of his age. No wrinkles showed around his smoky gaze. She had to be wary. He'd already made his intentions clear. He was a cad. He would attempt to seduce her with empty promises. At least Simon had treated her like a lady with parlor manners during their courtship. She examined her frayed hem. Her gown was worn and faded but modest over the short corset, bloomers, and petticoat. She dressed for comfort aboard the *Irish Rose*. She hadn't expected a reckless passenger.

He'd been bold to invite her to share the bunk in the stern cabin. How many women had said yes? He had insulted her by thinking she would agree. She recognized the hungry look in his eyes and, having two married sisters, understood what it meant. Plenty of men had attempted to seduce her, and in spite of gossip and rumors to the contrary, she had managed to maintain her virtue. A woman had to walk a fine line between encouraging a man's attentions with her charm and wit and discouraging his uncontrolled desires.

Simon had bestowed words of flattery and adoration upon her. He had called on her every Sunday for the past six months, behaving properly in the parlor but stealing a kiss or embrace when opportunity allowed.

Simon's family owned a boiler company, and he had graduated from nearby Western Reserve College. He was well-spoken, versed on the latest subjects, and handsome by most standards. She had allowed more than one kiss but with tears and words of admonishment so he would respect her. He often declared his love and desire.

Cole expected a proposal and had practiced her shocked but flattered acceptance speech. She had suggested training Cass and Jules to replace her on the canal boat in anticipation of her wedding. Now, there was no need.

Everything had changed when Simon had gone with his parents to New York on business. He didn't write a single letter, and when he returned, he missed his Sunday visit. This morning she had purchased the weekly *Summit County Beacon* to read an article on the latest dress styles while waiting for the *Irish Rose* to reach Mustill Store. On page two below the social news heading was the announcement of Simon's engagement to Miss Margaret Radcliff, the daughter of a rich New York textile merchant. She had memorized the newspaper announcement. *Mr. and Mrs. Darius*

Radcliff are proud to announce the engagement of their daughter, Margaret, to Simon Blackwater, the son of Mr. and Mrs. Stanley Blackwater. A fall wedding is planned.

Simon was marrying another woman. He'd lied with words of love and deceived her with promises of marriage. She had been jilted. Not at the altar, but the wound of betrayal ached in every part of her body. She had yet to share the news with anyone, even Jess, who had been her confidante and chaperone throughout Simon's courtship. Why had she bragged about Simon buying her a ring in New York? Her enemies would throw her premature plans in her face, and her friends would pity her for being in love with a man who didn't return her affections. What had she done wrong? Did Simon think he could forego marriage because she had allowed a few kisses? Was Margaret more beautiful, more talented, or more accomplished? She had given her heart to Simon, something she never did to any man and would never do again.

She swiped at a tear. Blake stared from the bow cabin. Pride stiffened her spine, and she threw her most charming smile in his direction. Why tie herself to the attentions of one man when there were so many to enjoy? He wasn't *that* scruffy looking.

Blake stared at her, a look of confusion on his face, and then a frown slowly broke into a broad grin. Did he think she was agreeing to his outrageous proposal in the stern cabin? She turned her attention to the crew.

Cass was feeding the mules in the center cabin. She stood when Cole joined her. "Should I help Grandpa?"

"You call him captain when you're aboard the *Irish Rose*."

Cass looked tearful at the harsh reprimand. Cole tugged her braid. She had no right to take out her anger toward Simon on her sisters. "You only have to call him captain when strangers are around."

Cass nodded, a shy smile playing on her lips.

"If you ask, he may let you steer the boat."

Her face lit up, and Cass joined her grandfather beneath a cloth canopy.

"I've known families who lived aboard canal boats, but I never met one like this." Blake's deep baritone voice echoed behind her.

Cole turned to face him. "The captain helped build the Ohio canal."

"Worked from sunup to sundown for thirty cents a day, a jigger of whiskey, food, and shelter," Michael announced from his platform in the stern, his hand on the tiller. "All we had were picks and shovels to dig this hole."

Blake looked over the side. "How far down did you have to dig?"

"Four feet in most places," Cole said.

"It looks deeper."

"You don't have to worry about drowning, but you need to fear the leeches," she warned. "So big they can suck a man dry before he can wade to shore."

Blake removed his wide-brimmed hat and ran his fingers through thick black hair. "I didn't know canal brats were prone to tell tall tales. I hope you don't expect me to believe that whopper." He looked past her to the captain. "You were telling me how you built this ditch."

"The labor wasn't in digging the depth but clearing the width," Michael said. "The canal had to be twenty-six feet wide at the bottom and forty feet wide at the top. We had to remove trees and brush twenty feet on each side of the canal for towpaths."

Blake whistled. "Was it worth it?"

Michael squared his shoulders. "You're a young man. You don't understand sacrifice and hard work. I was young when I built this ditch out of nothin' but wilderness. Now that I'm old, I can look back on my labors and take pride in them."

"You made a difference," Blake said. "I like that."

"Now I can enjoy travelin' with my grandchildren on my canal," he said. "While we can." He looked around. "The state neglected repairs and began leasing it to a consortium this year. They've made improvements though, and I'll keep travelin' my route as long as I can."

"How long have you owned a boat?"

"This is my third *Irish Rose*," Michael said. "The first was a packet back in 1827. My wife, CJ, and I raised three children on her. Then I bought a cargo and passenger boat. It's a good way to spend the summer."

"What do you do during the winter?"

"CJ and I run an inn in Peninsula with one of our sons. He's Paddy's father."

Blake crossed the gangplank toward Cole. "Where's Peninsula?"

"Half way between Akron and Cleveland," Cole said. "We spend the night at Grandma's inn."

"You don't sleep aboard the boat?"

Did he hope she would change her mind about sharing a bunk? "We do in Cleveland."

"Then we won't reach Lake Erie until tomorrow night."

Cole sat on the edge of the center cabin, her legs dangling over the side. "You should have taken the train if you were in a hurry."

Blake winked at her. "The train lacks the beautiful scenery this trip offers."

His flattery was wasted on her. Men were liars, and a woman was a fool to believe anything they said. "If you don't mind the smell of garbage."

Jess turned toward them from the bow. "The canal smells better when we're farther downstream."

Her sister had misunderstood her editorial on Blake's flowery words. She didn't correct her. She had once been innocently blind to the true nature of men.

"Look at the heron!" Cass pointed at a grayish-blue bird with a long neck and longer legs wading in the canal. It poked its long beak beneath the water and pulled a fish from its depths. The crane flipped it in the air and swallowed it whole.

"He didn't take any time to enjoy his meal," Blake said.

"Wait until he regurgitates it to feed the baby herons in the nest," Cole said. "Yum."

Blake made a face, and her sisters laughed. Their happiness reminded her of the misery Simon had caused with his rejection. Why couldn't she ignore her emotions? Why did such a deep disappointment follow high hopes?

Blake pointed to the river a short distance away shadowing the canal to provide water when necessary. "What is that waterway beyond the trees?"

"That's the Little Cuyahoga River." Cass stood beside her grandfather, his hand ready to guide hers on the tiller. "It joins the Cuyahoga River at Lock Twenty.

The name means crooked river."

Blake turned to the young girl. "Why is it called crooked river?"

"The Cuyahoga River flows south until it collides with the hills of Akron. Then it turns around and flows toward Lake Erie." Cass motioned with her free arm. "And the canal follows along beside it."

Cole swung her legs to the deck, sweeping her skirt out of the way, and stood. "We're approaching Lock Sixteen."

"What should I do?" Blake stumbled and bumped into Cole as Michael steered toward the lock.

She shoved against his immovable chest. "Stay out of the way." She motioned to Jess in the bow. "You take the starboard beam. I want to show Cass how to operate the leeward beam."

"Do we have headway?" Michael shouted to Paddy.

"The boat is coming out now," Paddy said. The wooden gates of the lock opened southward, and another boat headed toward them.

The *Dora Jean* had come into the lock on the lower side. The doors on both ends were closed, and the lock filled with enough water to make the boat rise to the higher level before heading south. The *Irish Rose* could go in without any water being added.

"Headway!" Captain Donovan hollered.

Paddy helped Jules stop the mules and allow the towline to slacken to the bottom of the canal. They waited as the mules for the *Dora Jean* passed. The boat neared the *Irish Rose*.

"Miss Colleen!" a big box of a man hollered. "You grow prettier every year. I have two sons who would make good husbands. Which one would you like?" Two men appeared on the catwalk, built like their father, their linen shirts were wide, their trousers short.

Cole pointed to Jess. "I'll have my sister take first pick."

"Even if Miss Jessica takes the better of the two, you won't be disappointed."

"Will you be at the Independence Day dance next week?" she asked.

"If they don't go off to war first," their father said before either son could answer. "A good wife would keep them at home."

"Will you save me a dance?" one of the sons asked, pulling his straw hat from his head.

"We'll save a dance for each of you." Cole waved as the boats passed. They would probably stomp on her feet, but she had a fondness for the shy, socially crippled canal laborers. The men were hard workers even if their education was limited and their manners uncouth by society's standards. Unlike Simon, their compliments were sincere.

"You're angels, Miss Colleen and Miss Jessica."

As soon as the *Dora Jean* was clear, Paddy moved the mules forward, and the towline grew taut. The captain aligned the *Irish Rose* with the lock. The doors had remained open, snug in the recess of the stone wall to maintain the full width of fifteen feet. Once inside the lock, Cole unhooked the towline and tossed it to Paddy. She attached a shorter bowline, and Paddy wrapped it around the snubbing post, tightening the line to halt the forward motion in the lock. Even with the captain's skill, the rub rails knocked against the large cut quarry stones stacked to create the walls of the lock.

Cole grabbed Cass by the back of her dress to keep her from falling. "You don't want to fall between the boat and the wall." The opening was large enough for a man's leg or a young girl to be crushed.

"On three." Cass grabbed Cole's hand, and they jumped to the edge of the lock wall. Her sister stumbled, but Cole held her upright. Jess had jumped to the opposite lock wall and stood by the balance beam, a large hewn log attached to the top of the canal gate. A pair of doors were placed on each end of the lock and angled on the edge to form a watertight seal. Cole showed Cass where to place her hands on the balance beam and shove to close the gate at the same time Jess closed her side. Once the mitered edges were tight, they moved to the northern gate.

"Do you think you can turn the wrench to open the paddle gates?"

A long metal wrench was attached to a rod that ran from the bottom to the top on the wooden panels of each gate. Jess waited for Cass to turn her wrench.

Cass gripped the metal handle with both hands and pulled.

"Turn the paddle control half way to open the sluice door."

The wrench opened the sluice gate in the lower portion of the wooden door and released water out of the lock and into the canal to lower the *Irish Rose*.

Cole examined her sister's hands. "Better wear gloves at the next lock, or you'll have blisters by the time we reach Peninsula."

"I don't know if I can learn everything."

"This is your first lock. You'll have plenty to practice on."

Cole watched Blake standing at the bow, his feet planted to adjust to the sinking movement as the water flowed out of the lock. He looked at home on the deck of the boat. He flashed them a wide smile. His white teeth contrasted against the dark growth framing his arrogant grin. Simon had made her heart flutter, but her whole body reacted to the sight of the swarthy figure gracing the *Irish Rose*. He was a handsome devil and probably accustomed to bedding fair damsels. She should have turned away, ignored him, but the brazen boldness in his gaze challenged her to stay the course.

"He looks like a pirate commanding his ship," Cass whispered.

For a brief moment she agreed but dismissed her romantic notions. "He's a poor man wearing a dirty, torn jacket and in need of a shave."

Paddy released the bowline around the mooring post to control the boat's movements. Blake grabbed a pike to shove against the stone wall when necessary. He moved with cat-like grace uncommon in tall, broad-shouldered men.

Once the water inside the lock was level with the canal water, the girls closed the sluice gates and opened the lock doors.

"Everyone aboard," Cole ordered, helping Cass jump to the bow roof. They used the pikes to push the boat forward out of the lock. Once clear of the doors and walk bridge across the canal, Paddy tossed the towline, and Cole attached it to the deadeye. "We're ready to go."

Blake pointed at the open north gate. "Don't you have to close it?"

"Boat is coming this way from the north," Cole

said. "It can go straight in."

"Headway," Blake said. "I forgot how much fun it was working on a boat."

"Why did you quit?"

"I grew up and had to forsake childish adventures."

Laura Freeman

Chapter Three

As much as Cole enjoyed spending summers on the canal with her grandfather, gentlemen didn't respect women who dirtied their hands with hard labor. She was saying good-bye to her childhood, too. Good-bye to dreams of knights, pirates, and men of daring. "This is my last summer on the canal."

Blake waved his arm to encompass the surroundings. "You're leaving the life of a canal brat?"

"I'll be eighteen in September." The years weren't as important as the life experiences. "It's time to think about my future."

Cass chewed on her bottom lip, her dark brows knit in worry. "Are you going to marry Simon?"

"I hope he's not one of the yokels you promised a dance to," Blake said.

Jess coiled a rope. "Cole has the parlor full every Sunday with men who want to court her."

Blake scanned the boat. "Is the parlor in the bow?"

Cass laughed. "No, silly. It's in a house. Men call in their Sunday best with flowers and candy."

Blake gazed into Cole's eyes. "I bet it's quite a parade of admirers."

Was it a compliment or skepticism? "Over the years I've discovered the ones wearing top hats and frock coats make the worst husbands." She plucked at his ratty sleeve. "I might save you a dance if you're in

24

town July 4."

"I plan to be in Cleveland by then, but I'm flattered you would consider a poor peasant worthy of the privilege of your exquisite company."

His words condemned her haughtiness, and she sought amends. "Clothes don't make the man, and your rags don't define you," Cole reassured him. "A little mending and cleaning, and you could be pleasantly presentable."

Blake removed his slouch hat and bowed. His long, thick hair blew in the summer breeze and erased years from his appearance. The man was a handsome rogue. If she wasn't a lady, she might be tempted to discover what secrets were hidden behind those stormy eyes.

Cass had joined her grandfather in the stern. "Twelve more locks before we reach Peninsula."

"Only twelve." Blake reached into his coat pocket and withdrew a newspaper. "I'm glad I bought this."

Cole couldn't see the front page. "What paper is it?"

"The *Summit County Beacon*."

The one with the announcement of Simon's engagement in it. What if he read it? Cole relaxed. Blake wasn't from the area. He didn't know Simon Blackwater. And men had little interest in social announcements.

He scanned the page. "The price of wool is high. Better buy more sheep."

Cass giggled from her perch in the rear. "It's easier to raise lambs."

Blake was handsome and charming. Cole danced along the deck, knowing his gaze would follow her movements. He might not be bad company for the long voyage north. Some frivolous flirting would restore her confidence and keep her mind off Simon.

"Does the paper have anything about hairstyles?" Jess met Cole midway on the gangplank. "I need some ideas on how to wear my hair for the dance."

Cole plucked a short chunk of hair loose from her sister's braid. "No style will help with your hair after you chopped so much of it off."

"I couldn't comb the burrs out," Jess said. "It's growing back."

"At different lengths."

"I like your curly hair." Cass left the stern and twirled on the narrow board above the hold. "I wish I was old enough to go to a dance."

"Next year," Cole reminded her. "We had to wait until we finished school before we could attend."

Blake lowered his newspaper. "You finished school?"

"All the way through eighth grade." She wiggled her toes in Blake's direction. "I can count to twenty when I don't wear my shoes."

"She's teasing you," Cass said. "Colleen passed the county test to be a certified teacher more than a year ago."

His surprised expression intensified. "You're a school teacher?"

He was shocked at her accomplishment. Most men saw a pretty face and nothing more. "I taught for a year. Then the school board decided to replace me with a man." Cole stomped across the roof of the bow cabin. All her hard work for nothing. Her lack of a job had turned her attention toward marriage. Now those plans had crumbled with Simon's engagement. Where was her life heading?

"I don't think he will be as good a teacher as you," Cass said. "Everyone loved you."

"But he wears trousers," Cole said. "The school board agreed it was the most important requirement for the job."

Blake rubbed his beard growth. "Did the man have a college education?"

"No. And it took him three tries to pass the certification test. I bet he was related to one of the men on the board. It's not always what you know but who you know." Cole pointed to the next lock, and they moved into position to travel through it. This time Cole directed Cass from the deck, letting her do the work alone.

Blake leaned against his pike. "Life has different plans for you, canal brat."

"Are you a seer? Can you tell me what my future holds? What path should I take to find happiness?"

"Only you can choose the course, but I hope it's smooth sailing."

"I've hit nothing but rocky shores lately." Cole helped Cass board, and they pushed the *Irish Rose* through the lock. "I worked hard to become a teacher." She tied off the line. "And they wanted me to help him learn the schedule. Hah! He knew nothing about teaching children."

Blake stored the pikes. "What do you mean?"

"After I showed him where the supplies were stored and what lessons the children were learning, he asked me to remain so I could benefit from his example."

Cass and Jess sat on the bow deck, their legs

dangling over the side as they faced Cole on the middle cabin.

Cole removed her bonnet and smoothed her damp hair from her face. "My students were well behaved and anxious to learn, but out of loyalty or the spring weather, they misbehaved. He wanted to discipline them, but I didn't agree with his methods."

"What were those?"

The memory was fresh. "He was a sadist."

"Sadist?" Cass repeated. "What does that mean?"

"A man who enjoys inflicting pain on others." Blake turned to Cole. "How was he a sadist? Did he hurt you?"

Cole shook her head. "Not me. And not one of the older boys. No, he picked a little boy of seven to inflict his punishment. But he gave me the switch and ordered me to beat him twenty times. I refused."

"He was a nasty dog," Jess said. "If I had been there, I would have shot him."

Blake's eyes widened. "Do you shoot every man who's a nasty dog?"

"I haven't found the need, yet." Jess stood and paced around the small space. "But I could. I'm a crack shot."

"She is," Cole agreed. "She won a five-dollar gold piece in a shooting contest."

Blake turned from Jess to Cole. "What did this school teacher do after you refused to switch the boy?"

She hadn't shared the story with anyone but her parents and Jess, but enough time had passed to ease the fear and anger from the experience. "He dismissed the students and had me remain behind. Then he backed me into the corner. Do I look like I'm wearing a dunce cap? He slobbered on me and promised he would recommend me for another teaching position if I was a good girl." Cole trembled with anger and humiliation. It hadn't been long enough to forget.

Blake clenched his fists. "Were you a good girl?"

A sobbed escaped her throat. "He said I was a temptation to any man, and I would never be able to control a class of boys."

Blake shoved his hat back and studied her for a long pause. "I would think they would do anything you asked."

His flattery softened any harsh memories. She'd had a few love struck boys in her class the year she had taught, but she had earned the respect of the entire class by being fair. "It was one of the worst kisses I've had to endure."

"I should have shot him," Jess said.

Cass stared, her face ashen. "He stole a kiss?"

"What happened after he kissed you?" Blake's voice was dark and frightened her.

"I hit him with the switch." Her hand moved through the air, imitating the motion. "I only meant to strike him once, but I was so angry, I kept hitting him. Twenty times like he had ordered for the boy. Then I broke the stick and threw it." She took a deep breath and swiped the back of her hand over her mouth. "I wiped off his kiss and left."

The cloud darkening Blake's countenance passed. "Good for you."

"Good? My teaching certificate isn't worth the paper it's printed on. He said I was incorrigible and no one would hire me."

"How can you be depraved?" Jess demanded. "I

would have noticed."

Blake chuckled, his gray eyes dancing. "It's nice you watch out for each other."

"I'm her chaperone," Jess said. "It's not an easy job. Men are always trying to kiss her."

Cole tilted her head back to capture some warmth on her face. "I could write a book about kissing."

"Tell us," Cass said. "I'm almost old enough for kissing."

"You're not old enough to hold hands," Jess said.

"Tell us how it's done." Blake's chest shook with silent laughter. Men thought they knew everything. They were praised for every accomplishment since taking their first step. Girls were warned not to show off, talk too loud, or the worst, act like a lady. They were kept in the dark until their curiosity drove them to make a mistake or agree to marriage with a stranger.

Courtship was meant to minimize mistakes to the altar, but some friends confided married life was not what they had anticipated. The same girl who bragged about walking down the aisle awaiting her first kiss at the altar was shocked when her husband shattered her virginity, claiming all physical intimacies in one night. More than one bride cried at dawn, wondering why reality didn't match her dreams.

If she had married Simon, would she have awakened to regrets? Cole's two married sisters were happy with their husbands. But their marriages were based on mutual respect. Most men seduced a woman with flattery and lies, hoping to capture her body without considering her emotions or her dreams.

But Cole had no dreams. Not yet. The slate of her life had been wiped clean. The chalk was poised above the surface, ready to write. She had claimed she could pen a book about kissing. Blake sat beside her, his smug smile challenging her to prove her words.

"There's the peck." Cole demonstrated on Blake's hairy cheek. The bristles were soft when she wiped the wet kiss from his face. "The kind of kiss you give to your grandpa or a cousin."

Blake's look of surprise was replaced by one of intense curiosity. "The man doesn't kiss you?"

"A man kissing you can be extremely unpleasant," Cole confessed, wagging her finger at her sisters on the bow cabin. "Avoid a drunk or a man missing teeth. Their kisses drool or slobber on you." Her body shook in revulsion. "Who wants someone to spit in your mouth?"

Cass made a face in agreement with her assessment. "Yuck!"

"Are there any men who are good kissers?" Jess was sincere. She competed with boys instead of complimenting them. She was sixteen and had yet to be kissed.

"A few men know how to kiss, but that could mean they've kissed their fair share of girls."

"I'm not going to let anyone kiss me unless they say they love me," Cass said.

Simon had said he loved her. "Declarations of love mean nothing to some men. You need to be wary of flattery."

"Then how do you know he's sincere?"

"Time will tell. That's why you shouldn't rush into marriage. Once you say 'I do' you're stuck for better or worse."

Cass smoothed her skirt over her crossed legs. "I

don't want it to be for worse."

Blake folded his paper. "Are you saying you've never been in love, canal brat?"

"I've lost count of how many men have proposed to fair Miss Colleen." Jess rolled her eyes and sighed. "I bet Simon Blackwater is going to propose on his next visit to our parlor. But first he'll give her flowers and candy. Then he'll recite some boring poetry." Jess yawned, fanning her hand in front of her open mouth.

"I don't plan on marrying Simon or anyone else," Cole announced in a loud, clear voice.

"But you've been bragging about him for months," Jess said. "His father owns a boiler company, and his mother is the hostess for three or four parties a year. Every girl in Summit County would be green with envy if you married him."

"A woman should marry for love not social standing."

"But you said you were in love with Simon."

Cole didn't answer. Blake was reading the second page of the newspaper. The notice of Simon's marriage was at the bottom of the page. What if he read the announcement? Now that Jess had blurted Simon's name to everyone, it wouldn't be difficult for Blake to make the connection and realize she had been thrown over for a socialite. He'd laugh at the poor canal brat.

No time to hesitate or think. She grabbed the newspaper from his grip, releasing it into the gentle wind. She wrapped her hands around his neck, trapping any escape, and pressed her lips against his, the smooth flesh of their mouths brushing back and forth in a tentative embrace. His cloudy eyes widened with surprise as he responded to her bold attack with mutual discovery. Warm lips caressed hers with tender strokes, building a response beyond any she had experienced. What began as a murmur of pleasure flashed like lightning striking a tree, exploding the bark into splintered shreds. A groan escaped her lips.

"Hey, none of that!" Michael commanded from the stern. "Stop canoodling my granddaughter."

Cole wrestled from Blake's embrace. When had his arms encircled her?

Blake's swarthy expression of satisfaction was bold. "You could write a chapter on that kiss."

Cole steadied her breathing and calmed her frantic heartbeat. She had always been reserved and in control when she allowed a man to kiss her, but with Blake, she had abandoned any restraint. Her mouth vibrated, and her body hummed from the experience. He wouldn't respect her if she didn't say something to put him in his place. "More like a paragraph."

His deep chuckle defied her words. She ignored him and strolled across the gangplank to the bow cabin.

"What about Simon?" Jess whispered.

"Simon who?" Her confusion was sincere. Several minutes passed before she remembered why she had kissed Blake in such abandonment. The newspaper, water soaked, sank in the distance. Blake wouldn't read Simon's name in the paper. He wouldn't know Simon was marrying another woman. Her dignity would be saved. Dignity? She had kissed Blake like a wanton seductress. If he had any respect for her, it had vanished like his newspaper.

"Simon Blackwater…" Jess said.

Cole opened the door to the bow cabin. "I need your help with something."

Jess obediently followed, but once secure in the privacy of the cabin, she demanded an explanation. "What were you doing up there? What if Simon finds out?"

"Simon won't care." Cole opened a drawer and removed several letters. "I bought the same paper Blake was reading when I picked up these letters at Wheeler's store."

Jess snatched the letters from her hand. "You didn't tell me Ed had written."

"I forgot."

"Forgot? You know I've been waiting for his letter." Jess shuffled through the envelopes but stopped when Cole shoved the newspaper article under her nose. "What's this?"

"Read it."

Jess gasped. "He didn't say a word about this at his last visit."

"Maybe he wanted to surprise me." Cole's voice trembled, and tears were dangerously near the surface. "I don't know if Blake read the notice or not, but if he said something, I was afraid I'd burst into tears." She rolled her shoulders back. "I don't want pity, even from a stranger."

"I don't think he qualifies as a stranger anymore." Jess bumped her hip. "Besides, I always thought you could do better than Simon Blackwater. He was too arrogant for my taste."

Jess was loyal, and Cole hugged her. "Let's hate him together."

She waved the mail in the air. "Can I read Ed's letter?"

"We'll read all the letters on deck. Now that I've

lost Blake's newspaper, we'll have to entertain him."

"I don't think any letter is going to match that kiss." Jess fanned herself with the mail. "How was it?"

Cole returned the newspaper to her hiding spot. "I'm sorry Grandpa interrupted."

"You make my job as chaperone so difficult…and so interesting."

Chapter Four

Cole and Jess divided the letters and returned to the deck. Cass was talking with Blake in an animated conversation. She was learning to hold her own with a man. She'd have plenty of beaus in her future. One of them would be worthy. She fearlessly joined Blake but maintained a safe distance between them. Cole displayed her letters. "Do you want to hear news from the boys?"

Cass clapped her hands. "Oh, yes!"

Blake leaned toward her. "I'd be happy to help with the big words."

Cole withdrew a sheathed knife from the folds of her skirt.

"Whoa! Where did you have that hidden?"

If they were to share a kiss again, she would decide. "My skirt pocket." She unsheathed the sharp blade and waved it in the air. "Grandpa gave us knives to use for cutting rope and other things."

"Like ending canoodling."

"You're smarter than you look." Cole slit open her letters while Jess did the same with a similar knife. They removed each letter and arranged them by date. "I have one from February."

"That beats any of mine." Jess unfolded the missives and smoothed them against the deck.

Blake pointed at the stack. "How many boys do

you write to?"

"Only the ones from our hometown of Darrow Falls."

"Do you think we should invite Jules to join us?" Cass sat cross-legged next to Jess.

"We'll read them later to her and Paddy," Jess said. "Ethan will want to hear about the war, too."

"Go ahead." Cass leaned forward as Cole perused her letter. "Who is it from?"

Cole checked the bottom of the second page. "It's from Arthur Herbruck."

Jess grunted. "I wish you wouldn't encourage him to write."

"We know how you feel about Art," Cole said. "So he caused you to lose a foot race when you were twelve. You can't win every competition."

"He did it on purpose."

"Stop holding a grudge."

"Some men deserve being treated like a pariah."

Like Simon. "Art isn't one of them." Cole read aloud.

"*Miss Colleen, I hope you and your sisters are well. It hasn't stopped raining since we arrived at Camp Kelly. We've tried everything to stay dry, digging ditches to channel the water and laying pine branches beneath our blankets, but I wake up soggy and cold. The boys in the Twenty-ninth Ohio and other regiments are sick with fever and chills. Ed and I are hardier stock. We hunted with our shoulder cannons and nabbed a six pointer.*"

"What is he talking about?" Cass asked. "What's a shoulder cannon?"

"A shoulder cannon would be his gun," Blake said.

"Instead of Enfield rifles, some of the boys were issued Pondir rifled muskets. They have a kick like a mule."

Cole squinted. "How do you know so much about soldiering?"

"I thought about joining."

So did other men, but a lack of volunteers and the high toll of disease had forced Lincoln to announce a draft from the militia rolls. Ohio boys would face their lottery in the fall. "Why didn't you?"

Blake's jaw tightened, and his voice growled, "I have responsibilities."

Had she kissed a married man? She scooted a few inches from him, the edge of the roof preventing any farther distance.

"What about a six pointer?" Cass asked.

"That's a deer," Jess said. "One with six points on its antlers."

Cole resumed reading.

"The Alleghany Mountains are pretty when we aren't freezing to death. I hate to ask, but could you send socks?"

Cole stopped reading and looked at her sisters. "We'll have to do more knitting."

Cass groaned but pointed to the letter. "Where's Camp Kelly?"

"In Maryland," Cole said. "That's where they were sent after leaving Camp Chase in Columbus.

"We have the Potomac in front of us and the Chesapeake and Ohio Canal behind us. Across the river is the camp of the Seventh Ohio."

"Cousin Jake is in the Seventh," Cass interrupted.

"Jake Donovan. He's first cousin to Paddy and us," Cole explained to Blake.

38

"The engineers have rebuilt the bridge crossing Patterson Creek that Confederate Major General Thomas Jackson burned. He tore up most of the Baltimore and Ohio Railroad last year in this area. We figure he's the reason we're here, although we haven't seen any Johnny Rebs. The mud keeps us from drilling, but we pass the time with Bible readings, singing, and listening to the regimental bands. At night they play taps. It's a haunting sound when it echoes in the hills. They're playing it now, and we have to extinguish our lantern. Respectfully, Arthur Herbruck."

"Not exactly a love letter," Blake said.

"We attended school together," Cole said. "Art carried my books home."

"He wanted to carry mine," Jess said.

"You should have been flattered. Art is two years older than me."

"But two grades behind," Jess said. "He wanted to copy my work, but I wouldn't let him."

"The boys missed school because of chores," Cole defended. "They had to do all the work around the farm with their pa gone most of the time."

"Doc Herbruck is a veterinarian," Cass said. "He lets me watch when he takes care of our animals."

"How many brothers does Art have?"

"Three," Jess said. "John was wounded at Bull Run, and Harry is too young to fight. Ed is fighting with Art in the Twenty-ninth Ohio."

"Read Ed's letter," Cole said.

Jess scanned the letter. "It's dated March 1862. No day.

"We left Camp Starvation."

Cass leaned over to read the letter. "What camp is

that?"

"I don't know." Jess continued reading.

"And headed along the B&O railroad to Paw Paw, better known as Camp Frozen."

"I think Ed is making names up," Cass said.

"Ed has a peculiar sense of humor," Blake said. "He means they're cold and hungry."

"We've learned to make camp with whatever supplies are available and divide up the work. Art and I stood in line to draw rations and boiled the beans over a fire for hours until they were tender. Ma would be proud of our cooking skills. Our biggest enemy is the wind. A man can't stand upright in it. The wagons finally arrived with our tents on the 17th of February. We were never happier to see those old rags from Camp Giddings after living in brush huts."

"Where is Camp Giddings?" Blake asked.

"In Ashtabula County near Lake Erie. That's where they formed the regiment," Cole said. "Three companies were filled by men from Summit County."

Jess rattled the page to interrupt.

"We joined Jake and the others from the Seventh Ohio to celebrate George Washington's birthday. They fired cannons, and we all dressed in our cleanest shirts and polished our guns and buckles before we assembled by brigades for Brigadier General Frederick Lander's review of his division.

"Lander made a fine speech and seemed pleased with the Twenty-ninth. We fired a thirteen-gun salute, one for each of the original colonies and had a supper of beans and hard bread."

"Lander died," Blake said.

"In battle?" Cass asked.

"No, he died in early March from an infection in an old leg wound, but they had a big funeral for him in Washington City," Blake answered.

Cole gasped, laying her hand on her breast. "Why, Mr. Ellsworth, you could write a book about the war."

"I would rather experience it firsthand."

Why would a man want to suffer the ways Art and Ed described? "What else does Ed say?"

Jess unfolded the second page and a band fell from the folds.

"What is it?" Cass examined the ring. "It's made from a twig."

"Ed sent you a promise ring." Her sister's face reddened. Simon had given Cole small gifts but never a serious token of his affection. Had she given too much credit to his attentions? "What does he say?"

Jess claimed her ring and turned her attention to the letter.

"We've been chasing Jackson up and down the Shenandoah Valley, but he always stays one step ahead. But we'll catch him, and when we do, we'll show him what Ohio boys are made of. My thoughts and prayers, Edward Herbruck. Enclosed is a ring made from laurel root. I hope you think of me when you wear it."

Jess slipped the ring on her finger. She examined the pages before folding them and slipping them inside the envelope. "Your turn."

Cole opened the letter from Jake.

"Dear Cousin Colleen, March 18 we marched out of camp north of Winchester to give chase to Stonewall Jackson, but he's a wily fox. No sooner had we abandoned Winchester then Jackson returned to recapture it. We arrived at the toll gate where Cedar

41

Creek Turnpike intersects the Valley Pike. We were finally introduced to Jackson's men. It was the first time firing my gun. I had to show some of the boys how to tear open the cartridge with their teeth and empty it down the barrel. You should have seen them trying to set the ball on the powder with the ramrod. I had to remind them to keep their finger off the trigger once they placed the copper primer. The Rebels tried to flank our line."

"What does flank mean?" Cass asked.

"The rebels were trying to sneak around the line behind them," Cole said.

"Colonel Erastus Tyler ordered us to take the Rebel battery."

"That's the cannon, right?"

Cole nodded to Cass. "They always start a battle with shooting cannons. A bullet may kill one man, but a canister shot from a cannon can kill half a dozen."

Blake raised an eyebrow. "Did you attend West Point?"

"No, and neither did any of the boys fighting on the lines." She found her place while he chuckled.

"We marched into a wooded area, but the enemy began shelling us, breaking trees and wounding some of the men. To our left was the Twenty-ninth. We were on the right with the rest of the brigade between us. The woods opened to a field with the enemy behind a stone fence. In between was a rail fence. Some of the men took it apart, and the Johnny Rebs opened fire. I was up front and dropped to the ground. Others panicked and ran for the trees. First battle always decides who's a coward and who fights.

"I gathered a group around me, and we fired at the

Rebels behind the stone wall. Every time we shot one, another took his place. They fired on command, sending up a wall of smoke so thick I couldn't see the man next to me. We fought for hours, and the sun was beginning to set when the order was given to attach bayonets and charge. I saw Ed and Art racing to the wall and told the Seventh we had to beat them. We chased the Rebels from the wall and would have pursued them farther, but we were exhausted. I collapsed on the ground to sleep, clutching my gun in case the Rebs returned. It felt good to show what we were made of. No one back home needs to be ashamed of the Seventh or the Twenty-ninth. Corporal Jacob Donovan."

"Corporal," Cass repeated with pride in her voice. She looked from Cole to Jess. "Any more letters?"

"One more from Ed." Jess unfolded the pages. "It's from late May. I wonder how his letter reached Ohio so quickly?"

"Maybe one of the officers delivered it," Cole said. "They can resign unlike the enlisted men who are expected to serve all three years unless they're wounded." She didn't add killed although more and more soldiers were listed in the local paper, buried in unmarked graves near the battlefields where they took their last breath. "Go ahead."

"Miss Jessica, I never marched so much in my life and hope I never have to walk so far again. Some of the men have called it quits and have slipped away. I can't blame them. The army has broken every promise it's made. If you could see us, you would have pity in your heart for our miserable state. Most of the men are barefoot, their shoes worn out from all the marching. Our uniforms are faded, torn, and patched when

possible. We were going to receive new uniforms at Falmouth, but they didn't arrive. Some of the other regiments made sport of our appearance. I was obligated to defend the Twenty-ninth's honor with a few flying fists."

Cole laughed. Ed was the biggest of his brothers and usually won any fight.

"President Lincoln was at Falmouth to review the troops."

Jess looked around. "He met the president?"

Cass pointed at the letter. "Don't stop reading."

"He looked like anybody, and most of the men liked him. He didn't put on airs like some of the officers. Hours after seeing Lincoln, news arrived that Jackson hadn't left the Shenandoah Valley like everyone thought. He attacked Front Royal and chased General Banks to Harpers Ferry. Instead of the Twenty-ninth joining General George McClellan to attack Richmond, General James Shields, who replaced Lander, was ordered to march back along the path we had taken before Jackson could attack Washington City. Lot of the officers complained, but we go where we're told. We passed through Manassas Junction."

"That's Bull Run," Cole said. "Where Ben was killed."

"Who's Ben?" Blake whispered in her ear.

"My sister Jennifer's first husband."

He looked around. "There are more of you?"

"Hush."

"Nothing much left," Jess continued. *"The Rebels cut down most of the trees to make fortifications. Art and I checked out the cannons facing Washington City, and they weren't nothing but painted tree trunks."*

"Why would they do that?" Cass asked.

After a long pause, Blake offered an explanation. "Fake guns are better than no guns. They didn't want Union troops to know they had abandoned the place. Sometimes they'll use scarecrows to make it appear as if men are still guarding the place."

"Can't you tell the difference?"

"Not from a distance."

Cass looked at the letter in her sister's hand. "What happened next?"

"We met Brigadier General John White Geary and his Pennsylvania volunteers in Thoroughfare Gap. Lucky they were heading the other direction because when we reached their abandoned camp, they had burned uniforms, tents, and weapons to keep the Rebels from taking them," Jess read. *"We were standing there in rags and barefoot. We would have throttled the whole band of them, but we were worried about the wounded we left in the valley. Jackson beat us to them."*

Cass gasped.

Jess scanned ahead. "They didn't kill them." Jess resumed reading.

"Most of the sick took the oath and probably are back in Ohio by now. Those well enough to travel were taken prisoner. After a week of marching, we ended up at the spot we started from, hungry, tired, and our feet aching. We were lucky to have a cracker and coffee for supper."

"Doesn't the army have any decent food?"

"They eat plenty in Washington City, but the supply wagons can't reach them in the mountains," Blake said. "That's why Jackson burns the bridges and tears up the railroad tracks. He wants to cut off the

45

Union supplies."

"The rain is pouring down constantly. We were issued shelter tents. You roll them up and carry them with your wool and rubber blankets instead of waiting on the wagons to deliver a larger tent. Art and I each have a half we button together. We build a frame with some sturdy twigs and pitch it over them. We have to tug it down and stake the bottom. It's small, but our humble home is better than sleeping in the open."

Jess turned to the next page. This is dated this month." Her hand shook as she read.

"We arrived at Port Republic June 8. The Twenty-ninth has about four hundred men in our regiment after all the illness and walk offs. The officers are trying to warn General Tyler it would be a slaughter to attack Jackson, but he's determined to fight."

"Jake wrote he was a colonel." Cole searched for his letter.

"He was promoted," Blake explained.

Jess coughed and continued.

"We piled our knapsacks by company, checked our cartridges and primer boxes, and lined up to the far right to march. We had to climb a fence, but no one was hit. Then we entered a wheat field to support Huntington's battery. The artillery tore the Rebels apart, but that didn't stop them from charging. They made a noise like a screech and holler that made some men stop dead in their tracks. We yelled back and fired. You would have been proud, Miss Jessica. We kept our lines, firing in volleys for three hours. My shoulder is still aching, but I rubbed some of Pa's horse liniment on it, and the pain is ebbing."

Jess looked up. "He made it through the battle."

"Keep reading," Cole urged.

"We drove the Rebels back, but smoke filled the sky. Jackson had crossed the bridge and burned it, cutting off General John Fremont from helping us. We had nothing in reserve. We realized we were all by ourselves in that wheat field with Rebs all around us. When the Rebel cavalry charged, we formed tight groups and made our way to the woods. I grabbed Art, and we headed for the thickest trees where the horses couldn't follow. We scrambled up one and hid in the branches. The Rebels had captured our big blue regimental flag and were parading it around. They rounded up prisoners and searched the dead for valuables."

Cass gasped. "They robbed the dead?"

"It's war, Miss Cassie," Blake said. "It cultivates the best and the worst in men."

"When it was safe, we climbed down and headed toward Union lines. We met Colonel Lewis Buckley and about eighty other men who had escaped capture and spent the night in an abandoned building."

Jess examined a new page and continued.

"We arrived in Luray safe and sound. We have about two hundred men left in the Twenty-ninth regiment. The officers are arguing about the mistakes and who is to blame, but all we soldiers want is to rest. Greet everyone back home for me. Bless you and your family, Edward Herbruck."

"War doesn't sound nice," Cass said. "They're hungry, and cold, and getting shot at."

"A man likes challenges," Blake said. "Between the complaints on those pages you'll find plenty of pride."

"I don't need them to be killed to be proud of them." Jess swiped at a tear. She fumbled to fold the pages and return them to the envelope.

"They sound like they could use some cheering," Cass said. "May I write to one of them?"

"You can write your cousin Jake or tell him to pass your letter off to someone in the regiment," Cole suggested. "A lot of the soldiers don't have anyone to write to."

"Must be awful lonely."

"They have each other," Blake said.

Chapter Five

Blake had read accounts in the newspapers about the war, but they were written by correspondents who had a jaded view of the war or took their information from officers, who didn't want to tarnish the faulty decisions of their equals.

The letters Cole and Jess had read were from the front line soldiers. They were honest and painted a brutal picture of starvation and exhaustion. But between the lines were pride and courage for doing a job no one else would volunteer for unless they were itching to prove their worth. How much longer would he have to wait? Once drafted, he wouldn't have any excuse to delay no matter what his stepmother and stepsister argued. He knew the reality of war. The properties he invested in would provide income and a home for him if he was crippled. They would fulfill his promise to his dying father to take care of his family.

Cole stood and stowed her letters in her skirt pocket. "I can't understand how the soldiers don't have new uniforms when we've been sewing jackets and pants all winter."

Blake remained seated, enjoying the gentle curve of heel into arch and the display of toes dancing on the boards as she paced on the narrow plank. Her words finally registered. "You've been sewing uniforms for the Union army?"

Cole frowned, pouting her lips in a gesture that reminded him of her warm and satisfying lips on his. Why had she kissed him? Did it have anything to do with the wedding announcement mentioning Simon Blackwater he had read before she ripped the newspaper from his fingertips and sent it to a watery grave? Did he need to know the answer? The memory was branded on his heart in spite of the reason.

Cole stood, feet apart, her hands resting on the swell of her hips below her small waist. Women strived for an hourglass figure with gathers and ruffles and a cinched waist. They would be envious of Cole's natural curves.

"You don't think we're making them for the Confederacy?" Her words were layered with disbelief and sarcasm.

The canal brat could read and write, handle a pike, and sew. "Are there no limits to your talents?"

She blushed. Had she included her kiss as a skill? The innocent attempt to distract him had bestowed shocking pleasure on both of them. She had ignited the burning desire poets wrote about in verse. He had tasted the forbidden fruit and wanted to devour the entire apple. He forced his attention on the topic of uniforms.

"They cut the fabric in Columbus and hire women to sew the pieces," Jess said. "I lost count of how many blue jackets I've sewn this winter."

As the capital of Ohio, Columbus was the location soldiers gathered before heading for their battlefields. Camp Chase was named for the former governor and current secretary of the treasury. Salmon P. Chase was in charge of paying for the war, which was costing more each day. Men on the march wore out their uniforms in a couple of months. Sooner if they were in battle. "Are you good with a needle and thread?"

"We use a sewing machine," Jess said, shaking her head. "It would take forever to sew that many uniforms by hand."

"I sew on the buttons by hand," Cass added.

"Do they pay you for the labor or is this volunteer work?"

"They pay us although we do plenty of volunteer work, too," Cole defended. "We support the men in blue."

He pointed to her faded and frayed gown. "They don't pay enough for a new dress?"

Cole twirled on the narrow plank of the deck, exposing more limb than society deemed proper. "Do you think I wear my best Sunday frock on the canal? This is a work dress."

The image of her shapely legs wouldn't disappear. "It's a bit worn."

"Criticism from a man wearing patched trousers and a holey jacket." Cole tugged on his sleeve where it was torn. "I could stitch your coat for a few cents."

Blake examined the tear. "My coat has seen better days, canal brat. Don't waste time mending it."

She studied him. "If you don't have any money, I'll do it for free."

Blake had thought her a gold digger, but it was her heart that was made of the precious metal. He had made an indecent proposal to her, another man had taken her job and blackmailed a kiss from her, and Simon Blackwater was marrying another woman after courting her for months.

He didn't know Simon, but he knew his fiancé.

51

Margaret Radcliff was his stepsister's best friend from Miss Wellington's School for Young Ladies. They were a twittering attack on a man's sanity. "My gender hasn't been kind to you."

"I don't expect kindness from men," Cole said. "They're stronger, and that allows them to be cruel."

"Cruel? Do you judge all men the same?"

"Some are sweet."

What man's memory had softened her features?

Cole sighed. "But lately my luck has run toward the disreputable."

The sadness he had seen in her eyes earlier had resolved into a hardness, a self-preservation not to be hurt. "If you classify me in the latter, I hope to redeem myself."

"Redemption can't be done in one act. It's a lifetime of change."

"But life can be cut short." His mother and two younger brothers had died of typhoid when he was at military school. His father had been traveling and had been spared, but his more recent death had left him alone. He wanted to be a member of a brotherhood, a soldier in the army. Marriage wasn't part of his plan. He had taken a bold chance earlier. Even though she had spurred his offer to share the bed in the stern, she had bestowed a kiss he would remember to his dying day. "Shouldn't we make the most of the time we have?"

"That's what Jake says, but we can enjoy life without breaking the rules."

"You don't seem to follow any rules. Where are your crinoline and stockings?"

"On the *Irish Rose* we make our own rules, but

everywhere else we must behave in a proper fashion. You should read the nonsense printed about social behavior for ladies." Cole tiptoed along the gangplank. "A lady's gait is measured, and she neither looks to the right or left to avoid a mistaken invitation toward a man."

Cass giggled. "It would take forever to get from the bow to the stern walking like that."

Cole twirled and lifted the right side of her skirt. "Only use your right hand to sweep your dress away. Two hands are vulgar and should only be used to avoid deep mud."

Her playacting was more believable than the behavior he had witnessed in the finest establishments. "I know women who attend schools to learn all those rules. You put them to shame, brat."

"For how long? A woman can have many accomplishments, but men only notice her beauty."

"I don't see you lacking in that category." Blake couldn't find any flaw in her features.

"But why is beauty valued above all other traits?" Cole leaned toward him. "Does it make me a better person by being young and attractive?"

"We're all young and attractive once." He winked. "It helps to propitiate the species."

"But it's a starting point for men. They grow wiser and more handsome, richer and more successful. For a woman, it's the height of her existence. She has to nab a husband before her beauty fades."

"Are you worried you've peaked and are tumbling down the backside of your life?"

"If a woman isn't married by twenty-one, she's a spinster."

"You have three years before you turn twenty-one," Jess reminded her sister. "Besides, you enjoy being courted too much to limit attentions to one man."

Cole pointed at the laurel ring on Jess' hand. "You should follow my example."

Jess examined the modestly made ring. "I measure other men against Ed and find them wanting."

Jess was in love with Ed. Probably her first love. She had not experienced the betrayal and heartache Cole had felt. Blake whispered a silent prayer that Ed would survive the war and return home to Jess. He had survived the first few months, which most soldiers said were the hardest. "It must be difficult to find a husband with so many eligible men fighting in the war."

"The best are gone and the worst prosper." Cole's voice was bitter.

"How do you tell the difference?" Cass asked.

"There are two types of people in the world, Cassie. Those who will do anything to be rich. They'll cheat their partners, rob their employees, and ignore their families to gather more wealth," Cole said. "Then there are those who are content, although they would like enough money to pay the bills, have a roof over their heads, and feed their family."

"But Scrooge was nice at the end of *A Christmas Carol*," Cass said. "People can change."

"And that shows the difference. Instead of keeping all his wealth, Scrooge learned to share it with those less fortunate. Love ruled his decisions not greed."

"Ed isn't rich," Jess said. "But he's always helping others."

"Ed is one of the good ones," Cole agreed, healing any rift her earlier criticism had caused.

"Who are the bad ones?" Cass stood with her sisters as they neared a lock. "Can you tell by looking at them?"

Cole unfastened the towline, ready to toss it to Paddy. "Don't fall in love with a gambler. He may be rich today, but he'll be broke tomorrow. Don't marry a drunkard. He'll beat you when he's in a stupor and apologize when he's sober. And beware of men who are full of flattery and gifts. Marriage is not on their mind."

"I hate men who smoke smelly cigars or chew and spit tobacco," Jess added.

Cass prepared to jump to the edge of the canal. "Sounds like the best men are already taken by Cory and Jem."

Jess turned, glaring at her over her shoulder as she prepared to jump on the opposite side. "And what's wrong with Ed Herbruck?"

Cass cowered under her sister's attack. "He's fine."

"Not every man has to go to college to be worthy of love." Jess looked at Cole. "Some college graduates aren't worth it."

In spite of their disagreements, the girls worked as a team to operate the lock. After finishing, Blake offered his hand to help Cass aboard and tossed the towline to Paddy, who attached it to the mules. Blake was snagged on an earlier comment. "Who are Cory and Jem?"

"Our married sisters," Cole explained. "Courtney is married to a Harvard lawyer, Tyler Montgomery. He has an office in Akron and helps families with sons or husbands in the war collect the eight dollar a month pension when a loved one is killed."

"Jennifer married Ben Collins, but now she's

married to Logan Pierce," Jess added. "He's a politician in Washington City."

Blake shook his head. Had he heard correctly? "Miss Jenny is your sister?" The resemblance had been in front of him all along, but Miss Jenny was a gentle, refined lady married to Salmon Chase's secretary. "We've met. They dined at the Mermaid's Mirth in Washington City when my cousin Hannah Smith was visiting."

Cole shoved her straw bonnet back from her face. "Deidre's mother was your cousin?"

How much did they know? "Yes."

"We heard Hannah died in January," Jess said. "She had such a sad life."

Cole studied him. "If you're Hannah's cousin, why didn't she name you guardian instead of Logan?"

"I guess uncles outrank cousins." If Logan hadn't agreed to become guardian of Deidre, Blake would have taken on another responsibility. Logan and Miss Jenny provided a more stable environment for a seven-year-old girl.

"We met Deidre at Christmas," Cass said. "She's sweet."

He nodded. "I visited Pierce House in the spring. Deidre was happy with Uncle Logan and Aunt Jenny." He smacked his forehead. "Deidre mentioned some aunts in Ohio giving her gifts. She must have meant you."

"We're practically family." Cole's smile was wide and flirtatious. "Our kiss doesn't count."

"Oh, I'm counting it."

She was modest enough to blush at his obvious compliment. "You mentioned meeting them at the

Mermaid's Mirth. What is that?"

"A small hotel I own in Washington City."

Cole stared at his ragged clothes. "You own a hotel?"

"Appearances can be deceiving, brat."

"Isn't your hotel profitable?"

"I've been making repairs for more than a year on the Mermaid's Mirth, and every time the army uses it for the wounded, I lose money."

Cole coiled a rope on the deck. "Don't they pay you?"

"Less than half a dollar per soldier. Other hotels are charging two to five dollars a night for a room."

Cole's mouth dropped. "That's highway robbery. How can anyone afford that?"

"Rooms are scarce with people flooding Washington City to nurse the wounded. The poorer guests share a room with others and split the costs. I put four soldiers to a room, and I'm still making less than two dollars. Thankfully, the army is building more hospitals. They won't need the Mermaid's Mirth anymore for the wounded, and I might stop drowning in debt."

"I hope your business does better."

She was sincere. "No matter how good a businessman is, he's one disaster away from ruin." Blake stretched. "I made a foolhardy deal in Tennessee I hope I don't regret."

"Do you own any property around here?"

"I hope to buy an inn in Cleveland," he said.

"With what? Your charm and good looks?"

Blake should have been insulted, but Cole considered him engaging and handsome. He didn't discuss business with others, especially a deal that wasn't finalized. But if she begged…

A high-pitched scream sounded from the towpath.

Paddy had his arm around Jules and was tugging her backwards. The mules fought the reins, braying in fear as a rattlesnake sunning on the towpath had been startled by them and rose to strike, its tail shaking a warning.

"Jess." Cole whispered, her gaze locked on the angry reptile. Jess opened a box on the side of the bow cabin and withdrew a revolver. The cylinder was loaded with the gunpowder, wad, and lead bullets in five of the six chambers. Copper percussion caps were placed on nipples on the other end of the cylinder to ignite a shot.

Blake reached his hand to take the gun, but Jess planted her feet and raised the pistol to shoulder level. She grasped the handle with both hands, her left supporting the right in an overhand grip as she steadied the gun and aimed down the barrel. Using her thumb, she cocked the hammer, exhaled, and pulled the trigger. The shot blew off the head of the rattlesnake, which dropped dead in the path.

Paddy took a stick and flipped the body of the snake into the woods.

Blake pointed at Jess. "One shot? How did you do that?"

Jess lowered the gun. "All it takes is a steady hand."

"Didn't you believe me when I said she's one of the best shooters in the area?" Cole said. "But instead of hunting, her husband will tell her to bake biscuits and churn butter in the kitchen."

Jess replaced the gun in the box. "Ed showed me

how to field dress a deer."

"A true romantic gesture." Cole's seriously spoken words ended in a giggle.

"He never tried canoodling me," Jess defended. "He taught me skills I can use."

Cole draped her arm around her sister's shoulders. "If you want Ed to think of you as more than a hunting partner, you might want to canoodle him the next time you see him."

Jess reddened. "I wouldn't know how to canoodle him."

Cole grabbed her chin and stared into her eyes. "You've been my chaperone for three years. Haven't you learned anything sitting in the parlor watching me?"

She freed her face from Cole's grasp. "I've learned how to avoid a kiss."

Cole laughed. "I am better at discouraging than encouraging suitors."

"I would disagree," Blake said.

Cole patted her pocket. "Have you forgotten my sharp little friend?"

She had kissed him once, but he would have to convince her to repeat the pleasure. Should he plead his case as the soon-to-be soldier? His plan of attack needed some thought.

"Time to eat," Michael announced as he turned the boat toward the towpath.

Blake grabbed a pike to push the boat toward the jagged bank. "I hope it's not rattlesnake."

The girls laughed at his comment. He had entertained his younger brothers with jokes and stories. He'd forgotten how much he loved to hear their laughter.

Michael dropped the anchor. "We'll switch out the mules first."

Cass headed toward the middle cabin. It would take one pulling and one shoving to propel the stubborn beasts out of the cabin and onto the towpath. They knew the dirt path meant work.

Jess and Cole lowered the gangplank for the mules, and Cass prodded the first one with Jess pulling. Paddy replaced each of the mules in harness with a fresh one while the girls disappeared into the woods for their toilette duties. When they returned, they led the mules aboard the boat where Cass fed them and added water to the trough in the cabin.

"I'll fetch the sandwiches." Jess disappeared down the bow cabin.

Paddy hobbled the mules and joined everyone in the shade of a tree.

The girls spread a quilt and unpacked the basket. Cole poured lemonade into tin cups and handed one to Blake. Their fingertips brushed, and his gaze locked onto hers. It didn't require a kiss to make sparks fly between them.

****

After eating and packing the basket, they boarded the *Irish Rose* and headed for the next lock. Cass walked with Paddy, and Jules joined the crew on the deck of the *Irish Rose*.

Jess retrieved a fiddle from the cabin and played a tune. Jules danced the heel and toe steps of the Irish jig in her bare feet. Cass had taken possession of her oversized boots for walking the towpath.

"What is that?" Blake asked when Jess finished

playing.

"I don't know. I made it up."

He shook his head. "Sounded pretty good to me."

"Play my song for Sunday," Jules said. "I need to practice."

"What are you singing?"

"The John Brown song."

"You're singing *John Brown's body lies a-mouldering in the grave* for church?" Blake demanded. It didn't seem appropriate even in abolition territory.

Jules giggled. "No, I'm singing the *The Battle Hymn of the Republic* written by Julia Ward Howe. Same tune, different words." She turned to Cole. "Will you sing harmony?"

"Give me a note."

Jules sang a high note, and Cole sang a third below it. Blake joined in on the chorus, harmonizing with the other voices. He clapped when the impromptu concert ended. "Your sister has a set of pipes. Although your voice is lovely, too," he added.

"I'm surprised you heard it above the caterwauling coming from your throat."

"You're supposed to reciprocate a compliment, brat."

Chapter Six

Her harsh words were necessary. Reciting the alphabet with his deep voice could make a female weak in the knees. It rumbled like thunder and settled on a woman's heart like a warm quilt. Her heart raced beneath her fingertips as she ran a kerchief along the opening of her dress. "Your voice is…seductive. I mean manly." Was it the afternoon heat or his intense stare causing perspiration to bead on her skin? She searched her pocket for her fan.

He leaned close. "You're blushing, brat."

Cole covered her ears as Jules shrieked in a high squeal. "You don't need to scream when you're on board the *Irish Rose*." She scanned the towpath for snakes.

"Over there!" Jules pointed to the opposite shore. "Men with guns."

"It's the Cassell brothers." Blake stepped forward on the roof.

Cole didn't ask how he knew them. She and her sisters had met the slave chasers two years ago at the Independence Day celebration. As abolitionists, her family had thwarted the plans of the two curs and rescued their captured slaves. The Cassell brothers weren't forgiving.

Buck and Clyde were stocky men with full beards and uneven dirty hair exposed beneath felt slouch hats.

Buck moved his broadcloth coat back to expose a revolver strapped to his thigh. He withdrew it and pointed the barrel toward the boat. Clyde had a long scar on the side of his face that left a white line of discolored hair in his long dirty beard. He raised a rifle to his shoulder.

"Tell your driver to halt the mules," Clyde shouted.

"Stay away from the shore." Blake grabbed a pike and shoved against the clay bottom to move the boat toward the opposite towpath bank. Cole's grandfather turned the tiller, but the canal wasn't wide enough to give them a safe distance from the men's guns.

Paddy and Cass were unaware of Clyde's order and continued to drive the mules forward. Clyde shot at the towpath in front of the lead mule. Paddy turned, and Cass screamed.

"Cassie!" Jules shouted, staring ahead at the towpath, stretching to see what had happened.

Cole grabbed the back of her dress and tugged. "Hug the deck."

Jules flattened her body against the bow cabin roof, a soft sob escaped her trembling lips.

"Get under cover!" Cole waved her arm toward the river. Paddy grabbed Cass, and they disappeared in the brush.

Cole motioned to Jess, who opened the gun box from a kneeling position. She exchanged her fiddle and bow for the revolver. Cole blocked her actions with her skirt. "Why have you returned to Ohio?"

Blake pointed at the two men, his eyes wide with surprise. "You know them?"

"Buck and Clyde Cassell are old acquaintances from their slave chasing days."

Buck squinted. He didn't remember her. It had been two years, and she had played a minor part in the drama. She knew they had joined the Confederate army but had grown tired of the rules and regulations and walked away.

"You have no business on the *Irish Rose*," Cole said.

"*Irish Rose*?" Buck looked at Clyde, who had drawn his revolver instead of reloading his muzzle loader.

Blake ceased shoving the pike. "They're not here for you."

If they didn't know who they were, what were they doing here? She looked at Blake. "Who are you?"

"A business man who made a deal with the devil."

Cole pointed at Blake. "What do you want with our passenger?"

"We're loyal Confederates," Clyde said. "And we've come for what that stinkin' polecat stole from the South. Hand it over, Ellsworth, or we start shootin'."

"Gentlemen." Blake stood on the edge of the cabin deck leaning against the pike. "Can't we be civilized about this?"

Cole turned to Blake. "You stole from them?"

"They're the thieves." Blake moved the pike to the opposite side. "Your dirty business is with me." He shoved the boat away from the towpath shore, and it drifted toward the Cassell brothers.

"No!" Cole grabbed the other pike and shoved on the opposite side to neutralize Blake's efforts.

"What are you doing?"

She clutched the pike. "I'm saving your life."

"Those are dangerous men."

"I know. Let's stay on this side of the canal."

Blake shouted to the men, "I'll wade across the canal, but you have to let the girls leave."

"I remember them now," Clyde shouted to Buck. "They're friends of Tyler Montgomery, that lyin' lawyer who stole our property."

"That red-headed boy with the mules looks like the one who tied us up," Buck said. "This is our lucky day."

"It's payback, brother." Clyde pointed at Blake. "After we kill you and the old man, Buck and I are goin' to have a party with those pretty young gals. They owe us."

In the stern of the boat, Michael was retrieving a loaded pistol he kept near the helm for trouble. He nodded. He would take Clyde, who was closer. "The captain is ready," Cole whispered.

"Let me know when I have a clear shot." Jess raised the gun.

Buck pointed his gun at Blake. "We'll let you join the fun if you hand over our gold, Ellsworth."

Gold? "He doesn't even have a few cents to pay for the repairs to his jacket," Cole said. "He's not the man you want."

"Liar!" Buck pulled the trigger on his revolver. The loud bang echoed in the trees, frightening the birds into flight. Blake flew back, his shoulder crashing onto the deck, and his body sliding to the edge. Cole dashed along the deck board, exposing Jess. She grabbed Blake before he slid over the side into the canal and threw her body over his.

"Buck, that ain't no warnin' shot!" Michael's shot barely missed Clyde. "Let's git!"

Jess shot at Buck. She hit him in the leg, and he stumbled.

"Clyde, I'm hit."

Clyde fired his revolver at the boat, grabbed Buck, and dragged him into the woods.

Jess and Michael kept their guns pointed at the bank, watching for movement in the trees, waiting to see if the men would reappear.

"I guess we scared them away," Michael boasted.

"I fired too fast," Jess said. "It's not the same as target shooting or aiming at a snake."

Cole rose from Blake's body, blood smeared across her dress. "Move the mules!" She tugged away his jacket. Blood stained his shirt over his left shoulder. She searched for an exit wound in back. None. She wadded her skirt and pressed the fabric into the bloody hole below his collar bone.

Jess shouted for Paddy and Cass to head up the mules.

Cole straddled Blake's chest, using her weight to press against the gushing wound.

His eyes fluttered open. "What happened?"

"Lie still." The blood wouldn't stop flowing. She wadded another portion of her skirt and pressed it against his torn body.

"The Cassell brothers?"

At least he was talking. "They're gone."

His dark brows knitted in confusion. "What are you doing on top of me?"

"You were shot." Cole looked at Jules. "Fetch some towels and the medical bag."

Jules remained sprawled on the deck, staring at Blake with wide blue eyes. She was pale, and her lip quivered. She was in shock. "Juliet," Cole said in a slow, calm voice. "The men are gone, baby. Can you fetch some towels for me?"

Jules nodded, scurried along the deck, and disappeared into the cabin.

Paddy and Cass had returned to the mules. The boat had drifted forward, and they were only a few feet apart. Paddy stroked the mules. "I heard shots."

"I missed the scarred one, but Jessie hit the other one. Good shootin', lass." Michael looked at Cole. "How's our passenger?"

Cole's hands were covered with Blake's blood as she maintained pressure on the wound the way her father had taught her. Doctor Sterling Beecher had instructed each of his daughters about medicine, taking them along on his visits to help with childbirth and other female ailments. They knew how to stitch a wound, leech a bruise, and other simple tasks, but removing a bullet was beyond her skill. She needed to minimize his loss of blood until her father could save Blake's life. "The bullet didn't clear. We need Papa."

Michael adjusted the rudder to turn the boat into the middle of the canal. "Hurry them mules along!"

Paddy obeyed, and the rope grew taut, groaning against the eyebolt as it pulled the boat forward. The woods had recovered from the disturbance. A woodpecker tapped the bark of a nearby tree, searching for insects. A bullfrog croaked and splashed into the canal.

"How far is the next lock?" Cole asked. Why couldn't she remember?

"It's Lock Twenty-six near Ira Road." Michael gripped the revolver in one hand and the tiller in the other. He scanned the shore for any sign of the Cassell brothers. Jess did the same in the bow.

Jules emerged from the cabin with several towels. She knelt beside Cole and handed over the top bundle. "Cassie should do this. Jem was training her to be a midwife."

"You're doing fine." Cole pressed a towel into the wound. "We'll need you to work the locks with Jess and Paddy. She couldn't leave Blake's side. Every time she eased the pressure on his wound, blood spurted. "Cass can borrow a horse at the next lock and ride to Darrow Falls for Papa. She's the best rider."

Jules clutched the unused towels in her trembling hands. "I know. She's good at everything."

"You're good at different things, Jules."

She dabbed at tears, her sobs catching in her throat as she glanced around. "Do you think they're coming back?"

"I'll be ready for anything they try." Jess planted her feet on the bow deck, her gun resting against the storage box as she scanned the horizon.

Cass had run back along the towpath to the boat. "What can I do?"

"When we reach the lock, you need to ride home and fetch Papa."

"I could run ahead."

"No!" The Cassell brothers could be waiting ahead, and Cass would be defenseless against the two brutes.

Jess pointed in the distance. "We're approaching the lock."

"Tell Papa we'll be at Grandma's inn. Better have Mama stay with Cory. And tell Sheriff Lane about the Cassell brothers." Had she forgotten anything? "You can do this, Cassie. You're the best rider among us."

If she was afraid, Cass didn't show it. Home was on the far side of the river, the opposite direction the Cassell brothers had headed. On a horse, she'd be safe. Cass nodded and joined Paddy, who was urging the mules forward at a record pace.

Cass crossed the bridge over the canal at Ira Road while Michael steered the *Irish Rose* into the lock. "Give her a horse to ride," Michael shouted to the man sitting on the porch of the farmhouse in front of the waterway. "She has to fetch a doctor."

The man stopped rocking and rang a bell on the corner post of the porch. "What's going on?"

"Two men attempted to kill one of my passengers," Michael explained. "They're chasers."

"Chasers? We haven't had chasers this far north since the war began."

"They're the Cassell brothers." Jess tossed the bow line to Paddy who wrapped it around the snubbing post. "One of them is wounded."

"Be on the watch for them. They're dangerous," Michael added. "We need to get through the locks at a steamer's pace."

Two young boys ran around the corner of the house. One had a wooden barrel hoop in his hand. "What do you want, Pa?"

"Saddle your horse," he said. "This gal needs to fetch a doctor."

The boys hesitated.

"Now!" The man clapped his hands to startle the boy into action. He pointed to the other boy. "Operate the far gate."

The boy and his father helped them pass through

the gates at Lock Twenty-six before the other boy returned with a horse. He helped Cass mount. She rode across the bridge toward the road to Darrow Falls. CJ's Inn was located a block before Lock Twenty-nine. The two boys climbed aboard to help with the two remaining locks. They stared at Blake's bloodied body. One gagged. "Better keep your eyes forward." Cole nodded to the bow. "Be ready for the next lock." She didn't need them throwing up on the deck.

Cole remained on her knees, her shoulders directly over the wound, her weight pressing a clean cloth into the opening. Warm red fluid stained the white cloth a rich crimson between her fingertips.

"Take my knife out of my skirt pocket and cut his coat off."

Jules retrieved the leather sheath and withdrew the blade. "Where do I start?"

"Begin with the left sleeve so I can see the wound."

Blake had been shot on the left side above his heart. A few inches lower and he would be dead. She wanted to remove the coat and shirt for a better view of the damage. The bleeding had slowed. A good sign.

Jules knelt beside Blake and carefully cut the threads on the seam of the sleeve.

"The coat isn't worth saving," Cole said. "Slice the fabric and rip it away. He's never going to wear it again."

Cole adjusted her position to give Jules more room and discovered the moneybag strapped to Blake's waist. Why was he dressed like a beggar and wearing enough gold around his middle to tempt the Cassell brothers to travel this far north to rob him? Who was Blake Ellsworth?

Jules had worked slowly, cutting the coat into pieces to remove it. The shirt beneath was stained. "Should I cut it off?"

They were nearing the inn. "No, but you can fetch a blanket."

Her eyes widened. "Is he dead?"

"No, Jules. We'll use the blanket to carry him to the inn."

She looked relieved. She left the knife on top of the clean towels and ran to the bow cabin door. The two boys were about her age. Neither one said a word. They stared as if she was the first girl they had seen.

No matter how much time boys and girls spent together, they were strangers. Would she ever understand why men were so different? She stared at Blake. He was pale and motionless. Cole remained straddled across his chest, her knees bearing her weight as she leaned closer, her head turned to listen for a heartbeat.

"I could breathe easier without you sitting on my chest," Blake gasped.

Cole faced him, her lips inches from his. "Good, you're still with us."

"Where would I go?" He raised his shoulders, but she held him down.

"What do you think you're doing? Don't you know you've been shot?"

He looked at her skirt and hands, covered with his blood. "Is that mine?"

"Buck Cassell put a big hole in you."

His breathing was labored. "How badly am I hurt?"

"Do you have a wife or next of kin?"

"That bad, huh?" He relaxed against the roof of the

71

center cabin and closed his eyes.

Cole spoke close to his ear. "Do you have anyone I need to notify?"

"Nancy Ellsworth." His breath was warm on her cheek. "She's staying at the Dutchman Hotel in Albany, New York."

He was married. She'd kissed someone's husband. She wouldn't take the entire blame for her mistake. Blake had blatantly invited her to share the bed in the stern. Didn't he love his wife?

His chest rose and fell in labored breathing. He reached for her. "Don't let her have the money bags."

He didn't want his wife to have the gold? "What should I do with them?"

"Keep them." He blinked. "Is it raining?"

"No, I'm crying."

Chapter Seven

Blake opened his eyes. Moonlight filtered through a curtain on a window to his left, but his surroundings were shadows and softened shapes in the darkness. He could discern the tall dresser and a washstand near the window. Beneath him was a feather-filled mattress and his head rested on a pillow. He shifted his hips, and the ropes creaked beneath his weight.

The window was open, and a soft breeze carried the sweet scent of flowers and the pungent odor of manure. He didn't detect the motion of the canal boat or hear any water lapping at the sides. He was on land.

He attempted to rise but couldn't. He waved his hands. They were free, but his upper arms and chest were tied to the bed. A large band of heavy cloth bound him to each side of the wooden frame. He kicked his legs. They were free but beneath a blanket tucked into place. "Hey, someone help me!"

He thrashed his head side to side until the dizziness forced him to stop. A jarring pain radiated in his left shoulder. He gritted his teeth to silence the scream. He'd been shot by one of the two men following him. Buck Cassell. The memory was blurry, but Cole knew him. Had they set an elaborate trap? No wonder Captain Michael Donovan had taken him aboard as a passenger, seducing him with his beautiful granddaughter. A siren of disaster. He reached for his waist. The money packet was gone. All he had on were his short linen drawers. "Hey, anyone, can you hear me!"

Bare feet pattered on the wooden floorboards and the door creaked open. A candle flickered as it moved toward him. "Hush, you'll wake everyone." It was Cole. She moved to the dresser and lit a lantern with her flame. "Stop moving, or you'll open your wound."

His eyes adjusted to the bright light amid shadows. She wore no robe, and her braids were undone. Her copper tresses cascaded in a fiery contrast against the white nightgown she wore. Modest in darkness, the light behind her illuminated the shapeliness of her figure underneath. The wide collar slipped to bare one shoulder. He groaned as his body reacted against his will.

Her hand rested against his forehead, and he inhaled the scent of her, a female aroma that tortured his self-control beyond endurance. "Your fever is gone."

Even in the dim light he could tell her figure was one a man could explore for ages and never discover all its secrets. "Where are your clothes?"

She toyed with the string tying the neckline. One tug and the whole gown would cascade to her ankles. "It's night time. I was in bed sleeping when your screams woke me." She stood and turned to leave. "I thought you were in distress."

The lantern behind her revealed her body's firm lines through the flimsy fabric. How could a woman have so many curves? He closed his eyes against the maddening sight. "I was not screaming." Jules had screamed at the sight of the Cassell brothers. Someone had been crying. "How are your sisters? The Cassell brothers didn't hurt any of them, did they?"

"No. They're fine." Her voice softened, and she sat on a stool by the bedside. "After Buck shot you, Jess wounded him in the leg, and he limped away with Clyde."

His shoulder throbbed. How serious was his injury? "Did a doctor examine my wound?"

"He removed the lead ball."

"Then why can't I move?" He flapped his hands on top of the covers. "Why am I'm trussed up like a roasted chicken?"

"When you were shot and fell on the deck, you broke your collar bone." She touched a band of cloth wrapped in front of both shoulders and around the back of his neck. "The doctor put this brace on you, but he didn't want you to roll onto your shoulder while sleeping, so we tied you to the bed."

"How long do I have to stay here? I was planning on being in Cleveland today."

"You mean yesterday."

"Isn't this Friday?"

"The doctor gave you a large dose of laudanum for the pain, and you spent yesterday sleeping. This is Saturday morning. Grandpa and my sisters will be returning from Cleveland this evening."

How could he lose a whole day? "Why didn't you join your sisters on the trip to Cleveland?"

She shrugged. "Someone had to take care of you."

Had she done it by choice or obligation? "But why you?"

"I was first mate on the *Irish Rose*. That makes me responsible for the welfare of the crew and passengers."

"I'm sorry you missed traveling with your sisters."

75

"There will be other trips."

"I thought you were giving up the life of a canal brat." He waited for her to bring up the topic of Simon Blackwater. Did she love him?

"I want to explore other opportunities. Who would have thought I would be in a bedroom in the middle of the night with a naked man?"

"Where are my clothes?"

"I had to throw them away. The shirt was torn and bloody, and the trousers were a maze of patches."

She rose and danced across the room toward the window where a notched board kept it open. "Are you cold? Should I lower the window?" A soft breeze ruffled her nightgown around her naked form.

He was sweating. "Leave it open." His clothes were gone but what about his gold. "What did you do with my money belt?"

"You gave it to me." She perched her well-formed hips on the stool beside the bed. "Don't you remember?"

He recalled his last words before passing out. "That was only in the event of my death. I want it back."

She pushed a loose curl away from her face. "You should be grateful I saved your life."

His hand was free enough to cover hers. "Tell me where my gold is, brat, or I'll turn you over my knee and spank you."

She freed her hand. "You couldn't swat a fly."

He struggled against the bindings but regretted his actions as his shoulder screamed. "Are you in allegiance with the Cassell brothers?"

She placed her palm on his forehead. "Are you delirious?"

"It can't be a coincidence you know them. Did your sister shoot Buck, or is that a lie?"

"You think I conspired with the Cassell brothers to take your gold?" She left his side and paced before halting. She tapped her bare foot on the floorboards and scowled. "I buried it where you'll never find it."

"What?" He kicked off the single cover, exposing a muscular leg tangled in the blanket. "Brat, I didn't escape near death at the hands of the Cassell brothers to lose my money to a mere girl."

"Mere girl?" She leaned over him and poked her finger in his face.

The gown gaped enough to convince him she possessed all the attributes of a woman. He strained to catch more than a glimpse of flesh, but she stood, disappointing him. What was his other desire? His money. "Return my gold!" His hands struggled to free the bindings.

She grabbed his hands. "Lie still. "Your money is in the safe downstairs."

He frowned. "Why didn't you tell me that straight off?"

"You accused me of conspiring with the Cassell brothers, and you lied to me."

He relaxed against the feather mattress. "I never lied to you."

"You made me think you were poor."

He chuckled. "I didn't want you to fall in love with me for my money."

"Fall in love with you?" She placed her hands on her hips, straining the cotton fabric of her gown. "Have you forgotten about your wife?"

He studied her breasts, outlined perfectly beneath

77

the thin layer of cloth. Her words slowly penetrated. Wife? What was she talking about? "What wife?"

"You said to notify Nancy Ellsworth in the event of your death." She stepped closer. "Why didn't you want her to have your gold? Don't you love her?"

He couldn't think clearly with her nearly naked body within arm's reach. He turned away, forcing his mind to decipher her misunderstanding. "Mrs. Ellsworth is my stepmother. One of my responsibilities." He tightened his jaw and grunted.

"You don't like her?"

"I inherited her and her daughter when my father died. I've had to make sacrifices to provide for them."

"You're not married." Cole resumed her seat on the stool. "Thank goodness."

He faced her. "Why is it important I'm not married?"

"I kissed you. I would never kiss a married man. It isn't proper."

"You're a moral seductress?" He studied her. "An odd combination."

"Me? You dress in rags but carry a fortune in gold. Are you a spy? Is that how you provide for your stepmother and stepsister?"

A spy? "No."

"A courier? Mercenary? Deserter?"

Her eagerness in listing the accusations was amusing. Now that she knew he wasn't married, her teasing playfulness had returned. "I hate to burst your romantic notions, but I'm a businessman, nothing more."

"But the bag contained gold coins stamped with a Confederate mark. The Cassell brothers accused you of stealing it."

"I am not a thief, a spy, or a candlestick maker. I sold a hotel, the Lucky Gambler, in Tennessee for gold. I signed over the deed so it was all legal and honorable on my part."

"But it's gold."

"Some business deals are done with gold, especially between the North and South."

"So why are the Cassell brothers after it?"

"The man who bought my hotel acquired the gold from the Confederate army."

Her jaw dropped and her eyes widened. "He stole it from the enemy?"

"The gold turned up missing when the Southern army retreated from Memphis." She filled in the blanks like the pieces of a puzzle, her brow furrowed in thought. "Both sides were looking for it," he explained.

"Then who does it belong to?"

"It belongs to me."

She pursed her lips. "How did the Cassell brothers find out about the gold?"

"The man who bought the Lucky Gambler hired the Cassell brothers to retrieve the gold once I was past the Union pickets. They confronted me in Kentucky. I told them I wasn't planning to return the gold to them or the Confederacy. They attempted to change my mind."

Her hand brushed against the hairs of his chest, tracing the dark thin line running down the center of his sculptured abdomen to his waist. She circled a scabbed wound across a few ribs. "Is that how you received this slash?"

His skin burned where her fingertips had marked a

path of heat on his skin. His mouth had gone dry, and he could only nod.

Her emotions played across her face and quickened his heart. She was worried about him. "But I escaped. They confronted me in Canton and beat me. I jumped from the train, but they were waiting at the Akron depot. I thought I had eluded them by traveling on the *Irish Rose*."

She stared at his chest. "I found the bruises and cut when I washed you."

How could he have slept through that? "You gave me a bath?"

"Only your upper half."

"You didn't peek?" His teasing harvested a smile.

"I thought you were a married man."

He winked, his grin wide. "If you want to peek, I won't tell."

She stared at the blanket, rumpled by his struggles. Was she curious? Yes. But would she look? She raised her gaze to his face. "I want to know who you are, Blake Ellsworth." She stroked the bristle on his cheek. "You can't be old. Your beard has hardly grown beyond the shadow you arrived with."

"I'm old enough to value life. Thank you for saving mine."

"You're welcome."

"I'm still not sure how you know the Cassell brothers."

"They were chasers, and we're abolitionists. Two years ago they were after some runaway slaves, and we helped the slaves escape."

"Isn't helping slaves escape against the law?"

"Slavery should be against the law."

"I think that's why we're at war." He sighed. "I can't believe they found me."

"When they were chasers, they traveled through Ohio." She examined the bindings but didn't remove them. "They attacked the *Irish Rose* before."

"How would they know I was on the *Irish Rose*?"

"If you didn't board the train, they may have gone to Mustill store. The owner probably told them you were a passenger."

"Now what?"

She rose, her gown taut against the full curve of each breast. Twin peaks strained against the thin fabric. Was she cold or aroused? Were women consumed like men by the urge to mate? Had she seen the bulge beneath the blanket? She checked his brace and a thick curl brushed his face. He inhaled the scent of her. "Stay." Had he spoken aloud?

"You need your rest, and I'm going to bed." She gathered the lantern from the dresser.

"Where do you think you're going?" he demanded. "You can't leave me like this. Aren't you going to take the straps off?"

"You need to be securely tied down." Cole stopped short of the door. "Do you want to open your wound?"

"But I have needs."

"Oh." She returned, placed the lantern on the floor, and reached beneath the bed. She retrieved a chamber pot with a spout for bedridden men.

The sight of the pot made him realize he needed to accept the container. "This is embarrassing."

Cole turned her back while he completed his task. "You don't know what humiliation is." Her voice was pained.

81

"Are you in love with Simon Blackwater?" Was he the source of the sadness in her voice?

Cole turned, and Blake covered himself and handed her the pot. She took it to the door. Was she leaving? She placed the pot in the hall and returned, washing her hands at the washstand. "How do you know Simon?"

"I read the notice in the paper before you tossed it overboard." When you distracted me with a kiss. "When your sister mentioned he'd been calling and you expected a proposal, I figured he had misled you to believe he was going to marry you."

"He's engaged now." She squared her shoulders. "I won't allow myself to be in love with him anymore."

"Sometimes we can't control how we feel."

She sat on the stool beside him. "How long does it take?"

"What do you mean?"

"How long will it take for me to forget Simon and all my dreams of a life together?"

He could help her forget. "Did you kiss me only to distract me and separate me from my paper?"

"I shouldn't have done that."

"I didn't mind." He relaxed. "I'm all tied up, brat. The perfect opportunity to do research for your book."

"What book?"

"The book on kissing."

"I said I *could* write a book." She stood. "It was a joke."

"That explains why your kiss was childish."

"Childish?" She leaned over him and kissed him hard on the mouth.

"*Tsk, tsk.*" Blake shook his head. "A woman takes

her time. She seduces a man with a look, a touch, and a kiss. She gives pleasure and receives pleasure."

Cole stared at him. "I've been warned not to tease a man. It could make him dangerous."

"You could tame a man instead." He waved his hands. "I'm not a threat tied to the bed. You can torment me, brat, and I won't be able to fight back."

Her hand moved along his bare skin between the brace. "You trust me?"

"You saved my life. Now it belongs to you."

Her fingertips played across the hard muscles of his chest. She stroked the short growth of beard and outlined his jaw, ending with her fingertips touching his mouth. He held his breath, waiting for her to decide. Would she kiss him or not? She lowered her mouth but hesitated. He fought any movement that could frighten her.

Her lips brushed against his before capturing them in a gentle embrace. He nuzzled back, softly before catching her lip with his and pulling her deeper, refusing to relinquish any hold. Someone groaned. Was it Cole or his reaction to a primal need he had denied? He reached with the limited use of his arms, resting his hand on the fullness of her hip, pressing her closer.

Every time she touched her lips against his, he suckled, holding them, wishing she wouldn't break away. He raised his head and begged for more, entreating her to return. His tongue teased her lips apart, seeking entry. She paused, surprised by the invasion and to his joy, opened herself to allow entry. He plunged, seeking the moistness, reveling in her playfulness as she joined in the parry and thrust of their tongues.

He fought against the ties, burning to touch her body, to explore more than her lovely mouth. "Untie me," he gasped between stolen breaths.

Her fingertips trembled against her bruised lips. "No. You may trust me, but I don't trust you. I don't trust any man." She blew out the lantern, crossed the moonlit room, and opened the latch.

Did she group him with all the other men who had wronged her? They didn't care about her the way he did. He was in love with her, but the timing couldn't be worse. She was holding out for marriage, and he was going to war. Those two didn't coexist.

Who knew what could happen to him on a battlefield? Death was only one option. He could be maimed, blinded, or disfigured. He didn't expect a young wife to sacrifice her future for a mangled man. If he survived the war, he could call on Cole. But how long would the war last? He couldn't expect her to wait, not knowing if a future existed for them.

Cole had saved his life, but it appeared bleak without her in it.

Chapter Eight

Cole paused at the tall free-standing mirror in the corner of the room at her grandmother's inn. Would Blake recognize her? Gone was the canal brat with a faded, worn dress. The yards of sheer gown decorated with a floral print flowed over the bell-shaped crinoline. The bodice crisscrossed in front over the chemise and corset cover and was secured by a broad emerald belt. The sleeves were wide beneath the elbow and trimmed in green satin ribbon. Her hair was parted in the middle and pulled to the crown, cascading in a wave of ginger curls.

She heard the bell at the inn's main entry and hurried down the stairs to greet her father.

Sterling Beecher was tall and lanky with dark hair and a touch of gray at his temples. He tossed his leather gloves into the long barrel of his top hat and placed it on a side table near the staircase. "How is our patient?"

"He's a horrible patient," Cole said as her father kissed her cheek. "He awoke during the night and wanted me to untie him."

His hazel eyes studied her. "You didn't?"

She took his arm as they ascended the steps. "No, and he wasn't happy about it."

"Sometimes we have to suffer to appreciate the good in life."

Cole paused in the hallway at the top of the stairs.

The tone in his voice alarmed her. "Is something wrong?"

He opened his medical bag and removed a newspaper. "I read an announcement concerning Simon Blackwater in the *Summit County Beacon*."

Cole waved away the newspaper he offered. "I read about his engagement."

"You expected it?"

Cole shook her head, not trusting her voice to betray her. She refused to shed any tears, especially in front of her father.

"I thought there was an understanding. He called often enough." Sterling returned the paper to his bag. "I'm sorry."

"It's not your fault he decided to marry someone else."

Her father looked tired. "Perhaps it is."

"What do you mean?"

"It seemed serious between you and Simon so I visited his father at his shop on Howard Street. He was surprised Simon was spending his Sundays in our parlor calling on you."

"Simon never told them about me?" Why keep their relationship a secret? "Was he ashamed of me?"

"No one could ever be ashamed of you, Colleen." Strong praise from her father. She was the daughter considered challenging to his patience. "The Blackwaters are ambitious. They have plans for their son."

She sighed. "And Margaret Radcliff is part of that plan."

"Some men improve their lot in life by working hard while others marry into wealth." He placed his hand on the latch to Blake's door but didn't open it.

"And the rich never marry the poor."

"Simon is the poor man in this marriage. He'll be indebted to his father-in-law. Two people stand a better chance at love if they start on equal ground."

"You married Mama, and she was poor."

"What your mother lacked in coin, she made up in so many ways I can't count them all. Besides, I loved her from the first moment we met."

"You fell in love that soon?"

"I'm sure your grandfather has told you how he broke his leg during a fight at one of the locks, and I set it. But I only remember your mother. Maureen Donovan was wearing a yellow dress with blue dots. She had a blue ribbon in the straw bonnet she wore. Her ginger curls reached her waist. She was mopping Michael's brow and trying to keep him from downing a pint of whiskey. When I told her to let him finish the bottle, she scowled at me. She didn't care that I was a doctor or a Beecher. She was my equal no matter what others said. No." He paused. "She's my partner and wants the best for me as I do for her. That's love, Colleen."

"You never regretted marrying Mama?"

"Every morning I wake next to the most beautiful woman in the world, and I thank God for the gift of her." He no longer looked tired. "She gave me six beautiful daughters who have grown into lovely young women." His hand caressed her cheek.

"Why aren't there any young men as perfect as you, Papa?"

He laughed. "I didn't realize I was setting the bar so high for my girls. Someday you'll meet someone who will appreciate all you have to offer and treasure you in a way that will make you feel valued and loved."

"I could have made Simon happy."

He gripped her chin and gazed into her eyes. "He's no good, Colleen. He's proven that. Don't waste time moping about it."

Her pride wouldn't allow it. "I won't."

Sterling opened the door. Rectangles of light decorated the floor where the morning sun was shining through the sectioned panes of glass in the window. Blake stirred in his bed. He opened his eyes. "I hear you're feeling better, young man. I'm Doctor Sterling Beecher."

Blake shifted, the ropes echoing his movements. "Forgive me for not standing."

Sterling approached him, placing his bag on the stool next to the bed. "Do you know your name?"

"Yes."

Sterling glanced over his shoulder at Cole, a worried look on his face. She moved toward the bed. "Say it."

Blake stared before uttering, "Who are you?"

Cole gasped and turned to her father. "He's lost his memory." She studied Blake. "Don't you remember anything?"

He scanned her gown from the wide hem to the sheer neckline, focusing on her face. "You can't be the canal brat I met on the *Irish Rose*."

Was her appearance so altered, he didn't know her? "It's the dress. He's only seen me in rags and braids. He doesn't recognize me."

"Do you know who you are?" Sterling repeated.

His gaze remained on Cole. "Blake Ellsworth,

blinded by the beauty of the morning sun."

"Blinded? What are you babbling about?" Cole turned to her father. "I told you he lost a great deal of blood. He may have hit his head in the fall."

"I believe you've made a startling impression on him." Sterling removed bandages from his medical bag. "Who is the President of the United States?"

Blake looked confused. "Why do you need to know that?"

"I don't need to know it," Sterling said. "You do."

"Abraham Lincoln unless we lost the war while I was unconscious."

"News travels slowly, but I think we would have heard if Lincoln had surrendered to Jefferson Davis."

Sterling untied the bindings. "I don't want you to sit, stretch, or move." He untied the harness around Blake's shoulders and lifted the bandage covering the wound.

Cole had retrieved an apron from the hook by the door and a tin bowl from the wash stand. She took the soiled bandages from her father and peered over his shoulder at the wound. She had expected a mangled mess, but the incision was small and clear of any yellow pus. Her father was a trained surgeon unlike some of the sawbones in the army.

Jem had written about the amputations following every battle. The end of the sawed bone sometimes was exposed after the skin shrank from a circular cut. The surgeons had learned to leave a flap to allow coverage and an opening for infection to drain. They were becoming better surgeons. Who wouldn't with thousands of patients to practice upon?

Blake turned his head, trying to examine his

shoulder. "It doesn't look bad."

"Not on the outside." Sterling pressed against his collarbone.

Blake winced.

"Do you know what happened to you, young man?"

"I was shot." He looked at Cole. "I couldn't breathe."

He was referring to her sitting on his chest. Cole took the basin to the washstand and poured water over the soiled bandages. She'd scrub them later and dry them on a line in the yard. Her father would reuse them on his next patient.

"Probably had the wind knocked out of you when you fell against your shoulder," Sterling said. "What is the last thing you remember before being shot?"

"The Cassell brothers. Do you know what happened to them?"

"They boarded a train in Akron heading south. The sheriff sent a telegram to the next depot to warn authorities, but the Cassell brothers slipped through. Probably on the other side of the Ohio River by now."

"Are you sure they're gone?"

"Yes. How do you know the Cassell brothers?"

"I bought a hotel in Tennessee from an unscrupulous thief. After paying me in stolen Confederate gold, he hired the Cassell brothers to take the money back."

"Nasty fellows." Sterling placed clean bandages on the wound and rewrapped the brace, tightening it around Blake's shoulders. "The wound will heal in a couple of weeks, but the clavicle bone will require nearly two months to mend. You're lucky the ball didn't shatter it. You'll feel a knot over the break after it heals. That's normal. Keep the brace on at all times. If the bone moves, it'll cause serious problems."

"Will it prevent me from fighting in the war?"

"Are you a soldier?"

"No, but I'm expecting to be drafted."

"That won't be until the fall. By then you should be able to carry a soldier's pack." He studied Blake. "Unless you don't want it to be healed. But you'll have to find another doctor to write you an exception. I won't."

"I'm not avoiding fighting. I want to do my part to win the war."

"Then I commend your courage. Some men are having accidents to avoid the draft. I had to bandage a man's hand after he *accidentally* shot off his trigger finger."

"That's horrible," Cole said. "Don't they want to win the war?"

Sterling closed his bag. "They would rather risk maiming than lose their life in a battle." He extended his hand to Blake. "Do you feel like sitting up?"

Blake gripped his hand and leaned forward. His bare back was wide, and the muscles rippled as he tugged on the blanket tangled around his legs. Blake searched the room. "Where is my satchel? It had my belongings." He tossed aside the blanket and swung his legs to the side.

"It's too early for you to stand." Sterling stepped between Blake and his daughter. "Do you know where his satchel is, Colleen?"

"Yes, sir." Blake had no modesty. Did he think because she had given him a sponge bath, she was familiar with his body? She had taken care of him like any other patient, detached and unaffected because she had believed he was married. Now, the body was alive, rippling with each movement, mesmerizing in its panther-like grace.

Both men stared, waiting for her to act. Cole blinked, averting her eyes from Blake's figure. She retrieved the satchel from her room and returned, placing it on the bed.

Blake searched the bag and extracted black broadcloth trousers and a linen shirt. He attempted to slip his arm into the sleeve.

"Put your left arm in first," Cole instructed as she grabbed the shirt from him and slipped the left sleeve over his hand and pulled it over his head to where he could slip his right arm into the other sleeve.

He inhaled. "You can't be the canal brat with bare feet and a rag for a dress."

"Brat?" Sterling repeated. "What does he mean, Colleen?"

"He's dreaming." The brace bulged beneath the shirt as she fastened the buttons beneath the collar.

"Was it a dream when you stole into my room last night and kissed me? The doctor has no medicine equal to your lips."

Sterling's eyebrow rose. It was the only indication of his displeasure. "You said the man requested to be untied. You said nothing about a kiss."

Cole stepped back from Blake. Was he trying to make her father angry?

"It was a kiss worth writing about." Blake winked at her as he stood. The blanket fell away, revealing his short pants below the bottom of his shirt. His legs were long, muscular, and well formed. He grabbed his trousers and attempted to step into one of the legs, wobbled, and put his arm around Cole's shoulder. "I may need some help."

"Wait outside, Collen, while I assist Mr. Ellsworth."

Colleen froze. The tone in her father's voice was reserved for his displeasure.

"She doesn't have to leave," Blake said. "No need to be modest at this stage of the game."

"What do you mean, young man?" Sterling turned to Cole. "Has this man behaved inappropriately toward you, Colleen?"

"He's a blubbering idiot, Papa."

Blake dropped the trousers, which pooled around his ankles. "What did you call the doctor?" He snatched the blanket from the bed and draped it in front of him.

He didn't know. Cole turned away, her hand covering her mouth until she regained her composure and faced them. "He compromised me, Papa."

Blake pointed at Cole. "I thought your name was Donovan."

"Her name is Beecher," Sterling corrected. "She's my daughter."

"One of six." Cole fought to keep from laughing.

"An abolitionist name." Blake was pale. "Do you prefer pistols or swords, sir?"

"I'd hate to put another hole in you." Sterling's voice was barely controlled. "Perhaps you could explain what happened."

"I was tied to the bed." Blake pulled up the trousers, slipping a suspender over his injured shoulder. "It wasn't much of a kiss."

Much of a kiss? "You should shoot him, Papa. He's a liar and a cad."

Sterling turned to his daughter. "Has this man done anything that warrants my intervention?"

"He tricked me into kissing him." She turned to Blake, jabbing her finger in his face. "Not much of a kiss? It was a wonderful kiss."

The blood drained from Blake's face. "Did I make it clear I was tied to the bed?"

Sterling groaned, a sign his patience was wearing thin. "Proper young ladies do not brag about their kissing skills."

Why was his judgment directed at her? "Yes, Papa."

"Your daughter misrepresented herself as an orphan working on a canal boat," Blake defended.

Cole stabbed him in the chest with her finger. "You're the one who dressed in rags with a fortune of gold wrapped around your middle." She stomped toward the dresser and tossed a small leather bag at him. "This was in your trousers. I wouldn't want you to accuse me of stealing your purse."

Blake had caught the bag with one hand. "How much do I owe you, doctor?"

"Two dollars and a half dollar for the nurse." Sterling folded a square of linen cloth and handed it to Cole. "Tie this sling around Mr. Ellsworth's neck."

Cole's actions were clumsy under her father's gaze. Did he have to watch her so closely? Her fingertips brushed against the bare skin near Blake's ear, and he turned. His smoky gaze made her throat dry. Memories of last night attacked her senses. Her body reacted against her will. What would have happened if she had remained?

"I've seen enough." Sterling grabbed his bag. "Remind your mother to talk to you about proper behavior between young ladies and gentlemen, again." He turned to Blake. "You are to do nothing more strenuous than reading a book." He turned to Cole. "Tell your grandmother what Mr. Ellsworth is allowed to eat for breakfast."

"Are ham and eggs on the menu?" Blake asked.

Sterling turned. "You will have to learn to control your appetite, young man. Toast and oatmeal is what you'll be eating for a while."

He swallowed, a bashful expression replacing his hungry one.

"Shall I help Blake downstairs?"

"He was not shot in the leg." Sterling turned to Blake. "But take the stairs slowly. You may be lightheaded."

Sterling offered his arm to Cole. "A word, Colleen."

She walked with him to the front door. "Are you angry because I kissed Blake?"

"You've always been impulsive, Colleen. But you need to be careful about bestowing your affections so freely. Some men do not practice self-control. And unfortunately, most men are stronger than any woman. I can't always protect you."

"Don't worry, Papa. Jess will shoot any man who forgets his place."

"I heard she received a letter from Edward Herbruck."

"Two."

"Serious?"

"She's in love, Papa, but don't worry. Ed is miles away. If anything, her romance will prevent her from kissing anyone until Ed returns home."

"Thank goodness," Sterling said. "I have enough worries with young men crowding my parlor to win your favor."

"I learned my lesson from Simon. I'm never falling in love again."

"I have a feeling that young man upstairs would like to change your mind."

"All he can think about is joining the army. All he wants to do is fight."

"Then when you kissed him, he didn't kiss you back?"

She didn't answer.

Chapter Nine

Cole opened the double doors with decorative etched glass to allow the morning breeze to blow inside. She stood on the porch with her father, hoping he wouldn't press for an answer. Not only had Blake kissed back, he had stirred emotions she didn't know existed.

A wagon loaded with freshly cut timber rolled along the dirt road from Akron to Peninsula. Beyond, the river flowed with the canal shadowing it on the far bank. Water rushed over the rocks and swirled near the mill on the other side of the canal. Peninsula was named for the bend in the river. The canal boats crossed the river at the Lock 29 aqueduct and continued their straight path north while the river wound to the western side.

She missed the *Irish Rose*. Her feet moved confidently on its worn deck. Her hands operated the locks with the familiarity of an old friend. A captain, guiding his boat into the lock, waved, and she returned the gesture.

"What am I going to do, Papa? This was going to be my last voyage on the *Irish Rose* because I was going to marry Simon."

"Do you want to go back to working on your grandpa's boat?"

"I will always have a special place in my heart for

the canal and the *Irish Rose*, but I was looking forward to marriage for the first time. I guess I'm destined to be a spinster."

Sterling chuckled. "Would you like a change of scenery?"

Cole followed him to his buggy. "What are you suggesting?"

"Jennifer wrote. Her morning sickness is not improving. I suggested she come home to improve her health, but she won't leave Logan. His work is too important at the Treasury for him to leave Washington City. I think an alternative would be for you to travel there and help her."

"Are you sure Jem is going to want me around? We've always been at odds with each other."

"You're both redheads." He laughed. "She's prim and proper, and you're a bit wild."

Cole stroked the nose of the horse pulling her father's buggy. "Only a bit?"

"Jessica can accompany you and guard against any impetuousness."

"Won't that double Jem's worries? She thinks we're hellions."

He secured his bag in front of the single seat. "She'll keep you so busy, I doubt you'll be able to cause any trouble."

"It might take a while to teach Cass and Jules to operate the locks."

"Ethan and Paddy have friends who can help your grandpa. Their parents will be happy to keep them occupied at home instead of dreaming of joining the battle. Cassie will help me, and Juliet can work on her cooking skills."

Cole glanced around at the familiar surroundings. "How soon do we leave?"

"I'll write Jennifer and tell her to expect you after the Independence Day celebration. You can enjoy the holiday and show everyone you're not grieving for Simon." He lifted her chin. "You're not, are you?"

"I promise to have a wonderful time."

"Your mother spoke fondly of her life on the *Irish Rose*, but she never regretted leaving."

"She had you."

"You'll find someone, Colleen." He hugged her. "Fate provides the opportunity, but you make the choice."

"What do you mean?"

"I met your mother because the captain broke his leg. That was fate. I married your mother because I loved her. That was my choice." He kissed her.

"Did anyone think it was wrong because Mama was Irish?"

"Yes."

The Irish were the serving class in English society. To many, her father had married beneath him. Did Simon consider her ancestry a liability?

"But true friends never questioned my decision. I've never regretted it. I want my daughters to be happy." He lifted her chin. "Sometimes that requires patience. You're young, Colleen. The world is changing, and women have more opportunities in life."

"I've tried, Papa. I taught school for a year, but the school board replaced me with a man."

"He was afraid he'd be drafted, and teachers are exempt."

Cole stomped her foot. "Why didn't they tell me? I

thought I had done something wrong."

"The truth would have reflected badly on the gentleman's courage."

"Well, it reflected badly on my ability to teach."

"The closer we near the draft in the fall, the worse it will become." He looked weary. "All the casualties are making the war unpopular. It's a man's choice when he volunteers to fight. But a draft forces men to show courage and fight or run away and hide. I was serious when I talked about some men injuring themselves to avoid being drafted. The maiming will increase as the date approaches."

"That's cowardly."

"As a woman you will never fight in a battle so don't judge a man who is afraid of dying."

"Jake writes that they fight in spite of their fears. He has no respect for the officers who fake an injury or hide when the battle begins. He says the men are hungry and tired." She shook her head. "Why don't they take better care of the fighting men?"

"The officers come from affluent families and think the poor are expendable." Sterling slipped on his gloves. "But the war has cost too many lives, and they have to use a draft to fill the ranks if men don't volunteer. The government has promised if a man joins a regiment that has already served a year, he only serves two years instead of three." He placed his hat on the single seat of the buggy. "Cowardice is a minor reason for not joining the regiments. War creates job opportunities, and more money can be made at home."

Her father talked medicine, politics, and current events with equal ease to his daughters. He didn't think the topics too lofty for their feminine ears. He had never proclaimed his support of women's rights, but his actions assured all his daughters he considered them equals and as such, valued their opinions. "It seems wrong to make money off of a war."

"Most decisions made by powerful men are based on wealth." He climbed into the buggy. "The South left the Union to keep slavery because the owners of large plantations would lose profits."

"You don't think President Lincoln will let the South keep slavery?"

"Men are divided here in the North about supporting the war and letting the South keep its slaves. If we don't start winning battles, the abolishment of slavery may never happen."

"But slavery is wrong, Papa."

"I agree, but white men are dying on the battlefields. Poor men are fighting for thirteen dollars a month." He put on his hat. "Families are weighing the freedom of black men and women against the lives of their husband, brothers, and sons."

"Isn't there a better solution than war?"

"President Lincoln proposed sending blacks to Africa or South America, but they consider the United States their home. Their ancestors have been here longer than most of ours," Sterling said. "When Lincoln freed the slaves in Washington City, he paid millions to compensate the owners."

"Isn't that a good thing?"

"I don't agree with paying men who have saved fortunes with free labor. We should have compensated the slaves."

"You're right. It doesn't seem fair for the rich to gain more wealth while the poor struggle to survive."

He shook his head. "Life isn't guaranteed to be fair."

"But does it have to be unfair? Women suffer the greatest inequalities, especially when it comes to love."

He had his reins in his hands but held the gelding firm. "Are you referring to Simon Blackwater?"

"He seemed so perfect, Papa. He was a college graduate and had a promising future in his family business. Why did he need to be so greedy? I would have been a perfect wife."

"You would have been an asset, but would he have been the perfect husband? Women in love tend to overlook a man's flaws. The next time you see Simon, take a clear, level-headed look. You may not believe me now, but losing Simon to someone else is the best thing that could have happened to you."

"You didn't like Simon?"

"I found it odd during our conversations when he called upon you, he never asked about your interests or friends. He usually bragged about his achievements or his family. A young man's focus should be on the woman he loves, not himself."

"I'm sure he was only trying to make a good impression."

"He failed, Colleen Josephine."

How could she have been completely wrong about Simon? Had he deceived her into believing he was in love with her? His feelings had appeared sincere. "I can't figure out what I did wrong."

"You didn't do anything wrong. Many men will cross your path, Colleen. You'll barely acknowledge most of them. But one of them will draw your attention. You'll measure each other, finding faults and discovering strengths. In the end, you'll know he's the one man for you. You'll choose him as much as he chooses you."

He paused. "And promise me, Colleen. No more kissing strangers even if they are tied to their beds." He slapped the reins on the hindquarters of the horse.

"Yes, Papa." But Blake wasn't a stranger. He was indebted to her because she had saved his life. Cole watched the buggy raise a trail of dust before she entered the inn. Blake stood at the top of the stairs. "Don't move." She lifted her skirt and hurried to his side.

He made a tsking noise. "You used both hands. A lady only uses her right. How do you expect to be treated like one of the gentry if you don't follow the rules, brat?"

"You're schooling me on proper behavior after the way you talked to Papa?"

He groaned. "Why didn't you tell me your name was Beecher?"

"Would it have made a difference in your behavior toward me?"

"The Beecher name is well known." He shook his head. "You said you were abolitionists. I hope you're not related to the author of *Uncle Tom's Cabin*."

"She's a distant cousin. We're descended from John Beecher of New Haven, Connecticut. Papa was born there but traveled to Ohio to practice medicine."

"I'm lucky I didn't tell him about you kissing me before he dug the lead out of my shoulder."

"Do you always brag about women kissing you?"

His smoldering gaze never left hers. "Only those worth boasting about."

Laura Freeman

She stopped on one of the steps. "Then why did you say it wasn't much of a kiss?"

"I lied." His smoky gaze swirled to show a spark. Her knees shook. "If I had told the truth, your father would have had every right to shoot me."

"I promised Papa I wouldn't kiss you anymore."

"I wish you hadn't done that." His deep voice was sincere.

"I didn't promise you couldn't kiss me."

Blake laughed, the rumbling sound echoing up the stairs. "Is Papa aware of the interpretation of your promises?"

"Only if you blurt it out like all my other secrets." She shook her head. "Don't you know it isn't proper to talk about a lady's behavior to other men?"

"Especially to her father. I must have looked like an idiot."

"I doubt if it was the first time."

Blake staggered. "You wound my pride, brat." He looked around the foyer, his arm around her waist. "This is a nice place."

She caressed the oak railing, tracing the intricate curve on the floor newel. "I love this place. Grandma has guests from all over the world." She laughed. "But you would know that from owning a hotel."

"You don't think I was telling the truth?"

"I don't know what is a lie or the truth from you."

"Let's promise to be honest from now on."

She shook off his words. Men couldn't be honest. They crossed the marble floor in the foyer to the polished oak floors in the dining room. Tables were spaced at regular intervals with guests enjoying breakfast. Along the sideboard were the remains of eggs, bacon, biscuits, applesauce, and ham slices.

"Did the other guests leave this all for me?"

"You're a patient. You have to be careful what you eat."

"But I'm starving."

"Sick and injured men eat oatmeal." She spooned some of the cooked oats into a bowl. "Would you like some jam?" She pointed at strawberry, blackberry, and apricot jams.

He reached for a slice of crisp bacon.

Cole slapped at his hand. "None of that."

"I'll waste away."

"How is our patient?" Grandmother CJ was a tall full-figured woman with only a hint of blonde in her white hair. Her voice revealed her German roots. She had traveled to America as a young woman and met Michael Donovan on the boat. Fate had joined them, and choice had made them husband and wife.

She wiped her hands on her apron and extended one. "I'm CJ Donovan."

"CJ?"

"Caroline Josephine. Easier to go by CJ."

"Must be a family trait."

CJ looked puzzled.

"Your granddaughters have nicknames."

"Courtney dubbed them with pet monikers because it was her task to round them up when Maureen called. They were lucky she didn't number them instead."

Blake pointed at Cole. "She won't let me eat your fine cooking."

"What is this, Colleen Josephine? The man is hungry. Let him eat."

"The man is causing trouble. Go ahead and eat the

bacon and sausage and fried potatoes and see what happens." She tilted her nose in the air and gave a huff of disgust. "But you're emptying the chamber pot."

He took the bowl Cole had filled. "The oatmeal looks delicious."

Chapter Ten

Sunday was a quiet day, but dark clouds were gathering and threatening to storm. Michael and CJ drove the girls home so they could attend church in Darrow Falls. Michael had been raised Catholic, married a Protestant, and had adopted a faith without religious practices. Cole returned to the inn with them after the services to check on her patient. She had left Blake in the parlor reading *Great Expectations* by Charles Dickens. At first she thought the man sitting in the shadows of the porch was Blake, but as she greeted him, she realized her mistake. It was Simon Blackwater.

Simon stood, leaving his stove top hat on the table. His straight brown hair was cut short, and he was clean shaven. The frock coat emphasizing broad shoulders was store bought with a mustard-colored silk vest beneath. A white ruffled shirt contrasted against the tan broadcloth. The lace-edged ruffle at each wrist was perfectly exposed. His trip to New York had polished his appearance. "I've been waiting for you." His horse was grazing in the side yard.

"I'll put the team and wagon in the barn." Grandpa helped CJ and Cole descend from the bench seat. "You have your dirk?"

His reference to her knife caused her to smile. The sharp blade was useful for cutting rope, slicing apples, and putting a safe distance between unwelcomed advances from men who didn't recognize boundaries. She removed her gloves and bonnet as she entered the inn. "Why didn't you call on me at home?"

"I did, but your father said you had left and were staying with your grandparents." He paused in the foyer, staring at his reflection in the large mirror. "I only arrived a few minutes before you."

CJ glanced inside the parlor. "I believe this room is empty. I'll bring some refreshments."

"Thank you, Grandma." Cole led the way. A fireplace was against the far wall but screened for the summer. A long table was set against a high back sofa facing the fireplace. Several books were stacked on a smaller table between two wing-back chairs. She had expected to see Blake in one of them, reading, but the room appeared empty.

CJ carried a tray with lemonade and pie and placed it on the table between the chairs they occupied. "If you need anything, I'll be in the kitchen."

Simon took a glass and surveyed the room. "It's not as elegant as the hotels in New York, but for a canal town like Peninsula, it's comfortable."

It was a compliment but cloaked in smug contempt. How long would it take for him to reveal his engagement? "You look well. Your trip to New York must have agreed with you."

He ran his fingers along the lapels of his coat. "Do you like the new suit? A successful businessman needs to look the part."

"You look dashing." She waited for him to return the compliment, but he sipped his drink instead. Her father had been right about his selfish focus. "Was your trip profitable?"

"My father negotiated several business contracts."

She pressed him for the truth. "You didn't acquire anything of value?"

"I made some important connections." He finished his pie and studied her slice, which she hadn't touched. "I see my prosperity increasing substantially in the near future."

She lowered her glass. "Marriage to Margaret Radcliff can do that."

His hand knocked the fork off the empty plate, rattling the china and landing on the table with a thud. "You read the announcement in the paper?" He coughed to clear his throat.

"Yes." Cole took a deep breath to keep from screaming. "It was a bit of a surprise."

Simon turned toward the window and gazed at the street. "I didn't know my parents would announce my engagement so quickly."

She barely contained her fury with her biting remark. "It must have been a shock to read you were engaged."

He faced her, a startled look on his face. "I knew I was engaged."

Had he always been so dimwitted? "And you forgot to tell me?"

Blood drained from his face, and his eye twitched. "It happened suddenly. I only met Miss Radcliff a few weeks ago."

"When you visited New York City with your parents? Hardly time to fall in love."

"It was a business trip."

"Did you buy her?"

He looked confused, his eye twitching several times in rapid succession. "No. I proposed."

"I was under the delusion you took your time making a decision. You've been courting me for more than six months, yet it took you only a few days to determine Miss Radcliff was suitable for a wife."

He dabbed at his mouth with the cloth napkin. "I know it may seem odd to a country girl that two people could decide to marry in such a short time, but Miss Margaret is a special woman."

"I'm sure she is." Cole gathered the dishes and placed them on the tray. "I would be insulted if you married an inferior woman."

He smiled with a familiar tenderness she had loved. "You will always have a special place in my heart, Colleen."

Cole threw her napkin on the table and stood. "Then you lied when you said you loved me."

"I do love you." He stood, taking her hands in his. "You have many admirable qualities, Colleen, but my family believes Miss Margaret will make a profitable union."

His palms were sweaty. She slid her hands free. "Do you love her?"

"Love is two people enjoying what life has to offer," he said. "Marriage is about social standing, wealth, and creating a future. She comes from a noble and respectable family."

"And I don't?"

"I have nothing against your father. He's a Beecher and a doctor, but your mother's family works on the canal."

"How does that make me a hindrance to your

success?" She paced the floor. "You have a college education and a family business to support you, and I'm a liability?"

"Miss Radcliff's father is a successful businessman," he said. "Darius Radcliff has already promised me a job in New York."

Her voice rose in volume as she faced him, stabbing her finger at his chest. "Everything you told me, told my family, were lies. You had no intention of marrying me."

"My parents didn't approve of you."

Didn't approve? What was wrong with her? "Why?"

He waved toward the street and the view beyond. "Your work on the canal was one reason."

"It's honest work."

"It's not dignified, especially for a young woman."

Cole's voice shook. "Were there other reasons?"

"I wasn't the only man in your parlor. You flirted with anyone wearing trousers. Your reputation for being reckless is well known." He moved closer. "You allowed me to kiss you on several occasions."

"Twice. Once was a peck on the cheek and the other..." She had been curious about her powers of seduction. It was chaste compared to the kisses she had exchanged with Blake. She touched her lips, the memory fresh.

"Your kisses betrayed your true nature." Simon placed his hand on her shoulders, trapping her in a loose embrace. "I would like to think my courtship was not in vain."

"How is it not in vain? For six months you declared you had feelings for me. You said you loved

111

me on several occasions. And I believed you."

"There are many ways to love a woman. I learned a great deal during my trip to New York. Mr. Radcliff is a man of the world. He took me under his wing and taught me what life has to offer to those who have the means to claim it. I'm fortunate he chose me."

"Congratulations, but didn't you choose Margaret?"

"He taught me that marriage has options."

What did he mean?

"A man marries a woman who can advance his career, but that doesn't mean he has to relinquish the pleasures other women offer."

She stepped back from the hungry predatory look in his eyes.

"Once I'm established in New York, I could make arrangements for an apartment for you and a generous allowance."

His intention was clear. He wanted a rich wife and a mistress on the side. She thrust her hands into her skirt pockets to hide her clenched fists. Her fingers bumped against the sheath of her knife. "Would it include a carriage, silk gowns, and jewelry?"

"I knew you would see the advantages. We could attend the theater and fancy dinners. I would have the best seamstresses fashion gowns to display your figure so others will be jealous I possess you."

He wasn't proposing marriage. He had reduced her to an object he would buy with pretty trinkets. "And how would you pay for all these gifts? Your wife's money?"

"It'll be my money once I marry her."

Poor Margaret. She gave him one more chance to

correct any misunderstanding. "You want me to be your mistress?"

"You seem surprised."

"I was anticipating a proposal of marriage."

"If marriage is what you want, I could find a token husband to retain your moral integrity. An old man. No, a soldier. A husband fighting at the battlefront would allow you to attend social functions openly. I'd give you the world, Colleen, my love."

He was serious. "I wouldn't know what to do with the world."

"You don't want to live in New York, London, or Paris?"

"I don't want to be your courtesan or whatever term the rich use for a kept woman."

"You little fool. I'm spreading riches at your feet, and you're trampling on them."

Cole stomped around him, emphasizing each heavy thud. "I'm refusing your offer."

"Colleen, you'll never do better than me."

She paused in front of him. "I could marry the town drunk and do better than you."

He grabbed her against his chest. She struggled against his iron-tight grip. She had never been afraid in the company of a man, but panic seized her. Where were her grandparents?

His fingers bruised her arms. "I've learned powerful men can do anything."

She fought to avoid his mouth as he attempted to kiss her. Instead of an anticipation of pleasure, it reviled her. She didn't have to tell her heart not to love. His insults had destroyed any tender feelings. "Take your hands off me!"

He laughed, his mouth capturing hers. She bit his lip. He released her, wiping his mouth with his silk kerchief. "I like a woman who fights back."

Cole retrieved her knife and slashed his sleeve when he reached for her.

"This is a two-hundred-dollar suit."

"Now it's a worthless rag."

"Why you little whore, I'll teach you a lesson…" He raised his hand to strike her.

"I've had enough!" Blake shouted from the tall-back sofa in front of the fireplace. "A man can't rest on a Sunday afternoon without being subjected to this decadent drama." Blake rose, his back to them.

"I thought we were alone." Simon turned and hurried toward the door. "I apologize, sir."

"Do you think your indecent proposal would have remained private?" Cole followed him to the porch. "Everyone will know what a cad you are."

"No one will believe you." Simon paused by his horse. "Everyone knows women use their wiles to seduce men and ruin their lives."

"Ruin your life? Men are congratulated on their conquests while a woman is ostracized from society with the tiniest hint of scandal." She grabbed a handful of pebbles from the road and threw them at Simon's horse. It jumped, nearly unseating him.

"You're a stupid girl," Simon shouted. "Someday, you'll beg me to throw you crumbs, and that's all you'll get."

Cole collided with Blake in the doorway. "Where is he?"

"Riding off." Cole waved toward the road, where dust marked his trail. "Did you hear everything?"

"I was awakened by the clanging of silverware. I would have made my presence known, but I didn't want to interrupt. Then he went too far."

"Did he? He made an offer."

"Not an honorable one."

"You dare speak of honor?" She searched for her handkerchief. "You and Simon are cut from the same cloth."

"You wound me, brat."

Tears coursed down her cheeks, and a sob escaped her throat.

"Don't cry."

"I can cry if I want."

"Not for a snake."

"For myself. For every woman who offers her heart but has the misfortune to be deceived by love's lies." She gazed at him through tear-filled eyes, judging, and condemning his sex before running up the stairs and slamming the door to her room. She flung herself on her bed and opened the floodgates to her shattered emotions.

****

Blake listened to the sobbing above, wondering how he could ease her pain.

CJ entered the foyer. "Is Colleen all right?"

Blake gingerly moved his right arm. Although not injured, it pulled on his wound, and he winced. "Simon is lucky I can't throw a punch for breaking her heart."

CJ gathered the tray from the parlor. "What about yours?"

"Mine? I'm not in love."

"I'm not too old to recognize the look of love in a man's eyes."

"She hates me. I'm a cad like Simon." Her words hurt deeper than he would admit. He stared at the ceiling. "Do you know when the train leaves for Cleveland?"

"Tomorrow morning."

"I'll be leaving then."

"Probably best. Colleen and Jessica are leaving for Washington City after the Fourth of July celebration."

"Washington City?"

"To help their sister, Jennifer, who's been ill." CJ paused in the doorway. "Colleen said you owned a hotel in Washington City."

He shook his finger at her. "Banish any romantic notions, Mrs. Donovan."

"I have too many granddaughters not to keep my eye open for possible suitors."

Blake retrieved the book he had been reading, *Great Expectations*. He would be in Washington City about the same time Cole arrived. Maybe she would be over Simon Blackwater, and he could prove he wasn't anything like the cad.

Chapter Eleven

Blake entered the Dutchman Hotel. It was the most lavish hotel his father had purchased, and he had lived with his mother and brother within its familiar walls. The place had dark memories of his dead family, and he preferred the Mermaid's Mirth in Washington City when he wasn't traveling.

The Dutchman's polished mahogany woodwork, thick carpets, and velvet draperies provided elegant furnishings for guests. It was the most profitable of the properties he had inherited and home to his stepmother, Nancy, and her daughter, Valerie Ferguson. Another reason to make his visits short.

Vincent Grey, the general manager, greeted him. He was in his fifties, a loyal employee hired by Loren Ellsworth. He had been a trusted advisor after his father's death. "It's good to have you back, sir."

Blake left the everyday operations in Vincent's capable hands, and the books never failed to show a profit. Except in one area. He had promised to provide for Nancy and Valerie, but their spending habits had expanded in the past few months.

Blake removed the bookkeeping journals from the office. "Have Mrs. Ellsworth and her daughter join me in the private parlor."

He mentally added the columns for gowns, bonnets, gloves, reticules, shoes, stockings, and an array of undergarments. Besides the clothing, bedding, cushions, a sofa, and a tea service had been charged to the family account.

Blake stood when the two women entered. Valerie wore her dark hair in an elaborate style of curls that required winding her hair around a heated rod. Her mother wore her hair in a more severe style and resembled Mary Lincoln in her plumpness. Nancy had passed her period of mourning for Loren Ellsworth and wore a deep blue silk gown trimmed with small black roses. Vincent had warned him a gentleman had been calling for his stepmother at regular intervals for the past month. Nancy knew the importance of being married for a woman of limited income and was wasting no time in obtaining her third husband.

Valerie was dragging her feet to find someone to take care of her. A white gown with layers of ruffles on the skirt and bodice added fullness to her rail-thin figure. She wore white gloves to hide the fact she bit her nails.

Blake did not enjoy his task of managing their financial affairs, but his father had asked him to take care of his wife and her daughter on his sick bed. How much could two women spend when they had everything they needed? The figures revealed they had no clue about money. They were in for a rude awakening. Luckily, Vincent had contacted him about their spending habits before they sent him into bankruptcy.

He took his seat once they were comfortable. "You have exceeded your allowance again," Blake said. "Not by a few hundred dollars but by several thousand."

"I'm no longer in mourning and needed a few

dresses," Nancy said.

"All silk?"

"What else should I wear?"

"Work dresses would be appropriate," Blake said. "If you want to continue to live at the Dutchman Hotel, you will need to participate in the running of the operations."

"Work?" She placed her hand on her bosom. "I wouldn't know how to perform menial tasks. Your father took care of me. I expect you to do the same."

"I know you only read the fashion news in the papers, but a war is raging in this country. And unfortunately, two of my hotels are in enemy territory."

"Didn't you sell the hotel in Tennessee?" Valerie asked.

"No," he lied. "I barely escaped with my life. He rubbed his shoulder. They couldn't miss the sling cradling his arm. I took a bullet during my journey. The property in Tennessee is lost."

"You were shot?" Both ladies appeared disturbed and yet disappointed. If he had died, they would have inherited. He had no heirs. Maybe he should marry before joining the army.

"I'm fine," he dismissed. "I had an excellent doctor." And an excellent nurse. Pleasant thoughts of a ginger-haired beauty dancing along the gangplank of the canal boat distracted him from his task.

"What will we do with only two hotels?"

"Only this one shows a profit," he clarified. "The Mermaid's Mirth has been converted to a hospital by the Union army."

"Can they do that?"

"They can do whatever is necessary during

wartime."

He was eager to return to the Mermaid's Mirth and call at Pierce House. He had left Cole without saying good-bye. She had remained in her room the rest of the day, nursing her broken heart. Blake was in love with her, but he wouldn't make promises he couldn't keep. He had a couple months before his shoulder would be healed, and he could join the army. He could help her forget Simon and redeem himself in her eyes. Maybe she would write. The letters from Jake and the Herbruck brothers had reminded him how alone he was in the world.

His recovery would allow him time to put his finances in order. The newly purchased inn on Lake Erie could be a profitable investment and tilt the profit margin higher into the black, but he didn't want Nancy or Valerie to know about the property. He was trying to build a future without them. But if the money was spent to obtain husbands, it was a small sacrifice to be free of his responsibilities.

He turned to Valerie. "And why do you need new gowns? Is there a suitor you're trying to impress?"

She pouted, a technique she believed made a man think of kissing her. She looked like a fish instead. "None of them measures up to you."

Since his father's death, Valerie had made it known she hoped her stepbrother would become more. Although there was no blood relation between them, he had never thought of her as more than a stepsister and made sure they were never alone. Another reason to keep his visits to a minimum.

"I will notify the storekeepers not to extend any credit to you," Blake said. "You are given a generous allowance, and I expect you to remain within its limits."

"But we have guests arriving."

"What guests?"

"Margaret Radcliff and her parents," Valerie said. "You know we attended Miss Wellington's School for Young Ladies, and she's my best friend."

And Simon Blackwater's fiancée. "When do they arrive?"

"Tomorrow. We were going to help her shop for her wedding trousseau."

"Make sure her father pays all the bills." Blake hoped he appeared surprised. "Who's the lucky man?"

"Simon Blackwater from some little town in Ohio." Valerie rolled her eyes. "Margaret thinks he's wonderful. Her father has big plans for him."

"You should follow Margaret's example and find a husband who will be more generous than me."

"If you're going to be stingy, I might."

Her threat fell on deaf ears. If she hoped to cause him to rethink his tight hold on her allowance, she was mistaken. Valerie believed she could convince a man to surrender to her desires by batting her lashes and giggling into her fan. Her charm had been taught through rules and practice at Miss Wellington's school, and most people admired her confidence, poise, and sense of entitlement. Thinly veiled contempt was hidden behind a frozen smile, but her lack of a fortune kept her manners in check.

Blake had been susceptible to her feminine displays of helplessness when he first took over his father's businesses, but he had grown weary of her tantrums when he didn't give into her demands. He braced for the onslaught of tears. She did not disappoint him.

He refused to extend any more funds or credit, but agreed to accompany them to a play with Margaret and her parents, who had booked rooms at the Dutchman Hotel with so much luggage it had to be stored in a spare room.

Darius Radcliff was a stocky man with a round belly and a penchant for smoking long cigars. He enjoyed any drink containing alcohol and every woman willing to tumble in the sheets for a few dollars. Amelia Radcliff was old money and claimed a duke in her ancestry. She was a bony creature with no bosom, protruding cheek bones, and a distaste for anything vulgar, especially her husband. Margaret overlooked her father's flaws because she was beginning to resemble him. Her delicate cheekbones would soon disappear in the chubbiness of her cheeks.

A carriage arrived with a surprise. Simon Blackwater greeted his future in-laws and wife. Margaret introduced him to Nancy, Valerie, and Blake. Simon did not recognize him. He had only seen Blake's back at CJ's Inn, and his clean shaven face and shorter hair had altered his appearance further. He studied Simon. The rich would admire his confidence and aloof disdain for everything, a camouflage for his arrogant self-indulgences. He wanted to thrash him but congratulated him on his good fortune.

The gentlemen were dressed in formal frock coats and top hats while the ladies wore silk evening gowns trimmed with ruffles, gathers, and lace. Their hoops crowded the carriage, and Darius ordered another carriage for Simon, Valerie, and Margaret.

Blake didn't mind sitting with the older women. He

wore a sling around his neck to support his arm, and they fussed about his injury.

"You need to take care of yourself, Blake," Nancy said. "I won't be around to give you motherly advice."

She had never given him maternal care. Their relationship was based on a formal politeness that required little interaction.

Nancy leaned forward. "I wanted to tell you the Reverend Dennis Lackey has asked for my hand in marriage. He was such a comfort after I lost your father. You know how much I loved Loren, and although we only had a few years together, I respected and admired him."

Whether she spoke the truth or not, he didn't judge her. "I'm happy for you, Nancy. Do you wish me to speak with him?"

"I would like you to meet him. I know nothing of my finances, and I wouldn't want to mislead him."

Would he cancel the wedding if he found out she had no fortune? It was a subtle hint to offer a dowry to the Reverend to take her off his hands. "I'd be honored."

"He'll be by tomorrow afternoon."

She was eager to seal the deal. "Will Valerie be living with you?"

"No, Margaret has asked her to be her companion."

"Even after she's married?"

Amelia cleared her throat. "Mr. Radcliff is giving them a home on the Hudson River, but it needs to be decorated. While Simon and Margaret are celebrating their honeymoon in Europe, Valerie and I will be searching the shops to furnish the house. Margaret hates to be bothered by details, and Valerie has excellent taste."

Expensive taste. Blake leaned against the cushioned seat. Nancy and Valerie would be taken care of. He had fulfilled his obligation to his father and could concentrate on his own life. But every time he thought of his future, he imagined Colleen Beecher reading his letters describing army life. Would she worry when he fought in a battle? Would she cry at news of his death? Would he leave this world with no one shedding a tear? Cole's harsh accusation comparing him to the cad Simon echoed in his thoughts.

The play didn't ease his guilty conscience. The melodrama told the story of an innocent young woman seduced by a rake who leaves her with a child. They shiver in the cold while the man parties to excess. He tosses her a few coins, thinking she is a beggar before turning his attention to another woman. The poor girl jumps from a bridge, her illegitimate child clutched in her arms.

"I didn't like it at all," Margaret said as they prepared to leave. "The girl was so depressing. But I liked the man. He was dashing."

"I thought he looked like Simon," Valerie said.

Margaret turned to Simon. "I see the resemblance now."

Simon offered his arm. "But I would never desert a lady."

"She wasn't a lady," Margaret said. "Women like that deserve what they get, don't they, Mother?"

"I believe that was the message of the play," Amelia answered.

Women were harsh toward their own sex. What would they think of Cole? A woman whose beauty was a liability as well as an asset.

When they reached the hotel, he offered the men a drink while the ladies retired for the night.

Darius handed everyone a cigar. "The night is young. Why don't we enjoy ourselves with some manly pursuits?"

"I'm game."

"You always are, Simon." Darius turned to Blake. "I bet you know where a man can find entertainment."

"When I'm here, I'm busy running the hotel." But he wanted to see what sort of man had broken Colleen Beecher's heart. "I know a few places guests like to frequent."

"After that boring play I need some excitement." Darius elbowed Simon. "What do you say, boy? Let's enjoy what this town has to offer."

"Do you need to inform your wife not to wait for you?"

"Amelia and I haven't shared a bed in years. She sleeps with Margaret." He turned to Simon. "Once you produce a grandson, you can join me again in the pursuit of happiness."

Blake shook his head. Was the man serious? His daughter was a vessel for an heir and nothing more? How could men treat women so callously?

Blake asked Vincent for some places men like Darius and Simon might find entertaining. He removed a hundred dollars from the safe. "It's for show, Vincent."

"I am in no position to judge you, sir."

Loren Ellsworth had preached hard work and clean living. He had never strayed from either of his wives, and it would have been easy in his travels. He wasn't forgetting his father's advice against a life of decadence, but he'd have to be cautious. Darius liked his companions to join in his fun.

They didn't bother changing their clothes but weren't the only gentlemen slumming. The poor neighborhoods of Albany could be identified from the stench of its trash and open sewers. The darkness failed to hide the crowded tenant buildings where women called down to customers, baring their breasts to entice someone to climb the steps.

"She has a nice pair of teats," Simon said about a woman leaning from a second floor window.

"You have to be drunk to bed that toothless hag," Darius said. "Let's find a tavern."

Blake ordered the drinks, asking the bartender to add water to his whiskey.

"I'll have to charge you the same." The bartender grinned, as if in on a secret.

Blake wasn't planning to rob his companions, but the tavern was crowded with unsavory types, willing to lighten the load of a gentleman's purse. He moved his money to an inside pocket.

Someone announced a cock fight, and everyone hurried out, following the crier to the pit behind a barn. The roosters had metal spurs attached to their legs, and by the time one had killed the other, they were both a pile of bloody feathers. Simon puked, and Darius laughed.

"You need a stronger stomach than that, boy. A man can't be afraid of a little blood."

"It must have been the oysters from supper. Seafood doesn't agree with me."

They spent another hour at a gambling hall where

Darius lost nearly four hundred dollars. Simon lost everything he had, but Darius loaned him another hundred. They threw their money away. The drinks had been supplied regularly during the card game, and both men were drunk as they headed to their next destination.

The Mounting Stallion was a whorehouse with a reputation of catering to any man's desires. Blake was uneasy sitting in the lobby as Madam Mimi paraded her girls before them. The seasoned ones were bold, strutting before the men in corsets that pressed sagging breasts into bulging mounds of flesh. Their faces were painted in bright colors to hide the look of death in their vacant eyes. The younger girls were frightened, wrapping sheer robes around their underfed bodies. An ugly bruise marred a girl's pale skin, and her wrist looked as if she had been tied. Prostitution was an ugly business.

Darius grabbed one petite girl and pulled her robe free. His hand cupped her breast. She screamed.

Madam Mimi struck her. The sound was disguised by the piano player's lively tune. The other girls looked away, blaming the girl for her misfortune. "Be grateful he's taken a bath." She held her hand out for payment. Darius smacked the girl on the butt as she led him upstairs. He turned and grinned at them. "Hope you enjoy your night as much as me."

A girl with red hair joined the other prostitutes. She bore a slight resemblance to Cole, and Blake sat upright.

"Now there's my Colleen," Simon said.

"What?" Blake turned to Simon.

"I like redheads."

Madam Mimi waited for payment. Simon dug into his trousers.

The girl giggled, revealing a missing tooth. The gaslight on the wall revealed her age to be older than he had first estimated. It didn't deter Simon. He paid his money and claimed the woman.

"You're such a cad," the girl told Simon.

Cad. He looked around the room. Cole would never accept any offer from a man but a marriage proposal. And she wouldn't like him being in a place like this, taking advantage of desperate women.

Madam Mimi studied him. "You're a handsome one. I have a young girl who would please you."

"Money can't buy the girl I want." Blake handed her a few bills. "Make sure my companions have a good time." He rubbed his shoulder. "My injury prevents me from enjoying your establishment."

"We can accommodate you," Madam Mimi said. "Lulu has a lovely mouth."

Blake hurried outside, gasping for clean air, and made his way to his hotel. If he wondered if he had missed anything in life, he no longer worried. He had shocked Cole by asking her to share his bed when they first met. She had mistaken him for a worldly man, but the only world he wanted was hers. She'd be in Washington City soon. He'd finish business in New York and call upon Logan Pierce, his lovely wife, and her visiting sisters.

Chapter Twelve

Cole and Jess stepped off the Baltimore & Ohio train at the Italianate-style depot at the foot of Capitol Hill. Barracks and a mess hall named Soldiers Rest had been built nearby. The long single-story and two-story buildings provided meals for thousands of soldiers on route to the battlefields or camps surrounding town.

A huge building of white marble was built on a rise, towering above the town. The Capitol Building's dome construction had continued through the first year of the war, and work had resumed on the extensions of the building. Scaffolding and cranes protruded from the roof in the central area.

Logan and Jem met them at the depot. Cole and Jess hadn't seen either of them since January. Logan's hair was bleached with blonde streaks from the summer sun and was a healthy contrast to their sister, who was thin and pale. They knew she was pregnant, but her narrow waist above a gathered skirt revealed no sign of her condition. Papa had been right to be concerned. This was more than simple morning sickness.

"I'm so glad to see you." Jem hugged each of them. "Did you bring supplies?"

"My goodness, aren't you the mercenary?" Cole laughed at her unease. "We have a whole train car full for the soldiers." Dark circles shadowed Jem's blue eyes. "We're here to help in whatever way we can."

Jess pointed to the Capitol. "What are they doing to the dome?"

"Trying to finish it," Logan said. "I don't know what will end first, the war or the construction on the Capitol Building."

Jess shaded her eyes with her hand. "It's impressive."

"Good," Logan said. "Washington City's goal is to impress its visitors."

"What's the dome made of?"

"Cast-iron. They had to reinforce the walls to support it and the Statue of Freedom which will be mounted on top."

"Is it open for visitors?"

"I'll take you for a tour later this week," Logan said.

Jess glanced around. "I want to see the statue of Andrew Jackson and the Smithsonian Institution."

"If you want a good guide for touring the sites, Ed and Art can show you around," Jem said. "They've been everywhere."

Jess stumbled. "They're in town?"

"Since last month," Jem said. "They have a camp near Alexandria on the other side of the Potomac River, but they've visited several times."

Jess searched the faces of the soldiers crowding the depot. "How long will they be in town?"

"They don't know," Logan said. "Could be a day. Could be months."

The women waited with the luggage while Logan found a black hack carriage for hire. They headed south on First Street before turning west on Pennsylvania Avenue. Hotels and shops were mixed with private homes in a staggering sequence of uneven heights and a myriad of construction materials. The large government buildings could be seen in the distance with the Treasury building where Logan worked at the end of Pennsylvania Avenue. They passed Seventh Street and stopped in front of Pierce House. The hack couldn't turn around to place them on the south side of the street because of the crowd of carriages, wagons, and people in the street.

Many of the faces were black. "I didn't know there were so many slaves in Washington City," Cole said.

"Former slaves," Jem corrected. "They have been pouring into the city since Lincoln abolished slavery here. Many of them live in Camp Barker, but others make homes from anything they can find. Too many people are crowded in too tight a space. The graveyards are filling with those who have died from disease."

"Aren't there any doctors or hospitals?"

"The entire city is a hospital. They've been converting barracks into hospital wards since the soldiers moved to the battlefields. They're empty until a battle. It begins as a murmur, a request for bandages. Then the wounded begin to arrive by boat or rail. They unload thousands and transport them to the hospitals in ambulances, on stretchers, or those that can stand, hobble on crutches. You'll see for yourself."

Cole looked around. "Isn't there a battle going on now?"

"This is a lull," Jem said. "You should have been here in June."

"The war would have been over if General George McClellan had taken Richmond," Logan said. "The men were trained with an army over a hundred thousand strong. He had good position on the peninsula between the York and James rivers back in March but hesitated to attack Yorktown, giving Joe Johnston plenty of time to position his Rebel forces. Without the Union firing a bullet, Johnston retreated in May to the Chickahominy River, ten miles from Richmond to defend the Southern capitol. And still McClellan hesitated. Johnston attacked May 31 but was wounded. Now Robert E. Lee is in charge of the Southern army, and that worries me."

"Is he a better general than McClellan?"

"A certain landlady thought Lee could walk on water," Logan said. "Only time will tell if she was correct in her estimation of his abilities."

They made their way across the sea of bodies shuffling through the street and reached the porch of the two-story building. A fresh coat of white paint contrasted with green shutters. A sign hung near the door. *Pierce House.*

"I like the name," Cole said. It had been called the Southern Belle by Annabelle Sharpton, the landlady who had a high opinion of Robert E. Lee. She had abandoned the boarding house and departed for the South when Alan Pinkerton and his security men began arresting spies. "You must plan on being in Washington City for a long time if you bought it."

"It was too good of a deal to pass on." Logan carried their bags and trunk inside. "Besides, rent has become unreasonable in the city."

The front of the house consisted of two rooms. One was a parlor and the other a dining room. A kitchen was visible in the back. Logan kissed Jem. "The wagon should arrive soon with the supplies from the train. I need to retrieve some papers from the office. Chase is urging Lincoln to sign the second Legal Tender Act so we can pay for this war."

"The second one?" Cole asked.

"The first one was issued in February and spent by June," Logan said. "This one is for one and a half million dollars. I hope it lasts longer."

Cole whistled. "How can anyone spend a million dollars?"

"War is expensive."

"Then why are we fighting one?"

Logan shook his head. "It was going to be over in ninety days, remember? But war never goes the way politicians plan."

Cole frowned. "Have we won *any* battles?"

"General Grant is making progress out west, but the graves in the cemeteries reveal the real price of the war," he said.

"Will our supplies make any difference?"

"They will to the men fighting the battles." Logan hesitated. "Do you want me to remain until the wagon arrives?"

Jem shook her head. "We have plenty of help unloading the supplies." She kissed her husband good-bye.

Cole looked around at the rooms. "You're storing the supplies here?"

"Warehouse space goes to the military, which has a priority over anything civilian," Jem said. "We use a spare room to store medical supplies and distribute the perishables as soon as possible."

"When do you think the wagon will arrive?"

"Time passes slowly when you're in a hurry. They

have to unload the train, load the wagon, and travel through the traffic. You have time for your toilette."

Jem led the way upstairs. Cole and Jess carried their trunk with their travel bags stacked on top. "Do you want to share a room? We have enough space if you'd like to be in separate rooms."

They had been sleeping in the same bed since toddlers. "Why start now?" Cole and Jess placed the trunk on the floor as Jem unlocked the door. "We'll share."

"Deidre is in the room next door, but she's a sound sleeper."

Cole glanced into Deidre's room. The bed had a lightweight quilt of pink and white squares, and a rag doll Jem had made was perched against a pillow. A small desk was near the window, and a cape and bonnet hung on a peg by a wall mirror. A low dresser and wash stand completed the furniture. "Where is Deidre?"

"At the neighbor's house. She has a little girl Deidre's age named Tammy. They're inseparable."

Cole joined the others in the guest room. The double bed had a quilt made from old dresses the girls had worn through the years. "I remember when you made this."

"I remember wearing most of these dresses and handing them down to you and Jess."

Cole ran her fingertips across the familiar fabric. "They never reached Cass or Jules."

"You two were difficult on clothes."

Jess had moved the trunk inside near a dressing table. She placed the two small travel bags on the bed.

Cole opened a drawer in the dresser. It was lined with paper but empty. The washstand had clean towels hanging from handles on each side of the flat top where a bowl and pitcher were placed.

"I'll fetch some water so you can wash." Jem grabbed the pitcher. "Hang your clothes on the pegs. I'll iron them later."

"We can do our own work." Cole took the pitcher. "We're here to help you not the other way around. You're pale and thin. What is going on?"

"Morning sickness."

"You're four months along. Something else is causing you to lose weight."

"I think it's the heat. I can't seem to keep anything down." Jem moved toward the door. "I'll make lunch while you unpack."

"No." Cole took Jem's arm. "You lie down, and I'll make lunch."

"But you're my guests."

"We're your nurses, and you better be a good patient, or we'll tie you to the bed."

What color she had, faded to pale white. "I know you're joking, but past experience makes me wonder if you might be serious."

"The only time we tied you to the bed was when you had poison oak," she said. "It was the only way to keep you from scratching."

"Logan would not be pleased if he found me tied to the bed."

Cole thought of Blake's behavior when he was strapped down and smiled. "Are you sure?"

"Colleen Josephine Beecher, does Mama have to have *another* talk with you?"

Cole groaned and ushered Jem out the door. She had Mama's talk memorized. It consisted of a lot of don'ts.

"There's smoked ham and potatoes in the cellar along with canned fruits and vegetables," Jem said. "I haven't had time to go to the market today."

Cole followed Jem into the master bedroom at the head of the staircase. The large bed was new, purchased by Logan before their wedding at Christmas. The quilt of blue, pink, and white was one CJ had made. "I could make soup. Do you have an onion and flour?"

"Yes."

"Where do you keep your cow?"

Jem laughed. "No cow, but there's milk in the ice box."

"No cow." Cole handed Jess the empty water pitcher. "You know what that means?"

"No milking!" she cheered.

"I hope I'm not going to have trouble with you two."

Cole put her arm around Jem. "You have judged us all wrong, sister dear. We're no trouble. We are your salvation."

Cole helped Jem undo her dress and remove her crinoline, corset cover, corset, and petticoat. She was unnaturally thin. She helped her into the bed.

Cole lifted a paper from the desk situated between the tall narrow windows overlooking the backyard. An important looking document was covered with Logan's neat handwriting. As a secretary, it was Logan's job to take the ideas and words of Salmon Chase, the secretary of the Treasury, and put them on official documents. The Pierce family had worked for the Chase family for many years, and Logan agreed with his opinion about abolishing slavery, women's rights, and public education.

Cory and Jem had married well. They had placed the bar high for their younger sisters' future husbands. Simon would have been a fine catch, a worthy companion of her brothers-in-law, if he hadn't been such a greedy schemer. She had accused Blake of being cut from the same cloth as Simon, but at that moment she had been embarrassed because he had witnessed the insolent proposition. Blake had appeared and disappeared in her life. She hadn't heard anything from him. He could have penned a thank you note for saving his life. Ungrateful rake.

Cole closed the drapes and headed for the kitchen.

The rooms flowed from the foyer to the dining hall to the kitchen with a pantry and a narrow hallway back to the staircase.

Jem was the most organized of the Beecher sisters, and it wasn't difficult to find the ingredients for soup in the carefully arranged crocks and tins on the pantry shelves or in the cellar. Cole began a fire in the stove and spooned a generous portion of butter in a deep cast-iron pot. She added chopped onion and peeled a dozen potatoes. She cut them in cubes and added the pieces to the melted butter and sautéed onions along with some water. Once the potatoes were cooked, she added milk and flour to create a sauce. She stirred to thicken and added cubed ham and a jar of canned peas.

Jess had finished unpacking and joined her. "Do you think Jem will be all right?"

"Papa said to feed her small meals that are easy to eat like soups, fruit, and breads. We'll put some weight on her." Cole opened the pie keep. It was empty. "We should make bread and rolls."

Jess found the flour bag. "I'll start on the dough. What about pies?"

"She has plenty of sugar and lard in the pantry and apples in the cellar."

Jess opened the trap door in the floor. She crinkled her nose. "It's damp."

"Logan said the city is built on a swamp." Cole lit a candle inside a tin lantern and gave it to Jess. "This should help, but be careful on the steps. They're steep."

Jess rummaged in the cellar and returned with apples in her apron and two jars. "I think these are peaches."

Cole grabbed the jars, and Jess emptied the apples onto the table. "They don't look too wormy."

"Let's get to work."

Sandwiched in the middle of the family, Cole and Jess had been constant companions since Jess was weaned. They didn't have to speak to convey what was needed. They moved in an effortless ballet as they transformed the flour into fresh bread and pies.

Jem entered the kitchen, her auburn hair neatly braided, and a fresh dress covering her underclothes. "What's going on in here?"

"You're supposed to be resting." Cole pulled a slotted chair from the table, and Jem sat.

"It's been hours, and I smelled something cooking."

"Ham and potato soup, but I think it's missing something." Cole winked at Jess and poured a ladle full into a bowl. She handed a spoon to Jem. "Taste it and see what you think."

Jem tried a spoonful and then another. "I think it tastes fine."

"Have some fresh bread with it." Cole smeared a generous layer of butter on the thick slice.

Jem swiped the remains of her soup with the bread, cleaning the empty bowl. She looked at the pot on the stove. "I think the soup needs some pepper."

Cole snapped her fingers. "I knew it needed something." She added pepper and ladled more into Jem's bowl. "How does it taste now?" She handed her another slice of buttered bread.

"Do you have any lettuce, carrots, or radishes?" Jess asked. "I was going to make a salad."

"I keep a small garden." Jem waved her hand toward the backyard. "But I neglected the weeding."

Jess borrowed Jem's bonnet hanging on a peg by the door. "I'll find something." She grabbed a basket on top of the pie keep.

"Not that one!" Jem snatched the basket from her hand. "This basket is special."

"It looks like the one Mama had."

"It is," Jem said. "She gave it to me for my trip last year to Washington City, and I took it to Richmond with me. I never had to worry about going hungry."

Jess made a face of disbelief but grabbed a basket without a lid. "Is this one special?"

Jem laughed and placed her special basket back where Jess had retrieved it. "I know it sounds silly, but Logan and I have some fond memories traveling with this basket."

Cole searched the pantry shelves. "I should go to the market. You're low on supplies. Is it far?"

"The Center Market is between Seventh and Ninth streets, but by now all the freshest selections are gone. I always shop early in the day."

"Then we'll wait to go to the market tomorrow," Cole said.

"That will give me time to make a list."

"You still make lists?"

"How would you know what to buy if I didn't?"

"I buy what looks ripe and tasty." Cole opened several drawers. "Where do you keep the cutlery?"

"It's in the dining room in the hutch by the table."

Cole put her hand on Jem's shoulder when she rose. "I'll set the table."

"Do you think the pies will be cool enough for dinner?"

"Apple pie is delicious warm or cold. Why don't you try a slice?"

Jem sliced into the apple pie. "I'll have a small piece."

It wouldn't take long for her sister to regain her health.

Chapter Thirteen

Deidre ran through the front door. "Aunt Jenny!" The girl was the spitting image of her Uncle Logan with blonde hair, caramel brown eyes, and deep dimples when she smiled. She had met the Beecher family seven months ago at Christmas. "Are you Aunt Courtney?"

"No, I'm Aunt Colleen."

Deidre looked around. "Where's Aunt Jenny?"

Jem appeared in the kitchen doorway. She examined Deidre's stained pinafore and messy braids. "You're missing a hair ribbon."

"Me and Tammy were playing a game."

"Tammy and I," Cole corrected. "Sorry, I'm no longer a teacher."

"What do you mean?" Jem touched Cole's arm. "I thought you enjoyed teaching."

"It seems a male teacher doesn't have to worry about being drafted." She shrugged. "When the war ends, I may be able to find a teaching position."

"You can help tutor Deidre." Jem lowered her voice. "With all the changes last year, she hasn't learned to read or write, and she's seven."

Deidre sniffed the fresh pie. "Can I have some?"

"You *may* have some after supper. First you have to wash."

Deidre headed for the back porch.

Jem gasped. "Where's my hug?"

141

Deidre ran to her, wrapping her arms around her waist. Jem tied a bow in the remaining ribbon at the end of one of her braids. "Did you have a good time playing with Tammy?"

"Yes, but she wouldn't let me play with her new doll. She said I might break it."

"I'm sure you would be careful, but it's difficult to share something new. After a while I'm sure she'll let you play with it."

Diedre skipped to the back door, nearly colliding with Jess as she returned with her harvest for a salad. She had washed the vegetables at the pump on the back porch and spread them on the kitchen table.

Cole snatched a small carrot and bit into it. "I wonder what happened to all my dolls?"

Jess removed the borrowed bonnet. "Are you looking for a doll?" She grabbed a knife and wooden cutting board to prepare the vegetables.

Jem watched through the window to make sure Diedre washed her hands and face. "You didn't have any dolls because you destroyed them."

Cole gasped. "Why would I do that?"

"You and Jess liked to send them on adventures." Jem scowled, her hands on her hips. "Most of the poor things didn't survive."

Jess sliced a radish. "Remember when we tied your rag doll to Mr. Wheeler's bull?" She waved her arms in the air and laughed. "That doll flopped its arms and legs until it was thrown off."

"Then the bull gored it," Cole added. "The sawdust stuffing flew everywhere."

Jem frowned. "I don't know if I should trust Deidre to your care."

Cole raised her hand in a solemn oath. "We promise not to tie her to a bull."

"From past history, that isn't reassuring. Which one of you threw Jules into the canal to teach her to swim?"

"She's the best swimmer in the family," Cole said.

"She nearly drowned."

"Nearly doesn't count."

Logan called from outside. "Are you ladies decent?"

Jem's expression softened, and she headed for the door.

"Aren't we suppose to calm her fears?"

"I couldn't resist. Remember how she was always bossing us around. Let her worry a little. But not too much." Cole followed Deidre through the open arched doorway into the dining room.

"The wagon arrived as I was returning home." He placed a large envelope on the dining room table. "Don't touch that," he warned Deidre when she reached for it with wet hands.

Jem grabbed her hands and wiped them dry on Cole's apron. "I hope you don't mind."

"It's your apron." Cole shrugged.

Logan stood in the doorway, grinning, displaying his deep dimples. "You might recognize the soldiers your sister enlisted to help with the supplies." Behind him appeared Ed and Art Herbruck. Ed was twenty-two, two years older than Art, who had barely made the age requirement of twenty when he enlisted. They had long, narrow faces with deep set eyes and light brown hair that curled in the humidity.

Jess dropped the carrot she was cleaning and

rushed to the front of the house. "Ed!"

"I should have made more food," Cole said under her breath as she smiled at their guests. From their letters, she had expected Ed and Art to be thinner, but the haunting look in their eyes frightened her. What had they not written in their correspondence home?

Ed's mouth widened when Jess appeared, and all the harshness in his features disappeared. Jess lowered her eyes and blushed under his intense scrutiny. Ed no longer bore any resemblance to the shy, bumbling young man who had left Darrow Falls less than a year ago. He stood taller and carried two boxes of supplies gathered during the Independence Day celebration. Folks back home had been generous and had sent food, clothing, personal items, and medical supplies to be distributed to Ohio soldiers.

"Where do you want these?" Ed asked.

"Upstairs in the room at the far end." Jem turned to ascend the staircase.

Logan lifted her off her feet and set her aside. "I'll show them."

"I'm not helpless."

Logan flashed her a dimpled smile that silenced any protest. Jem stared after her husband, a queer look on her face.

Jess grabbed Cole's arm, distracting her from her observations. "Doesn't he look grand?"

"Logan?"

"No, Ed." What was this strange spell her sisters were under? They were handsome men, but her pulse had remained steady, her breathing unlabored. The only time she had panicked about a man was when Blake Ellsworth had been shot, and blood was pouring out of his shoulder. And the time he kissed her in the bedroom. But that was a onetime passionate encounter she didn't plan to repeat.

Jess looked at the traveling gown she wore. "Do you think I have time to change my dress?"

"There's nothing wrong with your outfit." Cole shook her head. "Go ahead. I'll entertain them while you make yourself presentable."

Jess ran up the stairs, nearly colliding with Art and Ed as they returned for a second trip.

"I thought she was only writing letters to share news of home," Jem said. "When did she start having an interest in Ed?"

"Ed has penned several romantic lines to our little sister. But I think it's the hunting stories that won her heart."

"Do I have to play chaperone for them?"

"I'll take care of the courting," Cole said. "I owe her for all the boring hours she sat in the parlor while men attempted to impress me."

"You never did choose a favorite. If you're looking for a husband in Washington City, there are plenty of men, but the wife of a soldier or politician is not an easy one."

"I plan to return home, buy a boat, and live my days floating up and down the canal drinking whiskey and singing bawdy tunes."

Jem couldn't answer. She believed her.

"I've quit life on the canal," Cole reassured her. "I'm looking for a new career."

"You're too pretty to be a military nurse."

Her compliment caught her off guard. "Why, thank you."

"The head nurses think pretty young women are looking for husbands among the wounded. They won't hire them."

"I'm sure some are." Simon had wanted her to marry a soldier. A marriage of convenience for him.

The men entered with a second load. "Will you stay for supper?"

"That's awfully nice of you, Miss Colleen." Art tipped his kepi hat. "I'm getting tired of Ed's cooking."

"Are you sure you have enough?" Ed asked. "We wouldn't want to deprive you of your supper."

"There's plenty," Cole reassured them. If Jess wasn't reason enough, food would keep the Herbruck brothers around. She turned to Jem. "I hope you don't mind I invited them to stay."

"I was planning to invite them." She turned to the kitchen where Deidre was poking a finger at the apple pie. "I better hide the pie, or there won't be any dessert."

"I'll check on Jess. She should have been down by now."

Jess was stripped to her undergarments and crinoline. Several dresses were scattered across the bed.

She grabbed a blue and white checkered dress. "Do you think Ed will like this one?"

"That's my dress." Cole took it.

"Why can't I wear it?"

Jess was tall, muscular, and nearly flat chested. "You need to fill out a bit more."

Cole searched through the trunk they shared. She removed a red, white, and blue plaid sheer summer dress. "This looks nice on you."

"I wore that at the Independence Day picnic last

Friday."

"They don't know that."

Jess slipped the skirt over her head. "I hope Ed notices me."

"You nearly ran him over on the stairs." Cole tied the strings to the skirt and helped her with the bodice. It had a ruffle from shoulder to shoulder to add fullness. "Besides, I don't think he sees many women on the battlefield."

"Why am I so nervous around him?" Jess pulled away before Cole had time to finish hooking the belt holding the bodice in place. She searched her travel bag for the sleeves to wear underneath the bell-shaped ones. "We've known each other for years."

"He was only a friend in the past." Cole finished securing her dress and arranged the yards of skirt over the crinoline. "Now you're in love." She had seen it in her eyes. And in Jem's. Would she ever look at a man the same way?

Jess retrieved her brush. "I don't know how he feels about me."

"You'll find out." Cole changed into the blue and white checkered dress after washing off the dust from the train ride. She had more curves than her younger sister, but it hadn't been too many years ago when she had been a flat-chested redheaded brat. The term made her think of Blake. He owned a hotel in Washington City, but that didn't guarantee their paths would cross. How would he react if he saw her? Would he laugh about Simon? Or would he pity her? And why was Blake's opinion so important?

Jess pulled on a few short tufts of hair. "Do you think he'll notice how uneven my hair is?"

Laura Freeman

"Why don't you tell him about snagging burrs in your hair setting a snare for a rabbit? I bet he laughs about it."

Jess sat on the bed. "He might think I'm foolish and childish." Tears brimmed on the edge of her lower lashes. "How bad does my hair look?"

Cole examined a clump of short hair near the crown. "Your curls hide most of the unevenness."

Jess, who rarely cried, swiped at a tear.

"It's not a bob," Cole reassured her. "You have plenty of length in the back. The curls frame your face and emphasize how pretty you are."

"You're not lying?"

Cole helped Jess arrange her blonde curls high on her head, allowing them to cascade down her back. She added a few combs to keep the shorter lengths of hair in place. "Relax. Ed wouldn't notice if you were bald and wearing a burlap sack."

"How do you do it?" Jess asked. "You have two or three men courting you, and I've never seen you become flustered."

"I didn't care enough about the men to be nervous."

"Even Simon? You were serious about him."

"I thought Simon was in love with me, but his idea of love has nothing to do with marriage. That's why it's important a man places a ring on your finger before you allow any liberties." She was quoting Mama's familiar admonitions.

"Did Simon take liberties?" Jess studied her face. "I was supposed to chaperone."

"He stole a few kisses." She should have slapped his face. How could he believe she would consider

148

becoming his mistress?

"How do I let Ed know I like him?"

Was she kidding? "I think he knows."

Her face reddened. "I bet he thinks I'm silly."

"You? Most men are afraid of you." Cole fastened a necklace around Jess' throat. "You've beaten nearly all the boys in the county in every contest possible."

"I don't believe in pretending to be helpless so a man will like me." Jess bit her bottom lip. "Should I?"

"We do the cooking and cleaning, and we're expected to build their pride, too? Grandpa talks about building the canal, and the boys talk about fighting in the war. I'd like to do something worthy of bragging about with my life."

"Don't you want to marry and have children?"

"I want those things, but will it be enough?"

"Cory and Jem are happily married."

"They married for love. Besides, Tyler and Logan respect them. That's what I want. A man who values me as a person. But how can he value me if I haven't done anything worthwhile?"

"Do you think Ed will think less of me if I allow him to kiss me?"

"You can't tell if he's the right one without a kiss," Cole said. "What if there's no passion?"

"Can that happen? Even with someone you're in love with?"

"It's more likely the spark goes out. I don't think I would feel a thing if Simon kissed me now. I wouldn't allow myself to react."

"You can do that? Turn love on and off?"

"I didn't think so, but I know differently since Simon," Cole said. "No matter how much you were in

149

love with a man, when you think of his horrible behavior, you don't allow any loving feelings to surface."

"How long can you bury your feelings?"

"Until they die." It hadn't taken long with Simon.

"I like being in love," Jess said. "It's exciting."

At one time it had been fun and exhilarating, but Simon had tarnished the magic of falling in love. Not even eighteen and she was a cynic. But how did a woman risk her heart after being hurt, knowing so many men were willing to repeat the process?

"How do I encourage Ed to kiss me?"

"Make your lips available."

"How do I do that?"

"When you say good-night, turn your head a little and close your eyes. Most men know that's an invitation for a kiss." She grabbed her arm. "If he does kiss you, act shocked. Cry."

"Why?"

"So he doesn't take kissing for granted, and some men think if you allow a kiss, you'll allow more."

"So I need to be outraged." Jess smiled, but her words were serious. "Should I threaten to shoot him?"

"You want him to practice self-control not run for the hills."

The girls hurried down the steps, striking casual poses near Jem when Ed and Art made a final trip up the stairs. Jake Donovan followed them inside. Jake's long ginger curls were an unruly mass around his sunburned face. His blue eyes sparkled as he surveyed the three sisters. "I'm in heaven."

Cole wrapped her arms around his neck and kissed his cheek. He twirled her around and then took Jess into his arms. Jem held up her hands when he attempted to spin her. "My husband might protest."

Jake kissed her cheek instead. "You're looking well, cousin."

Ed paused on the stairs after delivering the last boxes. "Typical of the Seventh Ohio to show up when all the work is done."

Jake surveyed Ed and Art. "I thought you boys in the Twenty-ninth Ohio were issued new uniforms."

"We just got 'em," Art said.

"Them are fightin' words, Jake Donovan." Ed raised his fists, exposing a white shirt beneath the sleeves of his blue jacket. Jake raised his fists and squared off with Ed.

"What is going on?" Cole demanded. "I thought you boys were on the same side."

"Regiments compete against one another, Cole, darlin'."

Jake sounded like Grandpa with a touch of Irish in his voice even though he had never set foot in Ireland. Of all the grandchildren, Jake favored Michael Donovan the most. He was tall, strong, and handsome with a bit of swagger. No matter who led the army, it was fighting men like Jake, Ed, and Art who would win the battles.

"No one is fighting in my house," Jem announced, grabbing a rug beater leaning against the staircase wall. She raised it in a threatening manner.

"We've had Johnny Rebs shooting at us for months, and Miss Jenny thinks a rug beater is going to scare us," Ed said.

"I'll uninvite you to dinner," Jem said. "And my sisters have been cooking fresh bread and pies."

Jake lowered his fists. "Home cooking means a truce, boys."

Chapter Fourteen

The dining hall was large, able to seat all the guests in comfort. Cole had to add more milk to the soup, but no one complained. Jake had brought freshly caught fish which Cole fried. Jem and Logan sat at each end of the table with Jess between Ed and Art on one side and Cole between Jake and Deidre on the other.

A knock on the door interrupted prayer. Logan said a quick "Amen" and opened the main door. "Add a plate to the table, Mrs. Pierce. We have another guest."

Cole rose before Jem could and headed for the hutch for another service. Blake Ellsworth strolled into the dining hall and flashed her a toothy grin. Logan made introductions and added a chair between Cole and Deidre.

Cole arranged the silverware on each side of the plate. He held her chair and sat beside her. "What are you doing here?"

"I'm visiting my cousin."

She scooted her chair in and bumped his arm. She recalled his injury. "How is your shoulder?"

"Fine until someone jostles me."

"I barely grazed you. Are you wearing your brace?" She ran her hand along his shoulder, seeking the tell-tale bulge. "Where is your brace?"

"I didn't think I needed it."

"Why don't men follow doctor's orders?" She

stared into his smoky gaze. "Did you throw it away?"

"No."

She calculated the time from his injury. "You should wear it at least six more weeks."

"I'll put it on this evening."

The others stared at Cole.

"He was Papa's patient," she explained.

"Were you wounded in a battle?" Art asked.

"No, one of the Cassell brothers shot me. Broke my collar bone in the fall. Doctor Beecher removed the bullet but said I should wear a brace for two months." Blake shrugged. "I feel fine without it."

Cole groaned. She had agreed with Jess not to tell their sister about the Cassell brothers. Jem and Logan had been captured in Southern territory last year, and the Cassell brothers had beaten Logan and threatened Jem. They had barely escaped their clutches.

Husband and wife exchanged worried glances. "Where did you encounter the Cassell brothers?"

"I was on the *Irish Rose* heading for Cleveland…"

Jem's hand went to her throat. "The Cassell brothers were in Ohio?" She stared at Logan at the opposite end of the table. "The last time we encountered them, they had joined the Confederate Army."

"They deserted," Blake said. "Turned mercenary."

"What did they want with you, Blake?"

Jem called him by his first name. How well did Blake know Logan and Jem?

"I sold a hotel in Tennessee and was paid with Confederate gold."

Jake interrupted with a long whistle. "You stole a Rebel payroll?"

"I didn't steal it," Blake defended. "The Cassell brothers were the ones attempting to take it from me."

"Buck shot him," Jess said. "Then I shot Buck in the leg. Grandpa missed Clyde, but they high tailed it into the woods."

Jake leaned forward. "Then what happened?"

Blake turned to Cole. "What did happen? I don't remember much but you sitting on top of me."

"I was trying to stop the flow of blood," Cole defended. "Cass rode a borrowed horse to fetch Papa and warn the sheriff about the Cassell brothers."

"Cassie?" Jem was closest to Cass.

"You'd've been proud of her," Cole said. "She rode home in record time to fetch Papa."

Jem removed a handkerchief from her sleeve and swiped at a tear. "I keep thinking of her as my little sister who loved to draw horses not ride them."

"Then everyone was safe?" Logan asked.

"They didn't go near Darrow Falls," Cole said. "With Buck injured, they boarded a train and headed south. We won't see those two vipers again."

Jem furrowed her brow. "What was Cassie doing on the *Irish Rose*?"

"We were training her and Jules to operate the locks."

"If they're helping Grandpa on the canal, who is helping Mama?"

"They are. When Papa asked us to travel to Washington City, Ethan and Paddy's friends volunteered to help Grandpa."

Jem dabbed at her mouth. "I can't imagine Cassie or Juliet working on the *Irish Rose*."

Cole pointed at Jess. "We did for years."

"Too many years," Jem said.

Jem didn't approve of their behavior or working on the *Irish Rose*. She had chosen to help Papa with his doctoring and was now the wife of a politician. "You can teach us how to behave like proper young ladies of high society in Washington City."

Blake smirked. He hadn't missed her sarcasm. "How long do you plan to stay?"

Cole knew better than to argue with her sister in front of others, but Jem had a way of riling her. "Long enough to snatch an officer or senator for a husband." Let Blake mull that declaration over.

"I don't want you changing, Miss Jessica." Ed smiled at her. "I like you just the way you are."

Jess beamed.

Cole turned to Ed. "Do you think Miss Jessica has changed much since last fall when you said good-bye?"

"She's prettier if that's possible."

Jess blushed. "You look like soldiering agrees with you."

"You should have seen me before our new uniforms were issued. I looked like a ragged scarecrow."

"I read your letters telling how you were starving and your clothes falling apart," Jess said. "How can the army neglect the men fighting its battles?"

Ed didn't answer.

"You still short officers?" Jake asked.

"We don't need them," Ed said. "When the fighting starts, most of them act wounded or ill. We charge forward into enemy lines because we have no one to order us to stop."

"Aren't most officers West Point graduates?"

Logan asked.

"Some. Others graduated from college, but book learning doesn't make a leader," Ed said. "I always thought a rich man or an educated man was better than me, but I don't care how rich a man is or what college he attended, he has to earn my respect. I'm not tipping my hat and bowing because his suit cost more than I earn in a year."

"That sounds like a demand for equality," Logan said. "Dangerous thing for a soldier to think for himself."

"More dangerous to listen to a fool who sends you to your death," Ed said.

Blake leaned forward. "But don't you have to obey orders?"

"When they tell us to march, we march. When they tell us to fight, we fight," Ed said. "But when they abandon us in the field, we have the right to defend our lives and do whatever it takes."

"You don't respect any officers?"

"We have a few men we trust, but we've learned to take command of our own lives," Ed said.

"Ed is right," Jake agreed. "We're as good as anyone in command. The men making the decisions aren't fighting the battles." His voice was bitter and angry. "They commission their friends or family as officers, and when the battle begins, they run."

"When you see your fellow soldiers drop to their knees, clutching their innards as they pour out on the ground, you forget the rules of polite society," Ed added.

"Innards? Yuck." Deidre made a face.

"How was everyone's Independence Day?" Jem

changed the subject. "We had lovely fireworks here."

"We had fireworks at Darrow Falls," Cole said.

"How was the picnic on the square back home?" Art spoke for the first time. "Was my ma and pa there?"

"Yes, and John, Harry, and your sister Lara attended. They donated some of the supplies you carried upstairs."

"Golly, I wish I'd been there." Art had a sad expression. "Did they decorate the square with flags and lanterns?"

"Red, white, and blue. Plenty of food and games." Cole laughed. "Harry won the pie eating contest."

"Our little brother?" Ed demanded. "He was the runt of the family."

"He's not so little now," Cole said. "Probably because he doesn't have to fight you two for food."

Ed touched the laurel ring on Jess' finger. "How was the dance?"

Jess couldn't answer, and Cole responded. "There was a shortage of men, but your ma allowed John and Harry to dance."

"John danced with his bum leg?" Art demanded. "He wouldn't re-enlist after being wounded at Bull Run even though he barely has a limp."

"Don't judge John too harshly," Jem said. "His scars run deeper than his leg."

"I can't believe Ma let him dance," Art said. "She thinks it's immoral."

Martha Herbruck preached fire and brimstone to her four sons. The Beecher sisters had taught them how to dance in secret. The boys had taught the girls how to shoot, build a fire, and ride a horse bareback. They kept each other's confidences and had been like brothers and sisters. The war, separation, and letters had turned their friendship into something more. Two sons fighting in the war, one wounded, and one yearning to join had softened Martha as well. "She was his first partner," Cole confided.

"Ma dancing?" Art stared at Ed. "I told you John was always her favorite."

"Harry was Pa's favorite," Ed said. "He was teaching him to be a veterinarian."

"Still is," Jess said. "He's pretty good according to Cass. She's always peppering him with questions about how to care for animals."

"Harry always liked Miss Cassie," Ed said. "Did he dance with her?"

"Cassie is too young," Jem interrupted.

"She can't wait to lower her hem," Cole said. "She wanted to know all about hand holding and kissing."

"Kissing?" Jem's face reddened. "I hope you told her she should wait until she was engaged."

"Engaged?" Cole looked at Jess. "No one ever told us to wait that long." She turned to Jem. "Did you wait until you were engaged to Logan to kiss him?"

Jem stood and gave Logan a stern look when he chuckled. "I'll fetch the pies."

"Sit," Jess ordered. "I made them. I'll serve them."

"I thought you were sent here to help your sister not torment her," Blake whispered in Cole's ear.

"You knew we were visiting?"

"Your grandmother told me about your plans. She likes me."

He had sought her out. Why? He didn't have any sense about what topics to avoid. Would he reveal what he knew about Simon? "How long are you visiting?"

"I own a hotel here."

"I thought your family was at the hotel in New York."

"That's why I'm here." He accepted a slice of pie from Jess. "With my gold, I bought the Pirate's Cove in a quiet inlet near Sandusky. You can sail to some of the islands from it."

"How many hotels do you own?" Jake asked.

"Four now. One on Lake Erie, the Dutchman's Hotel in Albany, the Mermaid's Mirth on Maryland Avenue near Seventh Street, and one in Richmond I wrote off when the war began."

"Is the Mermaid's Mirth near the Smithsonian?" Jake looked at the Herbruck brothers. "Have you seen the castle?"

"I can see it from my back yard," Blake admitted.

"Your hotels have a nautical theme," Jake concluded. "Are you a sailor?"

"My grandfather worked on a whaling ship," he confessed. "I've been sailing a few times. No feeling like the wind in your face as you crash through the waves."

"Beats working on a canal boat."

"Jake! I thought you loved working on the *Irish Rose*."

"Child's play. A man likes to face tougher challenges, Cole, darlin'."

Cole gathered the supper dishes. "I think you've had your share of danger fighting in the war."

"I don't think you're living life if you play it safe," Jake said.

"Or settle for ordinary," Cole agreed. "I want to do something special with my life, too."

"That's a Donovan for you."

"She's a Beecher," Blake said. "Her father made that clear."

His words sparked a memory. "Papa and Mama sent presents!"

"Presents!" Deidre clapped her hands.

The adults enjoyed dessert in the parlor while Deidre opened her gifts. Grandma Donovan made her a dress, and Grandpa Donovan made her a replica of the *Irish Rose*.

"You're spoiling her," Jem said as Cole and Jess took turns handing her another gift to open.

"We haven't seen her since Christmas. Everyone wanted to give her something. There's also some gifts for you and Logan."

Sterling had given Deidre a book of nursery rhymes. Maureen had knitted pink slippers and filled them with hard candy. Cory and Tyler had sent a store-bought porcelain doll. Cole had purchased chalks and a slate. Jess had bought embroidery threads, fabric, and a frame. Cass sent several watercolors of Darrow Falls she had painted, and Jules sent a puppet with a painted face.

After Deidre examined each of her presents, the women helped her carry her haul upstairs and put her to bed.

Logan waited for them to return to open the remaining gifts. Sterling has sent Jem medical supplies. Maureen had sent baby clothes, and CJ had sent a maternity dress although Jem would have to put on several pounds before she needed to wear it.

A soft breeze blew through the open windows of the parlor. The traffic on the street had slowed with an occasional horse clipping along on the cobblestones. Cole poured coffee for the men.

"This is the best coffee we've had in a long time," Art said.

"Tell us what happened since your last letter," Jess urged Ed, who was seated beside her. "You were at Luray resting. How did you get here?"

"About a week later we finally received our uniforms." Ed ran his hands over the blue wool fabric of his coat. "Didn't change the minds of the men who walked away or returned home on furloughs because of sickness and never returned. Morale was low."

"We had the same problem in the Seventh," Jake said. "One man called it natural selection like in Darwin's book. Only the fittest remain in the army."

"Or the dumbest," Art added.

"I think it takes a sense of honor to serve under such trying circumstances," Cole said.

Art sipped his coffee. "Wish more men believed in honor to country."

"No disrespect, Logan," Ed added. "You have an important job in Washington City. The money, when it arrives, helps motivate us."

"Sometimes the leaders in Washington forget about the men fighting and dying in the war."

"You remind them for us." Ed continued his story. "We left the valley June 21 and marched to Bristoe Station where we boarded the railroad cars on the Orange and Alexandria line." Ed motioned toward Art. "When we reached Alexandria, we thought we were going to board a steamer to help General George McClellan attack Richmond."

"Is that the battle you told us about?" Cole asked

Logan.

"Yes. Seven days of fighting, and McClellan lost his chance to take Richmond and end the war," Logan said. "I wish Joe Johnston was in charge instead of Lee."

"Joe Johnston was the darling of Manassas," Jem said.

The men exchanged looks of surprise.

Jem cleared her throat. "I used his name when I traveled to Richmond to look for Ben."

Logan put his arm around her. "That's when I met the Cassell brothers." He cupped his jaw. "They made an impression."

"They wanted to kill you." Jem snuggled against him. "I hope they don't find out you're alive."

"They think Logan is dead?" Cole hadn't heard this part of the story.

"Colonel Chauncy LaDonte told them he hanged him. The Cassell brothers buried another body in a coffin."

"Chauncy," Cole repeated. "Poor man saddled with a name like that."

"I like it," Jem defended. "I'm thinking of naming our child Chauncy."

"If it's a girl," Logan added. "Chauncy Theodora after the two Rebels who saved our lives."

Cole repeated the name. "I like it for a girl. What if you have a boy?"

Jem didn't hesitate. "Derek Logan Pierce."

A son would be named for Logan's brother and Deidre's father.

Chapter Fifteen

They had waited long enough to find out what had happened to the Ohio boys.

"We don't care about the Cassell brothers anymore," Cole said. "What happened when you reached Washington City?"

"Nothing. We helped load the steamers, but they didn't want us," Ed said. "Seems McClellan finally had enough men. Without orders, our regiment resided on a hillside in Alexandria with a nice view of the Potomac. Most of the officers in the Twenty-ninth Ohio had gone home, were sick, or had been taken prisoner. Captain Wilbur Stevens of Company B is in charge until they find someone to lead the regiment."

"We have plenty to eat, and we've been taking in the sites of Washington City," Art added. "We've seen Mount Vernon, the Capitol, and the Patent Office."

"We plan to have our photographs taken at Brady's office tomorrow," Ed said.

"I'd like to have my photograph taken." Jess looked at her sisters. "May we go?"

"I think Mama and Papa would like having your photographs." Jem retrieved a picture with Logan, Jem, and Deidre. "Davy Cooke is an assistant at Brady's Studio. He took this one in May."

Jess rested her hand on Ed's arm. "What time will you be free from your duties?"

He patted her hand, playing with the ring he had created. "We have general inspection and drill most of the morning, but we'll be free early afternoon."

Cole turned to Jake. "Where is the Seventh camped?"

"Right beside the Twenty-ninth like we are in battle," Jake said.

"We're both in Tyler's brigade in the Second Corps in the Union Army of Virginia," Art explained.

"New name, same old men," Jake said. "Major General John Pope is in charge of the Second Corps. I can't wait to see what he does to Stonewall Jackson."

"That wily fox has our generals running around in circles," Ed said. "Most of the men in the Twenty-ninth were barefoot from wearing out their shoes searching the hills and woods for Rebs."

"Jackson keeps everyone in Washington City on edge," Logan said. "Do you think he might attack?"

Jem gasped, her face pale. "Let's talk about something more pleasant."

Logan put his arm around Jem. "What's happening in Darrow Falls?"

Cole and Jess updated everyone on the weddings, births, and businesses at home.

"Your brother John is learning how to make plows from Noah," Jess said.

Ed didn't disguise his disbelief. "John is a blacksmith?"

"I believe he calls himself a metalworker," Cole corrected. "He's doing good business. Families are heading west and need equipment for farming."

"Homestead Act," Logan said. "A man can gain land and escape the war."

"Who's taking care of our farm?" Art asked.

"Harry takes care of the chores," Cole said. "I bet he's as tall as you."

"We haven't been gone that long," Art said. "You make it sound like we won't recognize the place when we return."

The farm was the same, but their family wouldn't recognize them. They were lean with muscles sculptured from long hours marching and carrying heavy packs. Although clean-shaven, carefree youth had been replaced with lines around their eyes and a cockiness in their attitude. They had faced death, conquered it, and knew they wouldn't back down when it reared its ugly head again.

The sky was light, but the men had to return to camp before nightfall or face being shot by a sentry posted at the bridges entering Washington City. They promised to call after dinner and travel to Brady's shop.

Cole turned to go inside, but Blake blocked her retreat. "You're angry with me, brat."

"I hardly recognize you, Mr. Ellsworth, with your hair cut and your face shaved. You almost look respectable."

"You prefer scruffy looking?"

She hadn't decided what man she preferred. "What are you doing here?"

"I called at Pierce House because Deidre is my cousin. If Logan hadn't taken guardianship, it would have fallen to me. I like to check on her welfare."

Cole put her hands on her hips. "Logan and Jem are excellent parents."

"I agree, but I promised her mother I would help, and I keep my promises no matter what they cost me."

"Logan earns a good salary working at the Department of the Treasury."

"I was referring to a different promise. One I made my father."

"Like the promise I made my father not to kiss you again."

He stepped closer and lowered his voice. "But you said I could kiss you."

"No, I did not. You're twisting my words. Even though you made no promise to Papa you wouldn't kiss me, that doesn't give you permission to canoodle me whenever we're alone."

"What makes you think I want to make love to you? I came to visit Logan, Miss Jenny, and Deidre."

"The same day we arrive?" Cole shook her head and groaned. "And did you have to tell Jem about the Cassell brothers?"

"I didn't know it was a forbidden subject. Maybe you should tell me what topics to avoid in the future."

"You plan to be a frequent guest?"

He nodded toward the window. "Your sister is waiting for you." He put on his hat and headed down the road.

Cole stared after him. What was the man up to?

****

Jess chose a red skirt with a white blouse and small red jacket to wear to Brady's shop. Cole opted for a plaid dress of green, white, and yellow. They joined Jem and Deidre in the parlor. "Do you think these gowns will do?"

"They will have to do." Jem tied Deidre's bonnet. "The men are waiting."

"Where's Logan?"

"He has to work. They're reviewing the designs for the new currency."

Jess peeked out the window. "Don't they look handsome in their uniforms?"

Blake was missing. Cole dismissed her disappointment. She loathed the man. It was only a matter of time before he revealed all her secrets. And he knew too many of them.

Cole handed Jess a wide-brimmed bonnet. She grabbed her reticule and handed Jess a drawstring bag. The three men were generous with their compliments as they escorted them down Pennsylvania Avenue.

Brady's office was midway between the Capitol and the White House in the business district above a drug store. Although Brady took photographs of some of the more important customers, the only presence of him in the shop was his photograph on the wall above the sales counter. The large print captured Brady's angular features, accented by a mustache and beard and topped with a thick mass of unruly hair.

Brady had a crew of photographers he sent to the battlefields in box wagons to document the war. Davy Cooke minded the shop. His face was scarred from smallpox, and he had a nervous energy that made his voice squeak when he greeted them. "I'm so glad to see you."

"We didn't make an appointment," Jem said. "Do you have time to take our photographs?"

"All of you?"

"One each," Jem said. "Then Art and Ed together and my sisters with me."

Davy counted on his fingers. "I have someone coming in at three, but that should give us enough time.

Who wants to go first?"

Jem made the decision. "Jake can go first."

Cole examined the portraits matted on thick cardboard. Larger prints were framed beneath glass. Davy had left a collection of photographs from a battle on the counter. Officers posed in a row wearing double breasted button frock coats tied with sashes or belts. Some wore swords, and all of them had removed their caps, but she couldn't identify them. She turned to Art. "Do you recognize any of these men?"

"That's Little Mac in the center. The short one."

"McClellan? Why do you call him Little Mac?"

Art tapped the photograph. "Look at his pose."

He had his right hand tucked inside his coat. "Does he have a crippled arm?"

"No, he thinks he's Napoleon."

"I thought the soldiers liked McClellan."

"The ones under his command who have cots to sleep on and meals of oysters and fresh beef," Art said. "We nearly starved and froze to death in the Shenandoah."

The photographs of wagons and tents were from the Seven Day battle Logan had told them about in which McClellan had retreated, and Lee had replaced Johnston. One photograph showed a bridge made from cut logs.

She paused at a photograph of an open field. In the foreground were three bodies or what resembled bodies. She recognized the leg bone jutting from a boot and covered in a tattered pant leg. The remaining parts of the body were flattened from decay, the uniform shredded around the bones. Another body was face down, the high boot perched on its toes. A skull, whitened from the sun, was several feet away from the remains of the body.

The next photograph showed a man with both legs amputated mid-thigh, his face somber, his eyes expressionless.

She shuddered. Brady wasn't documenting the parades and celebrations. He was documenting the pain and suffering of the war. Who would buy reminders of death and mutilation?

Jess examined a photograph of a young soldier. "How do they make these?"

"Davy explained the process to me last year," Jem said. "He coats plates of glass with chemicals and then makes it sensitive to light with silver nitrate. He has to store the plates in a light-tight holder until he's ready to take a photograph. When he removes the cap on the camera, light makes the image."

"Can we watch?"

A large room on the north side of the building had large windows that provided light for the photographs. Jake was seated in a stiff back chair. He had removed his kepi hat but held it in one hand to identify his regiment by the number inside a bugle on top.

Davy stood by a view camera on a tripod. "Don't move." He stepped behind the camera, lifted the black focusing cloth, and disappeared beneath.

Davy reached forward and removed the lens cap from the front of the camera. He adjusted the accordion section of the camera to focus on Jake. Then he replaced the cap and disappeared under the cloth.

"What are you doing under there?" Jess asked.

"Don't lift the cloth," Davy warned. "I'm inserting the glass plate." Something grated in a sliding motion beneath the black draping. "Don't move!" Davy removed the lens cap, waited a few seconds, and replaced the cap.

Davy struggled to escape the cloth. His hair stood in static peaks. A box was in his hand. "Let me process this plate, and I'll take the next one."

"Let's have Deidre pose before she becomes restless," Jem suggested.

Davy took Ed and Art together and the three sisters before finishing with individual photographs of Jess and Cole.

Davy opened his ledger and recorded each plate number, name, and copies to be printed. "I'll make prints later today. You can pick them up tomorrow."

Jess studied a picture. "Is it difficult to develop the photographs?"

"It's all in the timing. You have to expose the plate to light on treated paper and then soak it in different chemicals to develop the image."

"Do you think I could learn?"

Davy stared at her, running his fingers through his mussed hair. "Why would you want to learn?"

"It sounds interesting. I might want to be a photographer."

He laughed, looking around at the other men for support. They remained stone-faced. "You're serious?"

"It doesn't look difficult," Jess said.

"But someone as pretty as you should be in photographs not making them," he stammered. "You could be on a collectible card."

"What are those?"

He opened an album of small photographs. "People collect and trade photographs of famous people like

Queen Victoria, Prince Edward, and General Scott."

"I'm not famous."

"Instead of officers, some men like collecting the photographs of beautiful women."

Jem covered Deidre's ears. "He means scantily clad women of ill repute."

"Oh, no." Davy's face reddened, and he knocked over a frame "All the women are clothed in my photographs."

"I don't think it would be a good idea," Jem said. "Do you want to be part of a collection and have strange men handing your image around?"

"Not all men are strange," Jake remarked.

"I meant strangers," Jem amended.

They stepped outside into the bright sunshine and gathered on the sidewalk. "What should we do now?"

"We have time to see some of the sites," Jem said. "Tomorrow we'll begin sorting supplies and delivering them to the troops."

Cole turned to the men. "We'll need your help."

"You had us carry all those boxes upstairs so we would have to carry them downstairs?" Ed asked.

"If it wore you out, Big Ed, let me carry your load," Jake offered.

"You would volunteer to carry them down the stairs," Ed said. "Just like the Seventh to take the easy way."

"Don't you like each other?" Jem asked.

"Of course they do." Cole put her arm around Jem's waist. "They fight like you and me."

Jem stammered a reply. "I thought you hated me."

"You're my sister." She squeezed. "I love you."

Jem stopped, a surprised look on her face. "We

don't say it often enough." She hugged her and Jess. "I love you, too."

Chapter Sixteen

Cole and Jess viewed the Twenty-ninth Ohio camp for the first time when Jake drove an army wagon with the supplies to Arlington Heights. Jem had supervised the sorting and packing of the supplies, and Cole had insisted she rest. Cousin Jake could serve as chaperone. Jess used the opportunity to hold hands with Ed in the back of the wagon.

The camp was on a hillside overlooking the Potomac River. Illness, the wounded, and the dead had left the Twenty-ninth Ohio with fewer than three hundred men, less than a third of the original regiment. Neat rows of small tents were arranged to allow the cool breeze to flow through the open ended canvas sheets. Two sections were stretched across a pole supported by two more. The bottom was framed with stacks of rocks or logs to form little canvas huts.

A few fire pits provided a place to warm coffee. A shallow trench ran down the hillside to the river. Boards had been placed over top of the ditch along the pathways to avoid the waste identified by its repugnant smell.

Cole peered inside the tent. The bottom was lined with a rubber sheet and two blankets made a bed. Knapsacks and supplies were jammed on each side. Their guns were in front of the tents and stacked upright, the bayonets interlaced for support, ready to grab in case of attack.

The tent cabins were barely big enough for one person. "You live in this?"

"Home sweet home, Miss Colleen," Art said.

"When you said they were little, I didn't think they were this small." Cole walked around the tent Ed and Art shared. "You both fit in here?"

"I'm getting the impression you don't think much of our grand accommodations," Ed said. "We affectionately call our shelter dog tents."

"More like pup tents." Cole shook her head. "I would think the army could provide better accommodations for its fighting men."

"We have a fine breeze off the Potomac and a splendid view of the city." Ed waved his arm in front. "Although wool would be my last choice for clothing in this heat."

Beads of sweat dampened Cole's undergarments. Most ladies retired indoors by lunch and remained until evening to escape the heat. "The weather is muggy in Washington City."

"You look cool and comfortable, Miss Colleen," Art said.

On the outside. "I'm wearing cotton. Purchased before the war," she defended her choice. Cotton was grown in enemy territory, and businessmen had to obtain special licenses to purchase it.

Art stared at the four yards of gathered skirt. "Lot of yards of cotton in that dress."

"Grandma CJ made this dress for me, and I have no intention of handing it over, even to soldiers, so stop looking at my frock," Cole warned with a smile.

Art studied Jake. "You don't look bothered by the

heat."

"Grandma CJ made me linen underwear," Jake said. "I have a linen shirt, too."

"I'll make you a shirt when I return home," Jess said to Ed.

Cole nudged her. "Better wait until you're engaged to make him any clothing."

She looked puzzled by the rule guiding gifts between courting couples. "We sew uniforms for the soldiers."

"We don't know the recipients personally."

"Well, if there's a linen shirt in any of the boxes, you can have it, Ed."

Ed ran his fingers through his light brown hair. "Aren't the supplies for the wounded?"

"Some, but the folks back home donated for the Ohio boys. I think you fighting men would enjoy some canned fruit and books to read," Cole said.

Jake looked around at the nearly empty camp. "Sid is around here somewhere. He knows where the supplies are needed."

Sergeant Sid Wilson stood by the wagon, examining what was in the boxes. Sid was a veteran from the original enlistment of men from Ohio. After serving ninety days, he signed up for three years with the Seventh Ohio and had been promoted to sergeant. His spectacles and receding hairline made him appear older than most of the men. He made notations in a notebook he carried.

Jake saluted him. "What would you like done with the supplies, sir?"

"Stop showing off, corporal."

Cole grabbed Jake's sleeve. "You weren't lying

when you wrote you'd been promoted." The stitches were large and uneven holding the two stripes. "But who taught you how to sew?"

"Grandma offered once, but I thought it beneath a boy."

"Next time you're by the Pierce House, I'll sew them on correctly."

Sid removed an oatmeal jar from a crate. "These need to go to the wounded at Mermaid's Mirth."

"Mermaid's Mirth?" Blake's hotel.

"The owner lets us use the place as a hospital for the convalescing men," Sid said.

"She knows Blake Ellsworth." Jake grinned at Cole. "They met in Ohio."

"Old friend?" Sid asked.

"He's not my friend."

"I thought you saved his life."

"I made a mistake." She ignored Jake's inquisitive stare.

Sid removed his glasses and wiped them with his handkerchief. "You're the troublemaker."

Cole put her hands on her hips. "Who told you that?"

"Your sister in her letters to Ben," Sid said. "She never wrote how pretty you were."

"You, I like." She looked at the ledger he was writing in. Mermaid's Mirth was written at the top of a page, which was nearly full with entries. "I'm surprised Mr. Ellsworth is allowing his hotel to be used as a hospital."

"He doesn't have much of a choice," Sid said. "The army comes first in Washington City. They take the trains, food, and shelter before anyone else."

****

The Mermaid's Mirth was a three-story wooden building with a balcony on the second floor above a porch on the lower level. Ornate trim braced each post and the roof line. Blake was making repairs to the floorboards on the porch. Every time he hammered a nail, he grimaced.

"You shouldn't do that." Cole offered to take the hammer.

"Did you write a book about carpentry?"

"I know how to swing a hammer," Cole said. "Someone had to make repairs around the farm."

"Why you?"

"I didn't mind dirtying my hands." Cole removed a nail from a wooden box. It was squared on the edges, tapering from a flattened head to a point. She tapped it into the board.

"That will take forever."

"I need to set it." She moved her hand to the end of the hammer handle and swung it in a smooth stroke, sending the nail into the wood nearly to the head.

Blake wiped his forehead with his kerchief. "Is there anything you cannot do, brat?"

"I'm accomplished in a wealth of useless abilities, especially for a woman."

Blake rubbed his shoulder.

"Are you wearing your brace?"

"I couldn't put it on."

"Fetch it."

Blake looked at the other men. They appeared amused she was bossing the man as if he were a child. "What are you standing around for?" Cole demanded. "We have supplies to deliver."

When Blake returned, Cole took the brace. "Remove your coat."

Blake gingerly removed his linen coat and placed it on the back of a chair on the porch. Cole lifted the brace. "You're too tall. Stand on the bottom step." She remained on the porch and stood behind Blake to wrap the brace around his shoulders and neck, tying it off in back. "How does that feel?"

"Tight."

"That prevents the bone from moving."

Sid lifted a jar of oatmeal from the box he carried. "Do you know how to make this?"

Blake examined the jar. "Is this what I ate at your grandma's inn?"

"Yes, you add boiling water and stir."

"And add some fruit or cinnamon to flavor," Blake added.

"How many wounded are left?" Sid asked.

"Half a dozen from the Peninsula Campaign," Blake said. "The serious cases were taken to Judiciary Square Hospital."

"We can split supplies between Judiciary and Mount Pleasant hospitals," Sid said. "How much do you want for your patients?"

"I don't need much," Blake said. "The doctor said he'd probably send these men home or back to their regiments in a few days. Then the real work begins."

"What work?"

"I can't rent any rooms until I clean the place from top to bottom. Do you know anyone who can do laundry?"

"Every company has three to four women to wash uniforms," Sid said. "I could ask around."

Cole tapped Sid on the shoulder. "Am I invisible?"

"What?"

"I can do laundry." She turned to Blake. "Providing the price is right. How much would you pay for the work?"

"I don't know." Blake looked at Sid. "How much does the army pay?"

"In companies not marching up and down the Shenandoah Valley, each serviceman pays fifty cents a month and each laundress handles at least twenty-five men plus a few officers. That's fifteen dollars a month."

"But that's for uniforms. You want me to wash sheets and blankets. And that includes ironing and making beds."

"No mending or buttons to deal with," Blake argued. "How about twenty a month and an extra four dollars for baking pies and cakes. I'll buy the ingredients."

"Don't you have a cook?"

"The cook married a soldier right after the maid married one. My general manager, Thomas Hill, is looking for replacements. He can scramble eggs and fry fish but not much more." He grinned. "It's only temporary. I'll pay you six dollars every Friday."

Working for Blake would throw them together more often than an occasional meal. Every time she saw him, her thoughts drifted to the night they had kissed, building a mutual passion that had been difficult to end. She should say no to his offer, but she had no source of income. Her money from teaching and working the canal was nearly gone, spent on supplies for the soldiers and material for new clothes. She didn't want to ask Jem or Logan for any. "Let's deliver these supplies while I think on your offer."

Jake was carrying a box inside and leaned in close to her ear. "That's a good deal. You should accept it."

"I'm negotiating."

"Cole, darlin', a soldier makes thirteen dollars a month. Take it before he changes his mind."

Blake led them inside. The wounded men were upstairs in three of the bedrooms. Each man was in a single bed. The illnesses ranged from sore feet to the loss of an eye.

The men were bored and grateful for the gifts Cole and Jess passed out. Cole was writing a letter for a man with his arm in a sling when Blake entered the room.

"I have two rooms that need cleaning. What did you decide about my offer?"

"I don't know if I can do it all alone."

"Hire your sister to help."

"Then I lose half of my wages."

"You have half the work."

He could be more generous, but extra money implied additional duties. The price was fair for the work and nothing more. "Jess and I agree." She extended her hand.

He took her hand in his, examining the palm instead of shaking to seal their deal. "What are you doing?"

"Finding my place."

"What?"

"In the palm of your hand."

His words were the romantic dribble she detested from men, but his rumbling deep voice made the nonsense sound sincere. Was she a fool to believe him or a fool not to? Her gaze locked on his, daring him to reveal the lie behind his words, but he remained stoic, standing by his declaration. Her legs wobbled beneath her crinoline as her resolve to remain indifferent floundered. She shouldn't work for Blake. He unleashed primitive feelings she had spent years controlling. She could flirt and tease as long as it meant nothing, but to declare any serious feelings scared her. It meant being honest.

Jess coughed from the doorway. "I heard my name."

"We have a job."

"Doing what?"

"Laundry. Blake will pay us six dollars a week."

"Each?" Jess clapped her hands.

"Three each," Blake said. "And that includes baking until Thomas hires a cook."

Her shoulders sank. "Doesn't Jem expect us to volunteer at the hospitals?"

"I'm not volunteering when I can earn money."

Ed leaned against the door frame. "How are you earning money?"

"We're doing laundry."

"It shouldn't take more than two days to do the work," Cole said. "One to wash and dry. The second to iron and fold."

"If you want to do laundry, there are plenty of enlisted men in our regiment willing to pay to have their clothes washed," Ed said. "Especially now that we have new uniforms. We took our clothes to Suds Row, and we were the ones cleaned out of our money."

"We can set up shop on Monday," Cole said. "Tell the men to drop off their belongings after drilling, and we'll have them cleaned and mended by Wednesday."

****

When Cole and Jess arrived Monday morning, Blake had two wooden oak tubs in the yard, two buckets, two scrub boards, and two iron cauldrons on fire grates to heat the water. "What else do you need?"

Cole shielded her eyes from the morning sun. "We should put the tubs under the shade of the tree."

After Cole checked that Blake wore his brace, he moved the tubs under the shade tree near the porch, and the sisters carried the remaining items.

"Should I build new fire pits?"

"No, we don't want them too close to our work area. It'll be hot enough." Cole looked around. "But we could use some stools."

Jess and Cole filled the cauldrons with water while Blake tied rope between two trees on the east side of the hotel for hanging the laundry. "Where are the clothes pins?"

Jess shook a cloth bag.

"Looks like we're ready for the laundry." Cole joined Blake as he tied off the final line. "Do you want to show me the bedrooms?"

"Should we take along your chaperone, or do you have your knife?"

"I always carry a knife. I don't know what unsavory characters might cross my path."

"Like Simon?"

"I don't want to talk about him, and if his name is mentioned in any conversation, you are not to say a word." She'd like to keep his immoral proposition a secret, especially from Jem.

Blake frowned but didn't argue. He led her upstairs to one of the rooms the soldiers had been using. He began removing the blankets and sheets.

"You don't consider changing sheets a woman's job?"

"As owner, I've stripped beds, served meals, and everything else necessary to keep guests happy. Running a hotel is difficult, especially with demanding clients."

"How long will it take for Thomas to hire someone?"

"He has a few good prospects. One is a black woman with two daughters. They're young, around thirteen, but willing to learn. Would you and your sister have time to train them?"

"Won't that put us out of work?"

"How long were you planning to stay in Washington City?"

"A few months." Cole studied his reaction. His shoulder would be healed, and he'd probably be gone, too. "We expect to be paid while training."

"You have a head for business."

Was that an insult or a compliment? Cole unpinned the sheets on the single mattress of straw resting on the ropes. The feather mattress had been removed with only a straw filled bag on the ropes for the soldiers. "When was the last time the straw was changed?"

"Before the soldiers arrived." Blake handed her the sheets. "I store the feather mattresses for guests. Sick soldiers tend to ruin them."

"No need to explain." Cole sniffed at the soiled bag covering the bed and recoiled. "It's easier to replace straw than feathers. The beds in the hospitals are metal with straw filled mattresses and pillows."

"I'll carry the mattresses outside."

He yanked at a corner. "Are they too heavy?"

He scowled. "They're filled with straw. I'm not an invalid."

Cole delivered the dirty bedding to Jess. They had braided their hair and wore large straw bonnets to shade their faces from the sun like they did when working on the canal. Each wore a long apron over a faded work dress with the sleeves shoved to the elbows.

Cole helped Jess fill the tubs with hot and cold water to create a mixture tolerable for them to immerse their hands in and scrub on the bumpy surface of the washboard. After scrubbing, the sheets were rinsed and hung on the lines to dry.

Jess nudged Cole. "Should Blake be pitching that hay?"

Blake had removed the soiled straw from the mattresses and was tossing it into a pile by the barn. Cole shook her head in disapproval. "Papa ordered him to take it easy."

She headed toward the barn, a stone structure with wide sliding doors on the front and a small door on the side. Openings beneath the roof eaves allowed air to circulate.

She grabbed the pitchfork handle. "What do you think you're doing?"

"I can't leave dirty straw in the yard."

"What about your shoulder?"

"It feels fine, and I'm wearing my brace."

"Do you have any clean straw?"

"In the barn." He led the way inside where two draft horses were standing in the stalls. They snorted and pawed at the ground as Blake stroked each one.

"Aren't you beauties?" Cole patted the nearest one

with a white blaze down his face. "What are their names?"

"Romulus and Remus."

"Rome's founders."

"You never cease to amaze me, brat."

"I know a few historical facts, and you're impressed." She looked around. "I don't see the straw?"

"In the wagon."

A wagon with a canvas top occupied the other side of the barn. Two stretchers leaned against the wall. "Is that an ambulance?"

"Not as nice as the military ones, but I help transport the wounded when they arrive. Other times I haul straw, hay, and oats for the horses and fresh vegetables and fruit for guests."

"I've never seen you at Center Market."

"I purchase my goods in Alexandria or the countryside where prices haven't been inflated."

"Aren't you afraid of being arrested as a spy?"

"I'm careful not to get too close to the Confederate lines."

Jess poked her head in the doorway. "If I'm going to do all the work, I expect to be paid more."

"Grab some of those mattress covers." Cole stepped toward Blake, whose back was against the stall wall. "You had ten minutes of unchaperoned time with me and didn't make an outrageous proposition."

"You're a hired hand, brat. And I make it a policy never to fraternize with the help. My pappy said there is nothing more despairing than an unmarried maid with child."

Cole narrowed her eyes. "You arrogant, blowhard. We shared a few kisses, and you think I'll crawl into bed with you. Try and seduce me and see who is despaired!"

Cole grabbed the remaining dirty mattress covers Blake had emptied of straw but dropped several. Blake picked them up.

"I can carry them." She tried to grab them, but he moved away.

"You are a prickly cactus." He carried his share of the covers to the tubs and dropped them. "I have other work to do. If you need any help, ask Thomas."

Chapter Seventeen

Blake kept his distance, whitewashing the porch while the girls finished the laundry. Cole glared at him a few times but didn't break the rhythm of scrubbing the linens up and down the board. She worked with Jess as a team, singing songs to pass the time.

They hung the last of the sheets to dry in the sunshine when the boys arrived from a morning of drilling.

Ed handed Jess a bottle. "My pa uses this liniment to heal red and cracked skin."

"That's so thoughtful." Jess removed the cork and sniffed. She made a face. "What's in this?"

"It's Pa's special recipe."

Jess poured some on Cole's hands and her own and rubbed it in. Both girls waved their hands in the air and blew on them. "It stings."

Ed looked distressed. "The horses never complained."

"Horses!"

"I have some lotion." Blake disappeared inside and returned with a jar of Lady Godey's cream. The girls rubbed the creamy mixture onto their burning skin.

"That's better." Cole examined the jar. "How did you come into possession of a lady's lotion?"

"A guest left it behind." He handed her the jar. "I have a box of forgotten items. You can take anything in it."

"I don't know if I should accept such a personal gift. I work for you."

"I'm not offering to rub it on." Blake raised a dark eyebrow when she gasped. "Put it with your other laundry supplies. You'll need it in the future."

The soldiers delivered their laundry to the girls, mostly shirts and socks. A few had added drawers. Most possessed one uniform and couldn't spare it for washing. Jess stitched the initials of the wearer along an edge while Cole marked the name down in a ledger Logan had given her. Instead of paying by the month, the soldiers paid per item. Sid determined a fair price. Once the clothing was properly marked, they stored it in a spare room to wash on Tuesday. The men loitered around, talking in the yard in front of the inn.

Jake pointed to the side yard. "Hey, Blake, do you mind if we use the field next to your hotel?"

"What for?"

"We play baseball with teams from different regiments, but it works better on flat ground. The field by the camp is on a slope. I don't know how many baseballs we've lost in the Potomac."

"Can we play?" Jess asked.

"A girl playing baseball?" A tall man with light brown hair and sour apple green eyes slapped his thigh and laughed.

"Why not?" Cole looked at Jake for support.

"I know Jess can beat about any boy, but these are my brothers in war," Jake said. "I got to side with them."

Cole put her arm around Jess. "I bet it's a dumb game."

"This is my property," Blake said. "The girls play or you don't."

Had she heard Blake correctly? He was defending them. "I thought you wanted to be a soldier. Taking their side would make you allies."

"Don't you want to play?"

"Yes, but…"

"Then play. If they give you any trouble, I'll throw them off my land."

No knight had ever been so chivalrous. She would have to reevaluate her opinion of Blake Ellsworth. "Aren't you playing?"

"I'm recovering from a bullet wound and resting per doctor's orders." He took a seat on the shady porch.

The soldiers found pieces of wood to mark the four bases and the spot for the pitcher. The men had a couple of sticks for hitting the ball. Jake showed her the ball. "It's made of rubber, wrapped in yarn, and covered in a two pieces of sheepskin stitched in this figure eight pattern."

"Fancy ball for a game."

Jake gathered the players together. "We're playing New York rules so no plugging the runner with the ball."

Cole looked at Jake. "What's plugging?"

"Throwing the ball at the runner. Some fellas aim for his head." Jake raised his voice. "You tag him or force him out at a base."

Cole played on the Seventh Ohio team with Jake, Sid, and Paxton Ravenswood, who wasn't happy about having any girl on his team. His sour disposition matched his green eyes. Jess joined Ed and Art's team.

"This is a friendly game isn't it?" Cole asked.

"Nothing is friendly between regiments," Sid said. "It's a matter of honor to prove you're better than the other men."

"But you're on the same side," Cole reminded him. "The Union," she clarified.

"If we act all sweet and cozy, we forget there's a Johnny Reb trying to kill us," Jake said. "A bit of rivalry keeps us alert and tough."

Cole was sent deep in the middle of the field while the rest of the players arranged themselves nearer the bases. The pitcher threw the ball and the batter swung. More often than not, he missed the ball.

Cole yawned. Beads of sweat dripped beneath her bonnet. Her arms ached from scrubbing all morning, and her clothes clung in uncomfortable folds. Even dumb animals knew not to stand in an open field in the hot sun. Blake looked cool and comfortable on the porch sipping lemonade. Maybe he hadn't been a gallant knight defending her right to play baseball. It appeared to be a dirty trick to teach her a lesson.

Jess gripped the bat like Ed showed her but missed the first pitch.

"Is the sun hot, or is Ed red from putting his arms around your sister?" Jake asked from his position in left field. "She's got her elbows too close."

"Tell her what she's doing wrong."

"She's on the opponent's team."

"She's your cousin."

"Pretend you're beating a rug," Jake shouted. "Swing your arms out and around through the ball."

"She's a girl," Pax sneered. "What can she do?"

"Don't you have any sisters?"

"No, and my little brother, Zach, could hit a ball

over your head swinging with one hand."

"I'd like to hit someone in the head," Cole growled under her breath. She cheered Jess, who had one more swing. She threw her arms out and around at the ball like Jake had instructed and connected, sending it over Pax's head at second base.

"Run!" Cole shouted.

"Cole, darlin'," Jake said. "You don't cheer the other team."

"You helped her."

"That was coaching. You're urging the enemy to score."

"My sister is not the enemy."

Jess ran to second base on Art's hit. Pax tagged her, calling her out, but Ed said she was safe. An argument ensued, but Blake intervened. "She's safe."

"What makes him the umpire?" Pax argued.

"I'm the land owner," Blake said. It helped Blake was taller than most of the men and in better health even with his wound.

"Let's finish the game," Pax suggested.

Everyone headed to their positions. Ed was up at bat.

Cole examined a stain on her apron. She had baked blueberry pies in the morning at Pierce House and spilled some of the filling. Wood connected with leather. Ed had smacked the ball, sending it high into the air toward center field. Her eyes followed the path of the projectile as it hurled toward her. What was she supposed to do? She wasn't going to catch the ball with her bare hands. She grabbed the corners of her apron and backed away, hoping it landed in the folds of the fabric.

Ed was rounding second when she raised the ball in the air. "I caught it."

"Is that fair?" Pax turned to Blake for a decision.

Blake was grinning as he ran out onto the field. "She caught it before it hit the ground." He took the ball from her. "I guess they'll think twice about not inviting you and Jess to play."

"It doesn't work that way. Boys don't like being beat by a girl."

"Grown men don't mind. Besides, none of them were wearing aprons."

"But aren't you trying to teach me a lesson?"

"What lesson?"

"Tricking me into standing in the hot sun for being prickly."

"That's no trick. That's part of the game." He pointed to the men in the Seventh Ohio sitting on the ground. "Better join your team. Remember, they stood in the sun, too."

Cole sat on the ground listening to the men repeat every miniscule detail of the game they had just played.

Blake joined them. He had brought her stool and carried a bucket of water. He offered her a ladle. "Maybe now you'll believe me if I say I wasn't punishing you."

"I'm not used to trusting men," Cole said. "I apologize if I insulted your integrity."

"Your flowery compliments make me blush, brat."

"Shut up." Blake was complimentary one minute, insulting the next, and a mixture of both that left her confused about his intentions.

Sid handed Cole a kepi with a seven inside a bugle. "You can't be part of the team without a hat." He tossed one to Blake.

Cole slid her bonnet back and examined the cap. She poked her finger through a gap in the fabric. "It has holes in it."

"So does mine," Blake said.

Cole tossed the kepi on the ground. "Did you take them off dead men?"

Jake retrieved the hat and returned it. "No, the men hold them in the air on sticks, and the Rebel sharpshooters fill them with holes."

"That's terrible."

"Better than filling a soldier's head with holes." Jake turned to Blake. "When they fire, their smoke gives away their positions."

"I'll remember that when I'm on the line."

Cole put on the cap. "How do I look?"

"You'd win the war," Blake said.

"I like my bonnet better, but I'll wear it for the Seventh."

"Ed gave Jess one from the Twenty-ninth," Jake said. "He's the romantic."

"Jess never had any fondness for flowers or candy. Ed won her heart by teaching her how to set snares for rabbits."

"What would win your heart, brat?"

"Ed figured it out for Jess. If a man wants to win my heart, he has to figure out what will cause me to fall in love with him."

Blake turned to Jake. "Why can't a woman be straightforward? If I want a woman to cook me a meal, I tell her my favorite dish."

"And if she can't cook it, I find another woman who can," Jake added.

"How open minded." Cole crossed her arms. "Forgive me for being a little particular about the man I spend the rest of my life with."

"I thought you had sworn off men," Blake said.

"Only those who propose something other than marriage."

****

By the following Monday, the number of men wanting their laundry done had tripled. Jess helped her wash, mend, and fold the laundry for the men to collect on Wednesday. Thomas had hired Amber and her daughters, Mia and Tia. They had been slaves on a plantation in Virginia, and the girls had worked in the fields. They knew nothing about keeping a house. Cole and Jess began training them on the simple tasks of dusting, sweeping, and cleaning the chamber pots. They helped with the laundry, but Cole limited them to the sheets. The soldiers' laundry was extra pay, and she wasn't giving it to the girls.

They played baseball again, but Cole and Jess remained on the sidelines in the shade instead of baking in the hot sun. Afterwards Amber served cold lemonade and pie. Both were delicious. Jake retrieved a large envelope from his haversack and waved it in the air. "I have another way for you to raise money."

"I hope it's not more laundry," Cole said. "We have more than we can handle."

He removed something from the envelope. "I had Davy print these."

He displayed a handful of miniature portraits, half of Cole and half of Jess. "What are you going to do with them?"

"When I showed the fellows your photograph, they

wanted a copy."

Cole put her hands on her hips. "You're going to give them my photograph?"

"Don't be silly. You can't make any money giving them away." He waved the photographs in the air. "Gentlemen, my beautiful cousins are raising funds for the Union cause by graciously providing several photographs, which I shall auction off."

"Hey, do you think that's a good idea?" Blake grabbed one.

"If you want one, you will have to bid," Jake said, snatching it back. "Bidding begins at twenty-five cents for your choice of one of the lovely Beecher sisters."

"Jem warned us not to do this," Jess said. "I don't know if I like strangers staring at me."

"It's only an image," Jake said. "We'll limit the trading cards to Ohio boys."

"It's only a handful," Cole said. "Think of it as your patriotic duty to maintain morale among the boys. Besides, you can put your money toward a new dress."

"Jake said it was for the Union cause," Jess said. "Isn't that deceptive?"

"Aren't we part of the Union?"

"Ed wants to buy a farm when he musters out," Jess said. "I could put the money toward that."

"You can't help Ed buy a farm," she warned. "But you can put it aside as a dowry."

"Isn't that the same thing?"

"A dowry isn't turned over to a man until after the wedding."

"I have ten copies of Miss Colleen and ten copies of Miss Jessica," Jake called out. "I'll auction them off to twenty lucky men."

"I want one," Ed said.

"Me, too," Art added.

"I'll give one to Ed," Jess said to Jake.

"The men were paid Saturday. Let them bid."

"Don't buy the first one," Jess warned Ed.

Ed paid nearly two dollars for his copy, but the highest bid was by Pax Ravenswood, who paid two and a half dollars for Colleen's image. Jake paid Colleen twelve dollars and Jess nine.

Cole put the money in her small purse and shoved it deep into her pocket. "We're in the wrong business."

Jess frowned. "I have a feeling this is on Mama's don't list."

"I think it's sweet the boys want to look at our photographs when they're camped far from home, waiting for a battle." Blake was talking to Pax, who was showing off his treasure. Blake hadn't bid on any of the photographs. The man could be attentive one moment and disinterested the next. He looked up and caught her staring. He flashed a smile. She spun on her heels and showed him the back of her head.

"To those who purchased a photograph, you also have won a dance." Jake motioned to Jess. "Did you bring your fiddle?" She fetched it from the porch, and Jake took possession. "I'll play. You can dance."

"Dance?" Jess looked at Cole for an explanation. She shrugged.

Jake turned to the men. "Anyone else remember to bring an instrument?"

A small band formed on the porch. "The highest bidder has the first dance."

Pax claimed Cole. He proved to be a capable dancer, twirling her around to the lively tune. He was in a better humor with her not on his team, and she laughed at several corny jokes he shared. Blake stood on the sidelines, his arms crossed, his dark brows knitted in disapproval. If he wanted a dance, he should have bid on her photograph.

Cole and Jess initially were the only dancers and would have been exhausted except Maryland Avenue was a busy street, and the soldiers invited women passing by to join them. It was a bold proposal, but many of them were nurses or clerks who worked in the government buildings. Their independence allowed them to accept the call to the impromptu ball without formal introductions or chaperones protecting their reputations.

Amber made sandwiches, and her daughters served lemonade.

Cole grabbed a glass. "This is what I like."

Blake leaned against the porch post. "Ball games, dances, and men bidding for your photograph?"

"Some women think sitting in a parlor sipping tea is the height of society."

"You might set a trend, brat." Blake bowed. "May I have the next dance?"

"I don't think I have to dance with you," Cole said. "You didn't bid on my photograph."

"I prefer the real thing." His voice was deep and filled with innuendo.

"How is your shoulder?"

"Let's find out." He took her into his arms and twirled her around.

Cole stepped in a hole, but his arm caught her from falling. He hugged her close. "You all right?"

Her heart pounded in her chest, her breath gasping

as his mouth hovered inches from hers. Would he kiss her in front of all these men? "Isn't this a violation of your employer and employee relationship?"

"My pappy never had you for an employee." He danced her around the yard.

Chapter Eighteen

Tuesday the laundry needed pressed. Cole and Jess showed the girls how to heat the irons on the stove and set up the board to press the sheets in the kitchen. After demonstrating how to smooth the wrinkles, they headed for the front porch where it was cooler.

Cole and Jess joined Blake who was entertaining a man named Tobias. He was a short man with a large nose with broken blood vessels forming a patchwork of blue lines beneath his sallow skin.

"Tobias is making a sign for the hotel."

Cole looked at the sign hanging from the post near the road. A plain white board with Mermaid's Mirth printed in uneven letters identified the establishment. "What's wrong with the old sign?"

"Boring." Bake unrolled the paper in his hand and showed them a drawing of a mermaid. The figure was half woman, half fish. She had a swirling mass of hair that barely concealed one breast. The other lay bare.

"I think she needs a sea shell."

"She needs some personality," Blake said. "Something that will attract guests."

"Clean sheets and good food attracts guests not a half-naked woman."

Tobias studied her as he sketched in his book. "You don't approve of the human body?"

She peered over the edge of the book. "What are

you drawing?"

He closed the cover. "I'm not finished."

She stepped back, looking from the artist to Blake. "I don't want a sign with a half-naked woman to look like me."

"This from the woman who auctioned photographs of herself to a bunch of soldiers."

"That was Jake's idea."

"You took the money."

"I'm not receiving any money for your sign."

"Isn't there a modeling fee?" Blake asked Tobias.

"Five dollars," Tobias said. "You have to pose."

"Bare breasted?"

"It would help."

Blake, who had been leaning back on two legs of his chair, fell forward with a thud. His anger was barely controlled. "All you need is her face. After all, she's half fish."

Tobias studied Cole. "I need your hair down, and you'll need to sit still."

"What if Jem recognizes you on the sign?" Jess hissed.

"How much can it resemble me?" She elbowed her. "Five dollars for sitting? I'd be crazy not to accept." Cole searched her handbag. "I need a mirror."

Blake motioned over his shoulder. "In any of the rooms."

"I'll check on the girls," Jess volunteered as Cole entered a bedroom on the main floor. It was tastefully decorated with a matching dresser, bed frame, and nightstand. The coat on a peg belonged to Blake. This was his room. She debated whether it was proper for her to remain but shrugged. He wasn't in the room.

A mirror was placed in a frame on the wall above the washstand. She removed the combs pinning her hair away from her face and brushed the curls with a stiff brush from her handbag. In the reflection of the mirror was a picture frame on the nightstand next to the bed. She moved a book aside and examined the photograph. It was her. Blake had purchased a large print of the photograph from Brady's shop. "No wonder he didn't bid."

She opened the book of poetry to its marker. It was a love sonnet. Blake had been treating her with polite aloofness since she had started working for him. If he had romantic intentions, why didn't he court her? He had called her a tease. She'd define the word. How long before Blake declared his love? She'd dismiss him like all the other men in her life. She laughed at her reflection as she arranged a thick lock of hair over one breast. "I bet he'd faint if I posed bare breasted."

When she returned to the porch, she was fully clothed, but her thoughts were anything but pure. Tobias pointed. "Your expression. That's the one."

Cole sat for Tobias as he made several sketches. She stared at Blake, studying his features as intently as Tobias studied hers. She didn't turn from his smoky gaze, daring him to blink. He brushed back his black hair. She preferred it longer. She also missed the shadow of his whiskers outlining his jaw and mouth. Those lips could work magic. She ran her tongue along her bottom lip.

"What the he..." Blake stood. "Aren't you done yet?"

Tobias stood and gathered his belongings. "I've been done for several minutes. I was waiting to interrupt."

"Interrupt what?"

"I am an artist. I make a living observing details."

Cole reached for his book. "May I see the sketches?"

"No, it is bad luck for a model to see the work until it is finished," Tobias said. He shook hands with Blake and handed Cole five dollars.

Cole examined the five-dollar note. "That was easy."

"You could make a fortune exploiting your beauty for money."

"Do you think a man can buy me?"

"Only with a band of gold."

"A bag of gold?" She balled her fist. "If you think I can be bought…"

Blake grabbed her. "I said band as in wedding band."

Her heart continued to beat rapidly even as his hands relaxed their hold on her. "A man usually courts a woman before proposing."

"I'm not in the market for a wife. My stepmother is remarrying, my hotels all have managers, and when my shoulder heals, I *will* join the army."

"Save yourself the cost of stamps." She turned away to hide the mist in her eyes. "I won't write you."

"I wish you would." It was a plea.

Her photograph in his room betrayed his true feelings. "You are the most frustrating man I know."

"Me? You make love to me while posing for Tobias."

She spun around to face him. "What?"

He grabbed a thick lock of her hair and wrapped it

around his hand. "Your hair ablaze, like a flame tempting a moth to its death." He inhaled the fragrance. His smoky gaze burned with desire. "Your eyes, playful and teasing, making a man wonder how you would respond if he kissed you. Only I know. Do you think I can resist while you look at me, licking your lips in anticipation of devouring me?" Blake pulled her against his chest and lowered his mouth against hers. His kiss was urgent, demanding a response. His arms crushed her in an embrace as his tongue penetrated deeper.

"I'm going to faint," she gasped when he took a breath.

"You're not the fainting type. Kiss me and no other." He brushed his lips against her cheek, nibbling on her ear lobe and feasting on her neck as he lips moved lower. "You played the temptress to perfection. Now you must reap the harvest."

Cole groaned, her arms clinging to him for support. Her body was drawn tight, throbbing with anticipation, the heat between them building to a climax she had never experienced. Had she gone too far?

Suddenly a flood of cold water washed over them. They pulled apart, hair and clothing drenched.

Jess stood at the bottom step with an empty bucket in her hand.

Cole turned on her. "What did you do that for?"

"I've been shouting at you for five minutes to quit canoodling. This was the only way to stop you."

Blake's shock and anger were replaced by a comical grin. "She is the chaperone." He removed his coat and shook droplets from the fabric.

"I need a towel," Cole said, leading the way inside. "Is the ironing done?"

"After three holes in the sheets, I made them quit," Jess said.

"Holes?" Blake paused in the hallway by his office door. A desk was placed between a pair of sectioned windows on the north side of the building. He had a view of the barn and pasture. "How did that happen?"

"They left the iron in one place too long." Cole took a towel from Jess and began to dry her hair. "They're young."

"What am I going to do with ruined sheets?"

Cole didn't hesitate. "Bandages."

Blake sat at his desk and stared at an open ledger. "Too bad my accounting problems can't be as easily solved."

Cole leaned over his shoulder. He had nice ears; small, close to his head and perfectly formed. "What are you working on?" She let her lips brush against his earlobe.

"My accounts." He closed the ledger. "The numbers don't add up."

She reached for the book. "Do you want me to look at it?"

"Solving the problem of ruined sheets has gone to your head. I've spent hours this morning going over the accounts. You'll never find the mistake."

Arrogant man. She moved around his chair. "I'm good with numbers. Don't you remember. I can count to twenty with my shoes off?" She snatched the ledger before he could stop her and stared at the last page. "Seriously, I check my father's accounts and Grandma's, too. It won't hurt for me to look."

Blake offered his chair. "I've added this row of figures a dozen times. It needs to agree with this number here." He pointed to the dollar amount on the bottom row.

"Here's your problem." Cole pointed to an entry in the middle of the page. "This is the wrong amount."

He stared at the page. "How do you know?"

"It doesn't look right."

"What do you mean it doesn't look right?" He pressed against her, studying the ledger. "You need to add the numbers to find the error."

"Your entries end in a nine, zero, or five. This entry ends in a four. I think it's supposed to be forty-nine not ninety-four." She leaned back in the leather chair. "Change it and see if the total is correct."

"That's ridiculous. You can't simply look at a page and see a mistake." Blake added the numbers, scratching subtotals on a blank piece of paper when they became too large to add in his head. He handed her the scrap of paper with his final calculation and pointed at the matching figure at the bottom of the page. "How did you do that?"

"I don't know." Cole shrugged. Blake's look of frustration was familiar. She couldn't explain how numbers jumped off the page when they looked out of place. "I've always been able to look at a row of figures and find the one that doesn't belong. Papa says it's a gift."

He leaned against his desk, studying her. "A hundred years ago they would have burned you at the stake."

"A hundred years ago I wouldn't know how to read or write. Women were kept ignorant so men could feel superior. Brute force wasn't enough."

"Have pity on us." Blake rested his hand on her

shoulder, his fingers playing with her loose hair. "We can't force a woman to love us. And although we don't always show it, our hearts can be broken, too."

Blake's heart was set on joining the army. He enjoyed spending time with the soldiers, listening to their battle tales. He and Jake had become best friends in the short time they had known each other. He had become her friend and more. "Then why fall in love?"

"Sometimes we…" Blake stopped when Jess entered the room.

"I hope you're behaving."

Cole showed her the ledger. "I humbled him with my mathematical prowess."

"You've always taught me to build a man's pride not tear it down," Jess said.

"All she has to do is stand next to a man to make him proud."

Blake's intense stare made Cole unable to respond. How could he say words of undeniable love and still want to leave her for war? She rushed past Jess to the front door. She gathered her belongings, crushing her bonnet on her head, and ran down the road.

Jess caught up half way home. "You mad at me for throwing water on you?"

"You keep throwing water on me. Wash Blake Ellsworth out of my hair."

"I thought you liked him."

Cole slowed her pace. "Worse. I'm falling in love with him, but all he can think about is being a soldier."

****

Thursday morning Jem was feeling well enough to accompany them to Center Market. Fresh produce was displayed in wagons, carts, and on tables. Cherries and blueberries were in season along with corn and zucchini. Fish, oysters, and lobster were offered by fishermen, while the butchers sold dressed chickens, turkeys, and quail. The two-block area was crowded with women, black and white, shopping for their households. Merchants shouted their bargains, enticing the buyer closer.

Cole peeled the leaves away to reveal yellow and white kernels of corn. "How about a dozen ears?"

Jem opened the strings on her reticule and withdrew several new greenbacks the Department of the Treasury had issued.

Cole grabbed her hand. "Who's that on the dollar bill?"

"Don't you recognize our former governor? That's Secretary Salmon Chase."

"Logan's boss? But why is his image on the one-dollar bill?" Cole asked. "Shouldn't he be on a ten- or twenty-dollar bill?"

"His daughter Kate suggested the one-dollar bill because it's the most circulated," Jem said. "More people see it, and Mr. Chase still has ambitions of being president."

"That's clever."

"Kate Chase is one of the most intelligent women when it comes to Washington politics and is equally ambitious. She'd be first lady if her father was elected."

"Are we going to meet her?"

"She's not in Washington City. Nearly everyone leaves for the summer, especially since Mrs. Lincoln is in mourning and isn't hosting any social events. There are a few small private parties and of course, Willard's."

Cole placed the corn in the large basket she carried. "What is Willard's?"

"It's a hotel, but the officers and politicians gather there to discuss the future of the country," Jem said. "Logan doesn't care for the place, but if you want to know what is going on in the city, you have to visit. We'll have Logan escort us some evening."

"I better finish my new dress." Cole's enthusiastic declaration turned to a somber nod as several ladies in black strolled past them, a stark reminder of the price of war. Happiness and sadness were interwoven in the tapestry of life. Even the president's family was not immune. "It was sad when Willie died in February. How old was he?"

"Eleven," Jem said. "Tad recovered from the fever but lost his best friend."

"I can't imagine how the President and Mrs. Lincoln bear so much."

"He's aged since his son's death," Jem agreed. "I'm afraid the war isn't helping. We need to win some battles, or the opinion of the people will turn against the war and demand a peace."

Jess turned from filling a bag with peaches. "Don't we want peace?"

"Without a victory, the North would give up half the country," Jem said. "Lincoln is determined to reunite the nation."

Cole tasted a cherry a vendor offered. It was sour but with sugar would make a good pie filling. "But what about abolishing slavery?"

"It's not a priority, and Mr. Chase isn't happy about Lincoln stalling on emancipation of the slaves."

"I don't understand why he's waiting either. The

South seceded." Cole added two baskets of cherries to her groceries. "What do we care if the slaves are declared free?"

"Because Maryland is a slave state and next door," Jem said. "The Baltimore residents rioted when the war started. It wouldn't take much for them to rebel and attack Washington City."

"With all the soldiers in town?"

"Washington City isn't as secure as it looks." Jem lowered her voice. "Do you know that the Treasury building is the last line of defense? The president and his family will be evacuated to it if the city is attacked."

"Where do we go?" Cole asked.

"The cellar at Pierce House."

Cole counted the number in the household. It would be a tight fit.

A woman with a wide face and dark hair smoothed over her ears and gathered in a chignon greeted Jem, who introduced Clara Barton. They had met last year and had become friends. Clara didn't waste time on pleasantries. "Do you have any lanterns in your supply room? The doctors operate late at night and need lights."

"We have a few we can spare," Jem said. "Do you have any socks? The Ohio boys march so much, they wear them out in a week."

"I'll trade you socks for lanterns. When can I send a boy to fetch them?"

"We're heading home now," Jem said. "Send him in about an hour."

"I can always count on you, Mrs. Pierce," Clara said.

"We're happy to do anything to help." Jem paused,

her voice barely a whisper. "Do you anticipate a battle soon?"

"I have my sources," Clara said. "Generals don't waste good weather sitting around the fire."

Cole waited until Clara left. "What did she mean?"

Jem was pale. "This is the season for war, and the generals are plotting a battle."

"Why don't we stop at the butcher and buy a few chickens to make a nice dinner for the boys tonight?" Cole searched her purse. "I have my laundry money to spend."

"You should save it."

"I can't think of anything better to spend it on than the boys," Cole defended.

Chapter Nineteen

Cole peered out the kitchen window to the back yard where the men were pitching horseshoes. Ed slapped Blake on the back after he rang the curved metal around a pole stuck in the ground.

Jess crowded beside her. "Aren't men wonderful?"

She nodded, afraid her voice would crack and betray her true feelings. Clara's words haunted her. Another battle was in the works. These men, laughing and enjoying life, would face a group of men, similar in age and background, and they would compete to possess a piece of land of little value except for the blood spilled upon it. And when the wounded and dead lay sprawled upon the soil, generals would declare a winner as if it was a game. And clerks would send letters of regret to the mothers and wives of those who lost and would never come home.

"Do you think we have enough?" Jem asked as she surveyed the food on the kitchen table.

"We could feed an army." Jess laughed.

"After hearing about their hardships, I don't mind feeding them," Jem said. "They looked so thin when they first arrived in the city."

Cole turned away from the window when Blake waved. "I don't know why anyone would willingly join the army and fight in a war."

"I think it's exciting," Jess said. "Not the dying

part. But to pit yourself against a worthy adversary and beat him. It gives a man confidence."

"I see that in Ed and Art," Jem agreed. "They were shy, quiet boys back home."

"Do you like the change in him?" Cole asked.

"Yes, I do. He's kind and gentle, but now he's a bit dangerous. Not toward me," Jess added, "but if there was trouble, I know Ed wouldn't back down. He'd fight."

"Have the men wash and join us." Jem lifted a bowl.

Cole took the bowl. "You tell them. We'll put the food on the table."

Jem removed her apron. "I'm tired of being treated like I'm incapable of the simplest task."

"You're not helpless," Cole said. "But you're better at yelling than we are."

Jem wadded up her apron and tossed it at Cole who laughed when it fell short of its mark.

****

The conversation eventually turned to talk of war. The fear of invasion was always in the thoughts of the residents of Washington City. As the capital of the Union, it was the prize for Southern victory. Lee was expected to attack.

Art leaned back after cleaning his plate. "You're spoiling us with your cooking. We won't be able to enjoy the beans and hardtack they like to feed us."

"I think it's disgraceful the way they treat the soldiers," Jess said. "They should feed fighting men better."

Ed patted her hand. "A man doesn't grow without hardships, Miss Jessica."

"No one asks for hardship," Cole said. "Nearly everyone wants a life of luxury."

"A man only needs a certain amount of money. He grows fat and lazy when he's too rich," Jake said. "He forgets what is important in life. But a war reminds us about the value of home, family, and friends. A soldier doesn't take luxuries for granted. He lives life every day. Something you should think about, cousin."

"I don't have to fight a war to appreciate life," Cole said.

"I think he means a man likes challenges to see what he's capable of achieving," Blake said. "It's like your grandpa building the canal. Men died of the fever or gave up digging that ditch, but he didn't. Even though it was backbreaking, he can look at the canal now and brag that he had a hand in building it."

"What are we building with a war?"

Ed's voice was quiet and confident. "We're setting slaves free, Miss Colleen."

"And they live in camps or makeshift hovels," Cole said. "Couldn't we have thought of a better way to accomplish the same thing?"

"Not as long as lazy, pampered men make the decisions," Jake said. "They don't want to lose a penny out of their pockets."

"Do you have something against a businessman making an honest profit?" Blake demanded.

"You're an exception, brother. You'd give a man in need the shirt off your back."

"Brother? He doesn't look anything like you, Jake."

"But our names rhyme. That makes us brothers."

Cole shook her head. "That's ridiculous."

"The men in the Seventh are my brothers, too. I'd die for them."

"I hope to join you soon," Blake said.

"And what's wrong with joining the Twenty-ninth?" Ed asked.

"He's too smart to join the Twenty-ninth," Jake argued. "He attended West Point."

Had she heard correctly? He never said anything about attending the military school. "When did you attend West Point?"

"I missed graduating by a year. I had to quit when my father died," Blake explained.

"You could still apply for an officer's commission," Logan said. "I could help."

"I'd rather enter as an equal with the men," Blake said. "Earn their respect."

"We need good officers who worry about us and not their own hides," Jake said. "I wouldn't mind taking orders from you."

"Me, too," Ed and Art agreed.

Blake nodded. "I'll think about it."

****

They sang songs in the parlor and packed some food for the boys to take with them.

Ed looked around. "Where's my kepi?"

"I think you left it in the back yard." Cole opened the front door for Jake and Art. "He'll catch up to you."

Jake kissed her cheek. "What are you up to, cousin?"

"A little romance for Jess. Keep Art occupied." Every time Jess was alone with Ed longer than a minute, Art interrupted them. Jake winked in approval of her plan.

Cole watched out the window as Jess and Ed searched for his hat. Blake joined her. "You were quiet tonight. Something wrong?"

"I thought joining the army was a way to escape a boring life, but if you attended West Point, you want to make it a career."

"My career is the hotel business, but I'd hate to have all those years of drilling go to waste."

"Waste is hiding Ed's hat." Cole ran her fingers through her hair, smoothing the loose strands into place. "I leave those two alone, and all they can think about is going on a scavenger hunt."

"What do you want them to do?"

"Ed might be going off to battle soon, and he hasn't kissed Jess."

The corner of his mouth turned upward. "Maybe we should encourage them."

How could a few words escaping his lips make her pulse pound? "How?"

Blake grabbed her hand and led her outside. "Where's his cap?"

"On the barn door." She pointed. "It's in plain sight."

Blake called out, "Have you searched the barn?"

Jess spied the hat and ran toward it. Ed joined her in the shadows of the barn opening. She handed him the kepi.

"What is he waiting for?" Cole demanded.

"Come here." Blake pulled her in close, crushing her body against his. He gazed into her eyes, his mouth poised above hers, hesitating, waiting for her approval. She closed her eyes, and his lips brushed against hers, sending a shiver through her body. His mouth captured her moan. She clung to his shoulders as every muscle collapsed beneath his onslaught and her body went limp in his arms.

When he released her, she expected a clever retort, but he was quiet, studying her. She couldn't think of anything to say. Her arms remained around his shoulders, the cloth of his coat clutched in her fingertips.

He nodded toward Jess and Ed. "I think it worked." They were kissing.

Cole sighed. "Her first kiss."

"Could almost renew your belief in love, huh, brat?"

Her head jerked at the familiar insult. Had the kiss meant nothing to him?

****

Cole couldn't sleep. Jess wouldn't stop talking about Ed. "Is it always like this?"

"No, not always." Cole thought of the men she had kissed. It was the anticipation, the breaking of rules that was exciting. The kiss was usually disappointing. Reality never measured up to the fantasy. Except with Blake. When he had kissed her tonight, her world had shattered. Every part of her body hummed. She let Jess put her feelings into words.

"It was exciting and scary at the same time," Jess said. "Like when you have a wild boar in your sights and you freeze, not sure if he'll charge or head for the brush. Everything builds within until you think you're going to explode. And then it happens. It's wonderful!"

"Hush."

"If you don't like hearing about Ed, say so…"

Cole placed her hand over her sister's mouth.

217

"Quiet."

She pulled her hand away. "What is it?" Jess whispered. The bed from the master bedroom creaked. "That's Jem and Logan."

"Listen."

Two bodies played a rhythm with the creaking of the ropes straining beneath their movements. Cole giggled.

"What are they doing?"

"Remember when we spent the night at Tyler and Cory's house?"

"They made so much noise, it was embarrassing." Jess covered her mouth. "You mean?"

They listened as Logan's cries echoed with Jem's fevered pitch for more. The creaking of the ropes increased as two bodies joined a mating dance. A cry of release, or ecstasy, or both echoed in the neighboring room.

"But she's already going to have a baby. Why would they do...you know?"

"Didn't you hear how much fun they were having?" Cole sighed. "I think our sister has recovered her health."

"That's pleasure? It sounds like an animal in pain."

"You've seen animals breed. Plenty of noise involved in mating."

As if on cue, they overheard Jem cry out in a final gasp followed by Logan's name. The noise was muffled, voices whispering until Logan's cries echoed his wife's. Silence.

"Oh, my goodness," Jess gasped.

Cole threw the covers over their heads to muffle their giggling.

****

Cole and Jess walked to the camp of the Twenty-ninth Ohio Saturday morning with baskets loaded with baked goods and supplies such as soap, handkerchiefs, and sewing kits, but the tents, guns, and men were missing. The stone and wooden foundations remained, each one marking the location of a former tent.

"Where are they?" Jess hurried to the rocks outlining the former home of Ed and Art.

Cole put her arm around her waist. "We knew they'd have to return to battle."

"So soon? We barely spent three weeks with them."

A stack of pie tins rested on the front rock. Cole lifted them. Several letters were wedged between two rocks below. She handed the mail to Jess.

Cole wedged the empty pie tins next to the fresh pies, bread, and supplies for the men. "What are we going to do with all this food?"

Jess couldn't answer. She was reading a letter, tears staining her cheeks.

Cole walked beside her as they headed across Long Bridge to Blake's hotel. They could sell him the extra baked goods for his customers.

Jess swiped her face and waved another letter. "This one is from Jake."

Cole's name was scrawled on the front. Jake was gone, too. The Seventh Ohio had left for war. "They always fight side by side."

By the time they reached Mermaid's Mirth, both were bawling.

Blake was in the yard and waved. Cole dropped the basket at his feet, her limbs weak, drained by the news that her cousin and neighbors would have to fight for their lives. Eventually their luck would run out. She couldn't think about what might happen.

Blake pulled her against his chest. "What's wrong?" He stroked her hair and made hushing sounds in her ear. His strong arms offered comfort. He pulled Jess close with his other arm.

"They're gone," Cole admitted between sobs.

"Gone?" He exhaled. "You mean they left. I heard bugles and drums yesterday, but I thought it was more drilling. They must have received orders to march out. Didn't get a chance to say good-bye?"

Cole waved a letter from Jake under his nose.

"Do you want me to read it?"

She nodded. They moved to the shade of the porch and sat side by side on the steps. Blake opened Jake's letter.

"July 25, 1862. Dear Cousin Colleen, We received orders to head south into Virginia. We're packing our gear and loading our cartridge boxes. Sid asked around and discovered we're heading for Culpeper Court House. We won't have to march. They have cattle cars to transport us. Made me think of trussing up the Cassell brothers in the livestock car in Akron. They were madder than a swarm of hornets. Strange the things we remember from our lives. I wonder what people will remember about me? I'll send word once we make camp. Jake."

Jess clutched the letter from Ed but didn't read it aloud. Her blush meant it wasn't for public hearing. She handed the letter from Art to Cole. "You can read this one."

Cole had recovered enough from the shock of the

men leaving to read Art's few lines of scrawled text.

"Leaving for the South. Sorry we didn't get to say good-bye. You made our stay in Washington City a pleasant experience. Your devoted servant, Arthur Herbruck."

"I wish I had gone with them," Blake said.

Cole didn't answer. He wanted to be a soldier. He'd attended West Point. He was trained to give orders. It would be cruel to stop him from living his dream. Even if it meant death on a battlefield. She calculated the time from his shooting. "Your shoulder won't be healed completely for another four weeks. But it seems silly to wait until you're healed from one gunshot to receive another."

"I don't plan on being killed."

"Nobody does."

His finger stroked her cheek. "Don't worry, brat. I'll mention you in my will."

She burst into tears, pounded futile fists against his chest. "Do you think I want your money?"

His arms encircled her tight against his chest, calming her sobs. His heartbeat thundered in her ear. His deep voice echoed within his chest. "Don't cry, darling. Please, don't cry."

Jess stood. "Oh, my!"

Cole raised her tear-streaked face. "We're not kissing."

"You're going to want to see this." She pointed at the sign swinging from a post in the yard near the road advertising the hotel.

"That's the new sign," Blake said. "I wanted to surprise you, but I didn't know about the boys leaving. I think it turned out rather well."

A scream caught in Cole's throat. Mermaid's Mirth was painted on a large circle painted to resemble a rock. Perched on the rock was a mermaid, her green tail shaded with blue shadows outlining the scales. The female torso was framed in ginger curls with a coral nipple crowning a jutting bare breast. But it was the familiar face of the sea creature that was most shocking, especially since the face of the mermaid bore an uncanny resemblance to her own.

"It looks exactly like you," Jess said, her eyes wide and worried.

Tobias had captured her features, including her seductive expression. She turned to Blake. "I hope your will is written because I'm going to kill you!"

His chest rumbled with laughter. "I thought you would be flattered. I think it's a good likeness although I don't think he captured your eyes."

She pointed at the uncanny likeness. "Everyone is going to know it's me."

Blake stroked the stubble on his chin. "I hadn't thought about that."

"You lying polecat. You did this on purpose. You wanted to humiliate me."

"Most women would be flattered by being immortalized in a sign."

"I'm naked." She gritted her teeth. "Shouldn't there be a seashell covering her…"

"Calm down. Tobias carved a seashell to cover your…I mean the mermaid's nakedness."

"Shouldn't you have added the shell before you hung it up for the world to see?"

"I saw you pass earlier and knew you'd see it on your return. Payment for torturing me." He walked to the post and removed the sign.

"I saved your life. I work for you. I feed you. And this is payment?"

"You charm every man in long pants, you treat the common soldier like a king, and you've unraveled all my plans."

"You're not joining the army?"

"I'm joining, but I'm not going to be happy about it." He studied the sign and compared it to the real woman.

"Don't even think it," Cole said. "You're never going to see me bare breasted, Blake Ellsworth."

Blake placed the sign on the porch table. "Then I'll always wonder." Cole extended her hand. "Where's the seashell?"

Blake handed her a carved clam shell.

She slapped it against the sign, but no matter where she placed it, the roundness of the bare breast swelled around it. "It's not big enough."

"We wouldn't want to cover everything." Blake turned from admiring the sign. "I'll fetch the glue and a brush."

"I don't know why he does this!" Cole clenched her fists. "He enjoys infuriating me."

"He's in love with you," Jess said matter-of-factly. "And you're in love with him, or it wouldn't make you so mad."

"I won't let myself love him. He's going off to war. Nothing I can say or do will stop him."

"Why would you want to stop him?"

"Aren't you ever afraid for Ed?"

"All the time, but war is only one way to die. Remember the man and his three children who were sledding on the river and fell through the ice? And the man who was thrown by his horse? War isn't the only way to die. But fighting for freedom is a good way to live."

Chapter Twenty

With the soldiers gone, the girls had lost a source of income. But Blake continued to pay them while they trained Mia and Tia. When Blake visited Pierce House, he didn't call on her personally. If he brought flowers, he gave them to Jem, and candy was shared by all. He had taken the boys' advice and asked Logan to help him apply for a commission.

They were in the same room, and yet he barely acknowledged her. The tension had built over the past week, neither one knowing how to diffuse it. "We received a letter from Jake." Cole retrieved it from the desk in the parlor and sat next to Blake on the sofa. The others had heard the news but listened again as Cole read it.

"Dear cousins, We have a new commander, General John White Geary took over for General Tyler, who was ordered to Washington City. We were sorry to see Tyler leave. He's been with us from the beginning. Geary arrived with his men from Pennsylvania. They outnumber all the men in the Ohio regiments in the division. Geary is a big man and rides a draft horse. All we can say is he makes a mighty big target. We've learned to keep our heads down during a battle.

"We had to listen to the words of General John Pope, our new high general. He's a vicious man and no gentleman. He's ordered us to burn any home that fires

on Union soldiers and arrest all male citizens in the area. If they don't take the oath, they have to leave. Anyone returning will be hanged as a spy.

"The fool doesn't understand Lee or Jackson. They won't stand for their citizens being mistreated, even if they deserve it. The war has turned ugly, cousins. Jake."

Cole folded the letter. "What does he mean the war has turned ugly? Hasn't it always been ugly?"

"Up to now the battles were limited to soldiers," Blake said. "The two sides lined up and shot at each other. Now, they're attacking civilians. Next it will be women and children who will suffer. War has a tendency to become messy."

Someone knocked on the door. Jem was nearest and rose to answer.

Cole peeked out the window with Jess and Deidre crowded around her.

Blake stood behind them. "Who is it?"

"I think it's Clara Barton."

"Oh, dear," Logan mumbled from his chair.

Cole turned to her brother-in-law. "What's wrong with Clara?"

"You'll find out." He didn't elaborate.

Jem returned to the parlor. "That was Clara Barton."

"Why didn't you invite her inside?"

"She's busy gathering supplies and has several places to visit. Doctor William Hammond has given her permission to travel with army ambulances to the battlefields."

"Who's Hammond?"

"The U.S. surgeon general," Logan said. "Miss

Barton finally wore him down."

"She's going to the battlefields?" Blake frowned. "Isn't that dangerous?"

"Clara Barton is insane," Logan agreed.

"She is doing it to save lives," Jem declared. "By the time soldiers reach a hospital, it's too late for medical treatment."

"She cares for the Confederate wounded as well as the Union," Logan said. "Some think that's treason."

"Clara doesn't look at the color of the uniform. She sees a man in distress and tries to relieve his pain," Jem said. "We've received help from Confederates, remember?"

Logan's features softened. He took his wife's hand. "Sometimes I forget there's good even in the enemy."

"We could help deliver supplies to the battlefield," Jess suggested.

"That is out of the question!" Logan said. "I'm responsible for you. I don't want to tell Doctor Beecher you were killed on a battlefield because I didn't keep you safe."

Jem rubbed his arm. "She wants to see Ed."

Logan calmed beneath Jem's touch. "I believe only Miss Barton has been awarded a pass, but we'll support her in whatever lunatic scheme she hatches. To a point."

Jem molded against her husband. "I'm sure we can find plenty to do around the city, especially when the wounded begin to arrive."

Cole returned Jake's letter to the desk. "Would anyone like some lemonade? I'm thirsty."

Jess followed her into the kitchen. "I'm not afraid of going to the battlefield."

"Neither am I."

"Then why didn't you argue our cause? What if Ed or Jake were wounded?"

"Haven't you learned anything from reading the boys' letters? You don't attack head on. You flank the enemy."

"Flank Logan?"

"By winning Jem to our side."

"How do we do that?"

"We don't. We wait and let Clara Barton show everyone she's right about women going to the battlefield."

A week later, August 10, news of a battle at Cedar Mountain reached Washington City. The Ohio regiments in Geary's brigade included the Fifth, Seventh, Twenty-ninth, and Sixty-sixth but barely numbered a thousand men needed for a single regiment. They were involved in the fighting that had started late in the day on the ninth. The wounded began arriving by train from Culpeper Court House. Ambulances and anyone with a wagon or large carriage headed for Alexandria where the men were being unloaded.

Blake drove his wagon to Pierce House loaded with water barrels, buckets, and stretchers. Cole and Jess packed bread, oatmeal, and medical supplies. Cole examined the blankets and sheets Blake had packed. "No wonder you're always buying linens."

"At least Tia and Mia stopped burning holes in the sheets."

They boarded, and he urged the team forward, merging with the traffic of teamsters, and they headed across Long Bridge to the railroad station.

The train had twenty cars and each one packed

with wounded men. The army had taken over the railroads out of Washington City. They transported soldiers and supplies to the battlefronts. They returned the damaged men.

Blake filled buckets for Cole and Jess, and they headed toward one of the cars to help unload the wounded. Each box car had been converted with four-by-four wooden posts. The posts had leather loops attached for the poles of the stretchers to rest within. The cots were stacked one on top the other three high on both sides with more cots on a bed of bloody straw on the floor. The stench was worse than any livery. The moans and groans of the men were pitiful. "Water," one man gasped.

"Cole," Blake called. "Fetch a bucket and ladle."

Jem had insisted they wear long aprons, cover their hair, and have several scarfs available to cover their faces. Cole pulled a scarf over her nose and mouth as she moved through the soiled, confined compartment. Her eyes burned, and she blinked tears. Beads of sweat soaked through her dress from the suffocating heat, which built to an unbearable temperature within the enclosed space. The air vents in the roof offered little respite.

"We ran out of water," one of the male nurses in the car explained. Cole began giving drinks to the men, their tongues swollen and dry. Jess followed and gave slices of bread to those who could eat. The men on the floor were removed first, but it was tight quarters as they moved between the stacks of cots, offering water, food, and encouragement. The car held more than thirty men, and an ambulance could transport four, two on the floor of the wagon and two more across the side boards.

The math made it a long wait before they could be transported to Mansion House or Marshall House hospitals in Alexandria.

The men rested in the train yard, in shade if available. Cole wrote the soldiers' names, regiments, and companies and pinned the information to their shirts. They had volunteered a few times at the hospitals to know the routine. When a soldier arrived at a military hospital, he had to wait until a bed was available. Then a nurse placed his personal belongings in a bag, marked his name on it, and stored it until his death or discharge. Orderlies would carry the patient to his bed where nurses would wash his face and neck. They would help him remove his clothes and wash his arms, hands, and feet. They were given nightshirts, and the nurses served food, mostly soup and bread.

The doctor made his rounds in the afternoon and prescribed medicines and determined if more surgery was needed.

They had asked about becoming nurses, but pay was forty cents a day. The low pay wasn't as bad as the fact male nurses made more than two dollars a day and had better accommodations.

She would rather volunteer her time when and where it was needed the most. She agreed with Clara Barton that the soldiers needed better care immediately after a battle. Even those who had arrived by train would have to wait hours before they were in a hospital bed.

Cole offered one of the wounded a drink.

"Miss Colleen."

The gaunt face was sunburned and streaked with black from gunpowder. "Art." She searched for his wound. His right arm was bandaged over a makeshift splint. He had another wound in his thigh, and he was lying on his side. His pants were torn, and the bandage was stuck on the wound, stained with blood and dirt.

"Can Miss Jenny see to my wounds?" Art wiggled his fingers. "I'd like to keep my arm."

"We'll load you in Blake's wagon," Cole reassured him. "Are there any other Ohio boys?"

"We were cut down by Jackson and some new Confederate general named Hill." He choked back a tear. "It was a slaughter. We lost half our men to bullets."

Jess handed him some bread. "Is Ed wounded?"

"A scratch. He helped me off the battlefield," Art said. "He penned a note for you." Art searched his pocket. "They gave the Twenty-ninth picket duty after the battle."

Jess chewed on her lip as he searched with his left hand. "Let me look." She found an inside pocket in his coat and retrieved the note with her name scrawled on the front. She shoved it in her skirt pocket. "I'll read it later."

Art was loaded into Blake's wagon along with Pax Ravenswood, the second baseman with sour green apple eyes. He had been shot in the abdomen. Normally a gut shot was a death sentence. Even if the wound missed any vital organs, infection would kill him. But Pax had survived so far.

On the ride to the Mermaid's Mirth, Art talked about the battle. It kept his mind off the pain caused by the jarring of the wagon on the rough road. "Our defeat started long before the ninth," he said. "That pompous Major General John Pope insists we carry twenty pounds of ammunition stuffed in our cartridge boxes and pockets and fifteen more pounds with a musket, knapsack, and full canteen for the march. Not a breeze and the sun beating down so hot, men dropped in their tracks, foaming at the mouth from the heat before we reached Slaughter's Farm."

"Slaughter?"

Art's voice was bitter. "Fitting name for a battlefield."

Blake turned from his driver's position. "I believe the Union is calling it Cedar Mountain."

"They can call it the pearly gates, but it's still hell." He hesitated. "Pardon me, ladies."

"I've heard worse on the canal." Cole mopped his brow with a wet kerchief. "Go on if you can."

"It took us six hours to march seven miles from Culpeper Court House," Art said. "When we reached Cedar Run creek, we jumped in for some reprieve. Major General Nathaniel Banks was in charge of our division. On the enemy's side was Stonewall Jackson with three divisions. His guns were lined up along Crittenden Lane where it intersected the Orange-Culpeper Road. We were about a mile north with a cornfield between us and the woods to the right."

Art took another drink. "They started the battle with the big guns firing at each other. We dug down on the back side of the ridge and covered our ears. Mine are still ringing from all the racket. It was six o'clock in the evening when they gave the order to attack." Art shook his head and made a guttural noise of disbelief. "No one starts a battle that late in the day. The Seventh Ohio began the attack with the Sixty-sixth on its left. Some of us crawled to the top of the ridge to watch, but all we could see was smoke from all the cannon fire earlier and the dust from the men's feet as they marched toward the Rebels."

"You should have been in the cornfield," Pax said from his cot. "As soon as we were in range, the Rebs fired at us. We halted and fired a volley back. Over and over again we fired our guns." Pax's breath was labored, and he began to cough. "I hate cornfields."

"We couldn't see the men, but we heard the firing, the screaming, and someone singing a song," Art said.

"Singing a song?" Cole looked at Pax for an explanation. "In the middle of a battle?"

"Jake has a mighty fine voice," he praised.

"Jake." Cole repeated his name. She wiped Pax's mouth. Blood spotted the towel.

"Some pray, some swear, and some sing." Art winced as the wagon hit a rut and jarred him. "I do a little of all three."

"Tell us more about your role in the battle, Paxton." Cole wanted to keep him awake.

"Artillery along Crittenden Lane fired grapeshot at us, tore our lines to pieces. We closed ranks and more Rebels approached. It was like they rose up from the ground and marched toward us. We had passed through the cornfield by then with our wounded and dead tangled in the mutilated stalks," Pax said. "We were fighting hand to hand with the Rebs. We needed help."

"We were finally given the order to charge," Art said. "As soon as we stood on the ridge, we were hit by Rebel fire. The sun and smoke blinded us. We were ordered to fire, but some of the Seventh Ohio were in with the Rebels in front of Crittenden Lane. I fired high, but some of the men hit our own."

233

"Is that when you were hit, Paxton?"

"I fell," Pax said. "But I was shot from the front. Had to be a Reb. Used the corn leaves to stench the flow of blood and waited to die."

"We marched over the dead, wounded, and discarded knapsacks from the Seventh, but we reached them," Art said. "It gave the Seventh time to gather their wounded and head back to the ridge."

"We were glad to see you," Pax said. "Jake carried me. I think he was the only one who escaped without a scratch. That boy has the luck of the Irish."

Jess turned to Art. "What happened to the Twenty-ninth?"

"We replaced the Seventh and had the Rebels beat until Stonewall Jackson appeared with his sword raised over his head shouting for his men to hold the line." Art's eyes widened. "I nearly fainted at the sight of him."

"He's become a legend," Pax said. "Wish we had a general like him."

"The Rebels attacked in full force, and we realized we were being shot at from three sides, but the worst was from the Rebels in front of us," Art said. "We started picking our targets and shooting at them. I thought we should have been moving back to Union lines, but no one was in command. After I was hit, Ed decided it was time to get out of there, and we worked our way back to the ridge. There weren't many of us left by the time we reached Cedar Run. Ed took care of my wounds. We wrapped our exhausted bodies in our blankets and fell asleep."

"You didn't go to a field hospital?"

"The Rebels were blasting them," Art said. "Their

lanterns made perfect targets."

"They shot at the hospitals?" Cole stared at Jess. "That's not fair."

"No rules in war," Art said. "Come morning we headed to Culpeper Court House. That's a sight I won't forget. Surgeons had worked all night and were still sawing off limbs when we arrived. Piles of arms and legs were stacked outside the courthouse. The wounded were taken to churches and hotels. Ed made sure I was put on the train when it arrived. He was anxious you received his letter, Miss Jessica."

"How many men are left in the Twenty-ninth?"

"About half," Art said. "Lot of them wounded like me. A few captured."

"How many did you start with?" Blake asked.

"Nearly two hundred."

"That's not a regiment," Blake said. "That's a couple of companies."

Chapter Twenty-One

Thomas helped Blake carry Art and Pax into Mermaid's Mirth. Jess hurried to fetch Jem and her medical expertise.

Cole washed the patients after Blake, for modesty sake, helped the men remove what remained of their clothing.

Jem took care of Pax first, examining the wound. Yellow fluid stained a cloth she applied to his midsection.

"What's that?"

"Bile from the liver."

"That ain't good," Pax said.

"Better than torn intestines," Jem said. "I'm going to clean the wound, pack it, and you're going to rest."

Cole unwrapped Art's arm. A bullet had smashed the ulna bone near his elbow when it passed through, but the radius was intact, keeping the forearm rigid. If both bones had been broken, the arm would have gone soft, unsupported by the bone structures.

Jem handed her tweezers and a probe. "Remove the bone fragments."

Cole glanced at Art's pale face. "Shouldn't we put him out?"

"We'll have to for the other wound," Jem agreed. "But I don't want him under too long. If it becomes too painful, Art, let me know."

"I can handle it," Art said.

Jem applied laudanum to the wound to numb the pain.

Jess took his left hand. "Squeeze my hand if it hurts."

"I don't want to hurt you, Miss Jessica."

"The only time you hurt me was when you tripped me in that foot race, and I ended up with gravel in my knees."

"It was an accident, Miss Jessica. I was wearing Ed's boots, and they were too big for me."

"You ruined my perfect record."

"Forgive him." Cole plucked a bone piece from the wound, wincing as Art jerked. "Bring the light closer."

Blake moved the lantern to illuminate the wound as Cole searched for more fragments. He touched her shoulder. It was an innocent gesture to signal he was passing behind her, but her skin vibrated beneath his fingertips. Her fingers shook as she removed another shard and added it to the others in a small bowl.

She concentrated on the wound. "What's that?" Cole held her palm out. "Hand me a probe." She used the straight metal stick with a porcelain ball on the end to search the wound. She removed a piece of cloth.

Blake peered over her shoulder. "Is that the wad to set the ball?"

"It's blue. Must be his coat." Cole searched for the fabric of his shirt. Both had been embedded in the wound when the ball had ripped through his garments and skin.

"Once you clean out the debris, we'll rinse the wound with whiskey. It seems to keep infection away." Jem turned to Blake. "Do you have some?"

"Down in the liquor cabinet. I'll fetch it."

By the time Blake returned, Cole had removed anything loose, leaving a gap between the edges of the broken bones. Jem offered the bottle of whiskey to Art. He hesitated.

"Go ahead," Jess said. "We won't tell your ma."

Art took a long swallow and handed the bottle back to Jem. "Thank you."

"Don't thank me, yet. This is going to sting." Jem poured the whiskey to rinse the wound. Art stifled a scream, but his eyes watered.

"Hey, I'm thirsty over here," Pax complained from the next bed.

"Not too much," Jem warned. "You might have holes in you we don't know about."

Jem arranged her instruments on a clean cloth while Cole and Jess placed a splint on Art's bandaged arm and secured it. He was turned on his side with his arm propped by several pillows. "Let's have a look at your leg wound."

Art's sunburn deepened.

"We'll drape you." Jem and Cole carefully arranged sheets over his leg and around the wound to limit the exposure to the soiled bandage covering his injury.

Jem soaked the bandage to remove it. A long gash oozed with pus and a mixture of blood and watery fluids. "Did they remove the bullet?"

"No, Ed slapped a kerchief on it and carried me to town in the morning. The sawbones were too busy for minor scratches."

Minor scratch? He had a deep cut in the muscle of his thigh. Cole helped Jem thread several needles.

Art strained to look over his shoulder. "How bad is it?"

"Not bad," Cole lied.

"I have some ether." Jem removed a tin canister from her medical bag. "We're going to have to search for the bullet, and that won't be pleasant if you're awake."

Jess held the wire mask over Art's face and applied a few drops of the ether to a cloth covering it. "Breathe deep."

"Keep giving him a few drops," Jem said. "I don't want him waking." She looked at Blake. "Open that window, or we'll start nodding off."

Cole helped Jem clean the bullet hole. She used two probes to open the wound while Jem searched for the bullet. "There it is." She used the large tweezers to remove the misshapen lead ball. "He'll have a souvenir from the war when he goes home."

"The wound is that bad?"

"No, his arm will send him home. He has a section of the bone missing. I don't know how much that will limit the motion of his arm, but he won't be able to support the weight of a rifle."

"Art is one of the lucky ones," Jess said.

Was she wishing Ed had been wounded instead? She wouldn't say it aloud. Some words were better left unspoken.

****

Doctor Will Martin, a friend of Jem's, examined Pax and Art after Jem patched their wounds. He prescribed opium and told them to make Pax comfortable. He died two nights later in his sleep. Cole wrote his brother, Zachary, who was attending school at

Western Reserve Preparatory School in Hudson, Ohio. Art wanted to return to the Twenty-ninth, but the doctor said his arm would never regain full strength and mobility and wrote a medical discharge. Blake obtained new clothes and shoes for Art to wear home. He wanted to keep his tattered uniform so Cole washed it and packed it with a razor, soap, and other items for his trip. Jem gave him a crutch to keep the weight off his leg. With orders to visit Doctor Beecher, they put him on the train to Darrow Falls.

The wounded were nearly gone from Mermaid's Mirth, and guests filled the empty rooms. Eight weeks had passed since Blake was shot. His shoulder was completely healed, but he delayed joining the army while he waited word on whether or not he would receive a commission. It allowed him time to consider the best way to ensure his businesses would continue during his absence. Vincent was old and Thomas inexperienced. The man running the Pirate's Cove was on a tight budget until he proved his trustworthiness.

He had confidence in one person, but would she consider the position? He called Cole into his office.

She had impressed him with her accounting skills, and she had taken the responsibility of caring for the wounded while convalescing at the Mermaid's Mirth. Each day he had given her another challenge to see if she could handle the numerous problems that arose in the hotel business. Her grandmother had taught her how to handle demanding guests and ways to stretch a meal for six to feed ten or more.

Cole smoothed the lace trimming the bodice of her mint and white striped gown. She looked like a piece of candy. Was he making a mistake? If he died, his plan could backfire. What if a man like Simon married her, not for all she had to offer, but for the wealth she would control?

"You must have learned a lot from your grandmother. You have a knack for managing my hotel," Blake said.

"It's a lot of work, but I don't mind."

"Good, I want you to take over my businesses while I'm gone."

"What?"

"I'm a practical man. I have capable managers at each of my hotels, but I visit regularly to audit the accounts and make sure the businesses are turning a profit. I won't be able to do that once I join the army. I'd like you to do it."

"Why me?"

Because I love you. "You've proven yourself. Thomas respects you. The other managers will, too."

"But what if you…"

"Die?" She sniffled. The brat had tender feelings for him, but they had avoided any declarations of love. No sense in making the situation worse. He was leaving soon. He wanted to take care of her but not in the way Simon had proposed. "Deidre is my heir, but she's too young to manage my properties, and Logan is too busy," he explained.

"Shouldn't you hire a lawyer to take care of your wealth?"

"What lawyer is going to travel to three properties in three states? Who can I trust?"

"You trust me?"

"I gave you all my gold once. You returned it after teasing me unmercifully." He chuckled at the memory.

"Why shouldn't I trust you?"

"I can't tell if you're serious or playing me for a fool."

"Remember the book I was reading in the parlor at your grandma's inn?"

"*Great Expectations* by Charles Dickens."

"Pip helped a convict and in return, the man provided money for Pip to become a gentleman. You saved my life. I would like to help you become an independent woman."

"What exactly would my role be?"

"Visit my properties and make sure my managers don't rob me blind. I'd hate to survive the war and end up a pauper. And if a bullet has my name on it, then Deidre will be a rich young woman."

Cole chewed on her bottom lip. Would she agree? "I'll pay you thirty dollars a month."

She stood. "You don't have to bribe me."

"It's for travel expenses and compensation for work I expect to be competently done. If you don't think you can do the job, I'll find someone else."

"I can do it." She placed her hands on the edge of the desk and leaned toward him. He tried not to stare at the gentle curves pushed upward by her tight corset, but his gaze lingered. Maybe he should marry her. What difference was there between being a widow and managing all his wealth? At least he would die with a smile upon his lips.

She snapped her fingers in front of his face. "Are you listening? I'll do it because Deidre is my niece. But I'll need thirty-five dollars. I don't like traveling alone."

"As long as your traveling companion is one of your sisters, I see no problem paying the extra expense."

She leaned closer, a beaded necklace dangling between him and her exquisite breasts. He grabbed a section, the back of his hand brushing against her bare skin. He ran his fingertips along the beads, following the smooth roundness, her breasts rising and falling as he examined the curved spheres. "Who gave you this?"

"One of my former students."

"He better have been six years old."

"Seven."

He released her necklace, but his fingers lingered, feeling the pulse pounding beneath his touch. "Pretty dress. Did you make it?"

She closed her eyes and sighed. "Yes."

"Then it's agreed. You'll be my representative while I'm away." He raised his hand.

She stared at it.

He preferred a kiss but didn't trust his self-control. "Shake on it?"

She placed her hand in his and sealed the agreement. "I'll have the paperwork drawn up."

She remained in the room, her body tempting further action. Blake concentrated on reading his mail. "Was there anything else you wanted?"

She stomped her foot. "No." She looked around, turned on her heels, and marched from his office.

Blake leaned back in his chair. That was close. He'd nearly dragged her across the desk to caress her tender flesh. Bedding the brat was tempting, but any sign of impropriety, and he'd be forced to marry her. A young bride demanded attention. The last thing she'd want would be a husband who could be absent for months, maybe years. He tried not to think about making love to the ginger-haired beauty but failed.

****

Cole and Jess walked along Maryland Avenue. Logan had reviewed the agreement between her and Blake, and she was returning the signed document. A closed carriage passed them and stopped in front of Mermaid's Mirth. The driver helped a woman exit. She wore a lavender silk gown, a large feather-decorated bonnet, and lace gloves. She opened her lace trimmed parasol and waved toward the porch. "Blake, dear!"

She said his name with a familiarity and affection that caused Cole to freeze.

"What's wrong," Jess asked.

The woman was young and fairly attractive. Her dark hair and eyes contrasted sharply against her ivory skin. The silk gown was expertly constructed by a dressmaker who knew how to tuck the fabric across the bodice to emphasize a tightly cinched waist. Lace edged each ruffle of the skirt. She swayed her hips as she walked toward Blake on the porch of the Mermaid's Mirth.

"Valerie."

The woman pressed her body against Blake and lingered longer than a casual acquaintance. "Darling, you don't seem happy to see me."

Darling? Who was this woman? Cole stayed behind a cluster of trees between the hotel and street, able to see the embracing couple but hidden from their view.

"Do you like my new dress?" She turned for him, twirling her parasol as she let her skirt swirl, exposing a lace trimmed petticoat. "I bought it with you in mind."

"I thought we had an understanding about your

244

bills."

"Don't you want me to look attractive?"

"Are you planning to stay, Valerie?"

"I have a room at Willard's."

"I don't own Willard's. I hope you don't expect me to pay for it."

Valerie took his arm, and they went inside.

Cole debated whether to return to Pierce House. She didn't trust her legs to carry her that far.

Jess stepped forward. "That woman was awfully friendly toward Blake."

Cole grabbed her arm and stopped any movement. "Didn't you hear what he said? He pays for her clothes and her room. She's a kept woman."

"But I thought Blake was in love with you."

"Lies. All this talk of handling his businesses is to keep me in reserve until he needs a replacement for her." Cole collapsed, sitting beneath the shade trees beside the road.

Jess tried to comfort her. "Please don't cry."

****

Blake escorted Valerie to the public parlor. She was a sharp contrast to Cole. Valerie wanted a man to pay her bills, a maid to dress her, a cook to prepare her food, and a household of servants to do her bidding while she complained about her poor, pitiful life. "What are you doing in Washington City, Valerie?"

She sat on the sofa, spreading her skirt to one side to invite him to sit next to her. "I'm traveling with Margaret. Her father has business with a few congressmen. He's looking for some business partners."

Blake remained standing. "Must be boring for you with no social season."

"Mrs. Lincoln isn't the only hostess in town. We've attended several dinners, and Darius is hosting a reception at Willard's tonight to introduce Margaret's fiancé to Washington politicians and businessmen."

Simon was in town. "What type of impression is he making?"

"Simon is utterly charming. You might take lessons, Blake. You could use a little polish."

Simon's kind of polish he could do without. "I prefer my rough edges."

"A woman wants a man who spoils her," Valerie said. "Simon dotes on Margaret."

"All the time or only when others are looking?"

"What do you mean?"

She appeared ignorant of the meaning of his insinuation. Did Simon have everyone fooled? "Darius Radcliff has a reputation for enjoying a festive time," Blake paused, "without his wife."

"Perhaps Mrs. Radcliff prefers it that way. She's descended from royalty."

What did one have to do with the other? "If that's true, why doesn't Margaret marry a prince?"

Valerie waved her fan. "Simon is her prince. She's in love. She wants to show him off."

"And why do I need to be informed of your best friend's dreams?"

Valerie closed her fan and smacked it against her hand. "I told you the Radcliffs are hosting a reception at Willard's tonight."

"What does that have to do with me?"

"I can't receive without a proper escort, and you *are* my stepbrother."

"Where's your mother?"

"On her honeymoon." Valerie laughed in a high shrill that made him cringe. "The Reverend Dennis Lackey took her to Niagara Falls." She quieted. "So you see, I must rely on you for an escort."

"Why me? Don't you know some other man who would be willing to stand by your side in a receiving line?"

"I'm attempting to snare a husband. As a stepbrother, you won't impede another man's advances." She tugged at her gloves.

"What role do I play in tonight's soiree?" Blake demanded.

"Help me make a good impression," she said. "Introduce me to a suitable prospect, and I'll do the rest."

"That gown ought to impress a few gentlemen."

"This is one of Margaret's cast offs. It's nicer than anything I could afford on your pitiful allowance."

He waved his arm around the room. "You see where my money is invested. Now that your mother is married, you can ask your new stepfather to support you."

"He's nearly as tight fisted with money as you are."

"You should practice frugality."

She batted her eyelashes. "Bite your tongue."

Her coquettish games were annoying.

"Besides, as a businessman, I would think you would want to maintain the connections of a wealthy man like Darius Radcliff."

"I had enough of Darius in New York." And the last person he wanted to see was Simon Blackwater. But more importantly, he didn't want Cole to know her former beau was in town. What if she wasn't completely over him?

Valerie waved her fan. "Well? Will you join us at Willard's or not?"

"I'll escort you, but it's the last time." He turned to face her. "I've applied for a commission, but if I don't survive the war, I'm leaving everything to my cousin Deidre. You and your mother will receive nothing."

"Isn't she a child?"

"I have someone I trust overseeing my properties. And now that your mother is married, I can stop supporting both of you."

"You'd cut me off completely." Valerie sniffled into her kerchief.

Blake sighed. "Stop crying. I'll provide an allowance for six months. That ought to be enough time to snare a husband."

Valerie removed her kerchief to reveal a dry face. He'd been played, but six months would ease any guilt for no longer supporting her.

Blake escorted Valerie to the waiting carriage. She turned her cheek to accept a kiss, and he gave a perfunctory peck. He offered his hand to assist her in the carriage. "I'll see you at Willard's at seven. Don't be late." She waved her kerchief out the window.

Blake noticed Jess and Cole standing near the road a short distance away. They appeared to be arguing. "What's wrong?" Cole's eyes were red and swollen. Had she been crying? He reached to touch her cheek, and she jerked away.

"I'm not feeling well," she excused.

"Why don't you come inside out of the heat?"

"We need to check on Tia and Mia." Jess searched

the yard. "Where are they?"

"Amber requested I move the laundry operation to the back near the kitchen so she could watch her daughters."

"Why don't you check on them," Cole said. "I have something to say to Blake."

"Have Amber bring some ice tea," Blake said.

Jess hesitated but left them. Blake offered her a chair on the porch.

Cole smoothed a loose curl away from her face. "I've decided not to accept your offer to manage your properties. I think you should find someone else."

Blake stared. Had he been too aloof lately? Had he disguised his true feelings too skillfully? "Why don't you want to do it?"

"It's a great deal of responsibility and would take up much of my time." Cole twisted the handkerchief in her hands. "I plan to return to Ohio soon, and I'll be rather busy with callers. Simon wasn't the only man in my parlor, and a girl my age has to think about marriage. I'm sure you understand."

An exploding canister couldn't have done more damage. Why had he thought he could keep her dangling? She wanted a husband. He wanted freedom. He should have prepared for her rejection, but his arrogance had assured him she would accept his generous offer.

Jess brought them drinks in tall glasses with lemon wedges perched on the rims. "The girls are doing fine. I don't think we'll have to check on them anymore."

"It seems I'm no longer your employee." Cole took a long drink and stood. "Good-bye, Mr. Ellsworth."

Blake choked on his tea. They were leaving. He

followed them into the yard, unable to find the words to halt their departure. He watched as their figures faded in the distance. He turned and saw the Mermaid sign taunting him with her smile. He hurled the glass, which broke against the wood.

Chapter Twenty-Two

Cole waited until they were out of sight before crying. Jess put her arm around her. "What did you tell him?"

"I'm not signing the agreement. I can't work for him knowing he has a mistress."

"Did you tell him that?"

"Not the part about a mistress. That would be vulgar." She wiped her tears. "He acted so innocent. Too bad I can't confront him about his lies."

"If only you could catch him with her at Willard's."

Cole grabbed her arm. "At seven." They had overheard the exchange. "Logan owes us a trip to Willard's, and Jem is starting to show. Let's convince him to take us tonight."

Jem readily agreed to a night at Willard's, and they spent the afternoon preparing their clothes and hair.

"It's nice to have an excuse to wear nice clothes." Jess twirled in her new dress.

Let's enjoy the evening," Jem said. "I wouldn't mind socializing before my confinement."

"But Willard's?" Logan frowned. "You know what type of people frequent that place."

"Don't you want to show off the women in your life?"

"We won't stay long," Cole promised. Long

251

enough to confront Blake with that woman and call him a liar and cad.

Cole plucked the delicate silk lace she had tatted to trim the hint of sleeve on her green silk gown while they waited for the carriage to arrive. She had chosen the silk material even though it was expensive and difficult to work with. Grandma CJ had taught her how to fit a pattern. Before cutting into the expensive fabric, Cole had made an exact copy from muslin, making alterations until the basted pieces fit perfectly to her figure. Then she had torn out the basting and used the muslin as a pattern. She was pleased with the results. The bodice molded against her body with the edge barely above her camisole, exposing a generous display of her feminine charms. Yards of gathered skirt with ruffles and flounces emphasized her tiny waist. What would Blake think about the canal brat now? Did he think he could have her and a mistress? She'd give him a vision to dream about on the battlefield. One he would never possess.

Jess had made a new gown of blue with a more modest neckline. "I wish Ed could see me." She had Ed's latest letter in her reticule.

Jess had shared Ed's somber thoughts. He missed his brother even though he wrote he was glad Art had returned home. *"Ma will have one less son to worry about."* He said the flag for the Twenty-ninth regiment had mysteriously been returned after being kept in a Rebel prison.

Jake's letter contained news of Sid, who had been overjoyed to see Clara Barton at Culpeper Court House after the battle of Cedar Mountain. She had arrived with supplies for the wounded. Sid had been her personal escort during her two-day stay.

"Like usual, the Union officers have underestimated Jackson. The wily fox hasn't retreated. He's heading north, and we are packing our supplies and heading after him. We're tired and hungry, but the countryside has been ravished by both armies, and we can't find anything but raw corn. I miss your cooking, cousin. Love, Jake."

"The boys probably won't return to Washington City before we go home."

Jess caressed Ed's letter. "Do we have to leave?"

Cole studied her hair in the mirror. "We can't stay forever."

"But shouldn't we help out with the delivery of the baby."

She had no excuse to remain. Jem had regained her health, and General McClellan's reluctance to fight meant she wasn't needed at the hospitals. Jess hoped Ed would return, but it was unlikely. The Ohio boys were deep in Virginia. It was time to return home. "Jem isn't due until December." Cole opened her reticule. Her fan, a lace-trimmed handkerchief, and a few pieces of peppermint candy were inside. "Do you want to miss Christmas at home?"

"What about Blake?"

"Logan said he had a good chance of receiving his commission." After tonight, Blake would be out of her life forever. She could forgive a man many faults, but keeping a secret mistress was not one of them. Blake Ellsworth was going to regret making her fall in love with him. Was she in love with him? No, she wouldn't allow it.

****

Willard's Hotel at 1401 Pennsylvania Avenue was strategically located a block from the Department of the Treasury where Logan worked. Beyond was the White House. The Willard Brothers had purchased the six-story hotel in 1859 and expanded it by purchasing the Presbyterian Church on F Street.

Logan helped the three ladies out of the carriage and offered his arm to his wife. Cole and Jess followed.

The foyer and main hallway were crowded with officers in their best trimmed uniforms and gentlemen in elegant frock coats, lace trimmed shirts, and an air of importance. Voices hummed with the static of excitement or murmured with shared bits of important information. Ladies whispered gossip behind painted fans or waved and shouted greetings to familiar faces across the way.

Many of the women, clinging to the arm of their escorts, had returned to town after spending most of the summer away from the heat and dirt of Washington City. Their gowns were crafted by the most skilled seamstresses, made of silk and trimmed with intricate gathers, ribbons, and lace. Some waited to be seated in the crowded dining hall while others retired to the ladies' parlor to wait for their escorts to finish business behind closed doors in the hallowed hall for men.

Cole's sewing skills were comparable, and at least one woman asked for the name of her seamstress.

"Couturier CJ." She elbowed Jess to end her giggling.

"I've never heard of her."

"She lives in Ohio and only sews for a limited clientele."

After the woman left, Jem confronted her. "Colleen

Josephine Beecher, I'm going to tell Mama on you."

"I didn't say anything that wasn't true."

Jem examined her dress. "Couturier CJ taught me how to make this gown."

"You've never looked lovelier." Logan's fingertips caressed Jem's bare shoulders. They gazed into each other's eyes as if no one else was around.

Jess giggled behind her fan, but Cole was envious of their obvious love. Logan would stay close to his wife's side. They weaved through the sea of ornate gowns and well-dressed gentlemen.

"Who are all these people?" Cole asked.

Logan pointed. "Government officials, military leaders, and businessmen gathered to discuss the future of the nation and make as much money as possible before the war ends." His tone was harsh.

"You sound cynical, Logan."

"Do I?" He gazed at Jem. "Sometimes I forget about the beauty in the world."

"You are a moral compass, the light that keeps the darkness at bay," Jem reminded him. His dimples deepened, their secretive exchange only understood by them.

A man with slick dark hair waved at Logan. He waved in return and whispered a warning. "Pete Burdett is heading this way."

Pete wore his black hair greased back from his face, which was beginning to show signs of over indulgence in the dark bags beneath his weary eyes. He worked with Logan at the Treasury building. But it was Pete's companion that drew everyone's attention. The woman on his arm wore a black silk gown draped upon white shoulders with plump breasts barely contained by the scandalously low décolletage. A necklace of gold and pearls decorated the wide expanse of naked flesh. "Who is that?"

"Lily Divine." Jem sighed and shook her head. "The merry widow of Pennsylvania Avenue."

The black gown was hardly modest. "She's in mourning?"

"Until she marries husband number four." Jem's blue eyes were frosty toward the approaching woman.

"Why don't you like her?"

"She's a horrible woman," Jem said. "I met her last year, and she wanted to recruit me."

"As a nurse?" Jess asked.

A snort escaped Jem's lips. "Let's say it was to comfort men for a monetary reward."

Jess gasped, her eyes widening in alarm. "She's a prostitute?"

"Jessica!" Jem glanced around for anyone who had heard her outburst, but no one had reacted. "She's called a courtesan in Washington City."

Jess shook her head, her curls bouncing with the gesture. "What's the difference?"

"The amount of money left beside the bed," Cole murmured. "I bet she makes more than two dollars."

"I'm going to pretend I didn't hear that." Jem fanned her flushed face. "Remember you're unmarried ladies. Try to act innocent and naïve."

"It's not like you can miss all the brothels in town or the soldiers and officers visiting them," Cole whispered behind her painted fan.

"Mr. Chase doesn't approve," Jem said. "Neither do most of the ladies of town, but no one can tell the soldiers how to spend their money. Logan says it's a matter of economics. Where there is a demand, someone supplies the service, and the greater the need, the higher the price."

"Sounds like an easy way to make money."

"You've never treated a girl who's been beaten and raped by her client," Jem said.

"Yes, I have." Cole shuddered. An image of a young girl flashed into her memory. One she couldn't forget. "It's bad enough when a man wants to kiss you against your will. To hurt and humiliate a woman so brutally takes a monster."

"Lily is worse. She makes it look glamourous to entice young women to join the sordid profession. She doesn't tell them the truth about the costs. Most end up with syphilis, and when they're treated with opiates, they become addicts. Then they have no choice but to sell themselves for any amount."

After making their way through the crowd, Logan made introductions. "This is my co-worker at the Department of the Treasury, Pete Burdett, and this is Lily Divine." Logan turned to Jem. "You know my wife, Jennifer, and these are her sisters, Colleen and Jessica."

"Don't your parents know how to have a plain daughter?"

Lily's compliment sounded sincere, but Cole took it in stride. She had flaws and five siblings to remind her of them.

"Thank you," Jem said. "My condolences on the loss of your husband."

"This is my first appearance in public since his death. I spent the summer in Maine." She fanned herself. "I should have waited until September to return.

I forgot how horrible the heat can be in late August."

"The humidity has been barely tolerable this summer," Jem agreed.

"You spent the summer in town?"

"My husband works here."

"Remind me to invite you to join me next summer."

"That's generous but I…"

"And your sisters must join us," Lily added before her invitation could be rejected. "You would love the beach."

"She speaks the truth." Pete's gaze was low, darting from one sister to another. "I was at death's door before joining Lily. "The beach is the place to recover your health."

"We're not sick." Cole turned to Jess. "Do I appear ill?"

"You are the picture of health," Pete said. "The beach offers many diversions, especially for young people. I hated to leave."

"I'm sure Mr. Chase will be happy you've returned from your sabbatical," Logan said. "You've been gone so long, I was beginning to wonder if you no longer required a job."

Pete laughed. "I haven't been so ill not to broker some business deals. There are fortunes to be made from war, and I have inside knowledge of what deals can fatten a man's bank account."

"You better be careful, Pete," Logan said. "Mr. Chase doesn't approve of his employees speculating on future investments."

"It's my money," Pete said. "Many businessmen come to Washington City looking for investments. One is holding a reception now."

"I hear he's wealthy," Lily said.

"And married," Pete reminded her. "But that has never stopped you."

"Married men tend to be more generous," Lily said. "What do you know about him?"

"He's from New York," Pete said. "He wants his future son-in-law to meet all the important people."

"Another profiteer?"

"He's grooming him for a political career," Pete said. "Old man Radcliff has dreams of having a senator in the family."

Radcliff? It couldn't be. Cole fanned herself. "Do you know the name of the future bridegroom?"

"Simon Blackwater." Pete grinned. "He knows how to have a good time."

Cole grabbed Jess' wrist. "We have to leave."

"Blackwater?" Jem repeated. "Is he from Ohio?"

"I believe so. Bragged about graduating from Western Reserve College as if it were Yale."

"That sounds like Stanley Blackwater's son." Jem turned to Logan. "He makes boilers in Akron. They're an important family back home. Grandpa transported some of their products for them."

Cole searched for the door but couldn't see past the pressing crowd. She couldn't escape.

"We should congratulate him," Logan said. "Seeing he's a family friend."

"Aren't you going to tell them?" Jess hissed in her ear.

Cole took a deep breath and smoothed her skirt. "We should say hello." Let Simon realize his engagement meant nothing. He was in her past and easily forgotten.

Jess stayed close as they headed to the reception room. "You're braver than me. I'd run for the street about now."

"Logan is one of the important people he'll want to meet." Cole glanced around for Blake. Was he in a room upstairs with his mistress? Was he making love to her?

Lily tugged on her lace glove. The seam near the thumb had been poorly mended. Her sleeve hem was frayed, and a stain marred the silk fabric, partially hidden in the folds of her skirt. Either she had limited mourning attire, or Lily had fallen on hard times. No wonder she was searching for another husband or caretaker.

Jess grabbed her hand as they entered the reception room.

The tall windows were framed with velvet curtains, and the wooden floor was polished, reflecting the gas lights in the wax. The elegant furniture was against the walls with a buffet table filled with meats, fruits, and desserts at one end of the long hall. The host party was standing on a raised dais at the other end of the hall.

Cole met Simon's gaze. He looked the same, young, handsome, and engaged to another. Margaret Radcliff stood beside him in a pink gown with puffy white bows decorating the hem and perched on each shoulder. She was a plump creature with birdlike features. Her large eyes dominated her face but failed to mask thin lips above a weak chin that doubled when she looked down. Her mouth moved constantly as she welcomed each guest through the receiving line.

Her mother was frighteningly thin with protruding

cheekbones and a stern visage. She wore black as if in mourning, but her husband stood beside her. Darius was the opposite of his wife with protruding girth and a jovial manner. His loud voice boomed across the room. His suit was black, but his vest was a myriad of bright silk colors embroidered in a hunting design across his belly.

Cole stumbled when she saw the next two people, Blake Ellsworth and his mistress. What was he doing here with Simon? Had he set her up to be embarrassed? He knew she must have overheard the woman reminding him about the engagement. She flashed a smile when his gaze met hers. His brows puzzled together, and a snarl marred his lips. What was he angry about? She'd shown like he wanted.

Pete and Lily were introduced first and then Logan and Jem. "These are my wife's sisters, Miss Jessica and Miss Colleen Beecher."

"Beecher?" Amelia Radcliff repeated. "Any relation to the Connecticut Beechers?"

"Distant cousins," Jem said. "Our father is Doctor Sterling Beecher."

"Doctor." Amelia nodded her approval. "You'll have to come and dine with us some evening."

"We would be honored."

"This was not a good idea," Jess warned Cole.

It was one thing to meet Simon and his future in-laws in a reception line. It was another to have dinner with them. What excuse would she invent to avoid an evening with the Radcliffs?

Simon didn't see Logan extending his hand, his eyes were riveted on Cole.

"Simon," Margaret nudged him. "Your manners."

He shook Logan's hand and nodded at Jem. "Miss Jennifer Beecher."

"It's Mrs. Pierce," Logan corrected.

"I'm sorry," Simon stammered. He removed his kerchief from his coat pocket and dabbed at his forehead.

"Mrs. Pierce." Margaret took her hand. "I don't know what's wrong with my fiancé. I hope you weren't offended by his *faux pas*."

Cole fought to keep the corners of her mouth from turning upward. Simon was a nervous wreck. It restored her confidence. He barely acknowledged Jess before his gaze locked onto hers. "I was unaware you were in Washington City, Colleen."

"We're visiting my sister and her husband. We've had a wonderful time seeing the sights. My cousin Jake and the Herbruck boys were in town. They'll be sorry they missed you." She had delivered her speech with the right amount of enthusiasm and lightheartedness as she had intended.

Simon's eyes widened. "I heard they were in the Shenandoah Valley."

"They were, but they were ordered closer to Richmond." She studied her handbag. "They dined with us several evenings and entertained us with amusing stories about the battlefront."

Margaret took Simon's arm. "Simon says the army needs officers, but we can't spare him." Her twittering laugh was high-pitched and painful to human ears.

"I was offered a commission," Simon bragged.

Commission? Simon would be the type of officer Jake and the Herbruck boys would chew up and spit out. Would he fake an injury or run away when the battle began? "But what about the draft? How will you avoid fighting?"

Margaret pouted and looked at her father. "Daddy dear will take care of it."

Darius Radcliff would pay another man to serve. Simon's courage would never be tested. Jake, Ed, and Art didn't have college educations. They didn't have wealthy fathers or a future father-in-law to buy their way out of the war, but they knew their duty to country, and their bravery had been proven.

"Anything to keep my little princess happy." Darius was staring at her in a way that made Cole shudder. Drool beaded in the corner of his crooked smile, and his eyes had a hunger that was unnatural for any decent man. She'd have to remind Jess not to go anywhere alone with the dirty old lecher.

"You must join us for an evening of entertainment," Darius said. "No one knows how to have a good time better than the Radcliffs."

"It's such a pity the social season was canceled because of Mrs. Lincoln." Margaret pursed her lips. "I wanted to go to the White House."

"She has to realize her continued mourning is ruining the social season," Amelia said. "After all, she has duties to perform."

"Her little boy died." Cole waited for a sign of sympathy. She looked at Jess, who was equally appalled.

"We know," Margaret agreed. "But a well-bred lady doesn't allow her personal hardships to prevent her from performing her obligations to society."

Jess nudged her. "Of course."

"I suppose it's for the best," Amelia said. "We'll be

too busy preparing for the wedding to attend parties and dinners."

"I'm so lucky to have Mommy dear and my best friend Valerie helping." Valerie turned at the sound of her name. So did Blake. "This is my best and dearest friend Valerie Ferguson. We attended Miss Wellington's School for Young Ladies in New York. Oh, and this is her escort, Blake Ellsworth. He owns the Dutchman Hotel."

Escort? The rich were brazen in their labels. Valerie wore a sheer beige gown with tiers of ruffles, each edge decorated in yards of delicate silk lace. Had Blake paid for the expensive gown? How long had he maintained a sordid relationship with her?

Chapter Twenty-Three

Blake took a deep breath to control his fury. What was Cole doing here? And what was she doing wearing a gown cut so low, she threatened to overflow its confines? Darius and Simon were openly ogling her breasts like hungry babes anticipating a warm meal. Wasn't she over Simon? Was this an attempt to seduce him into changing his mind about marrying Margaret?

"Miss Beecher."

"Mr. Ellsworth. Any relation to the first man to be killed in the war?"

Her anger matched his own. "No."

"But he has a death wish," Valerie said. "He wants to join the army, and I can't do anything to dissuade him." She squeezed against him. He stiffened in response.

"I think we've met enough guests," Darius announced even though there were several people in line behind them. He signaled for the small orchestra to play and offered his gloved hand to Cole. "As the host, I feel entitled to claim the first dance."

"You have to dance with me first, Daddy," Margaret whined in a little girl voice.

He turned to Simon, who had crowded next to Darius. "You should dance with Simon."

She pouted. "But you're my daddy."

"I'll take the second dance." Darius offered his

arm, and Cole shrugged her naked shoulders. She looked like a lamb being led to the slaughter. She was in over her head.

Valerie stored her fan and handkerchief in her beaded bag, which she hung on her wrist. "I believe this dance is ours."

No one offered to dance with Amelia, who turned her attention to the guests who had been abandoned in the receiving line.

Blake searched for Cole and Darius over Valerie's head as he led her through the country dance steps.

"You seem interested in Miss Beecher," Valerie said. "How do you know her?"

Blake frowned as Darius attempted to draw Cole close. Keep your elbows taut, brat. The dance was taking entirely too long. Valerie repeated her question.

"Her father removed the bullet in my shoulder."

"And she followed you to Washington City?"

"No. She's here to help her sister."

"What's wrong with her sister?"

"She's expecting a baby."

"How awful."

"Don't you anticipate motherhood, Valerie?"

"Since you're not a prospective husband, I'll be brutally honest. I don't like the little buggers. They cry and whine and ruin a woman's figure."

"No wonder you've been avoiding marriage."

"I'm beginning to think marriage is foolish," Valerie confessed. "Look at Margaret. Once she marries Simon, her life is over. She'll have to do whatever he says and put up with his mistresses and tight-fisted hold on *her* money."

Mistresses? Simon had his eye on Cole for his

mistress. "I would think Margaret would demand some attention."

"Simon will do his duty. Darius wants a grandson. Like most men, he wants to leave his wealth to a man of his blood. But once Simon produces the heir, he can do whatever he wants."

"Margaret won't complain?"

"A lady never shows disappointment in her husband or marriage."

"Did they teach you that at Miss Wellington's school?"

"Miss Wellington's lesson were about attracting a husband. Amelia Radcliff is the one with the lessons on how to survive after the nuptials."

"Wouldn't the real lesson be not to marry a man like Darius or Simon?"

"Where do you find a man who doesn't drink, gamble, or chase skirts?" She tipped back her head and laughed. "Oh, did I describe Mr. Blake Ellsworth?"

Her sarcasm was meant to anger him, but he took pride in his self-control. "Although I limit my liquor, hold onto my hard earned cash, and practice control with the ladies, it doesn't make me a Puritan."

"The beautiful Miss Beecher doesn't look like the type of woman to wait while you play soldier or have you changed your plans?"

"I intend to join. What are your plans? Will you be traveling to Europe to shop for the newlyweds' home?"

"And I'll shop for a rich husband while I'm there. I may not be returning."

"I hope you don't expect a generous dowry."

"Can I at least give the impression my stepbrother is wealthy?"

"You can say whatever you want to nab a husband."

****

Cole scowled at Blake. What was he saying to the dark-haired woman in his arms? He couldn't keep his eyes off her. And what was Valerie saying to capture his attention? She was smiling at Blake in a way that made her want to scratch her eyes out. Was he in love with her? Had all his playful teasing and attention been a meaningless game? All her promises not to fall in love with Blake crumbled under the realization she was jealous of any woman who garnered his attention.

Darius hadn't stopped talking since leading her on the dance floor. She barely acknowledged anything he said, her ears straining for any stray word from Blake or Valerie.

"You're a beautiful woman," he said.

She nodded.

"And vain."

She agreed.

His boisterous laughter broke her concentration. Blake and Valerie turned at his outburst. His dark eyebrow shot up, his gaze locked on hers. She turned to face Darius. "I'm sorry. I didn't understand the joke."

"Do you know Mr. Ellsworth?"

"He's a friend of Mr. Pierce, my brother-in-law."

"I knew Blake had connections," Darius said. "I've been trying to encourage him to join my team for years. Even offered him Margaret, but he turned me down."

"Blake was going to marry Margaret?"

"Didn't get that far," Darius said. "He called on her once and never returned. Can't blame him. She's an annoying child."

He was describing his beloved daughter, the one who adored her daddy. Was their sugar-coated affection in public a ruse? "She adores you."

"I spoil her." He licked his lips. "I spoil all the women I love."

How much longer was this dance? "You were talking about Mr. Ellsworth."

"The boy won't take my advice. If I owned his properties, I would have made a fortune by now."

"How would you accomplish that?"

"He has a hotel, the Mermaid's Mirth. He allows the army to house its wounded when he could demand top dollar from paying guests."

"He's doing his patriotic duty."

"Nonsense. War can be profitable to those who are smart enough to cash in on the opportunities. Have you noticed that rich men start the wars, but they never participate in them? Throw a patriotic speech or worthless cause to the poor masses, and they'll sacrifice their worthless lives and be proud to do it. I plan to triple my fortune by storing wool."

While Ed and Art wore rags, slept on the cold ground, and ate hard biscuits, he enjoyed every luxury. She curled her fingers into fists. How dare he ridicule them? "You withhold wool even though the army needs it for its uniforms and blankets."

"If they want to pay my price, they can have all the wool they want. That, little lady, is the world of business."

"I believe you're describing profiteering. You're withholding supply while demand is high in order to charge more and increase your profits. It's why the poor despise the rich."

He laughed. "They don't despise us. They want to be us. This country is based on capitalism. Those who are smart enough, seize the opportunity to make wealth."

"Like slave owners who claim slavery is a necessary evil to maintain their lifestyle?"

"I don't own slaves."

"You're in the textile industry. Do you employ women and children?"

"Yes, and they're grateful for the work."

"You force them to work long hours for low pay."

"I don't have to force them," he defended. "Plenty of workers are willing to take their place. I hope you're not a suffragette. I find the whole idea of equality ridiculous."

"You have a wife and daughter. Don't you want others to treat them with respect?"

"Others respect them because they belong to me," Darius said. "No one claims my possessions without my permission."

Could she spit in his eye?

Simon tapped Darius on the shoulder. "My turn. He handed Margaret to her father and took Cole in his arms. He regaled her with his latest adventures, and she pretended to listen, but her thoughts were elsewhere. Something was different. She no longer hated him. The thought of being jilted for another woman didn't make her angry. Her feelings were indifferent toward him. He had joined the ranks of the beaus she no longer thought about. She had been in love with Simon, and yet her heart wasn't broken. It wasn't cracked or bruised. She had survived losing him.

Valerie's shrill laughter interrupted her revelation.

Blake was dancing with her. This was the second dance. Why hadn't he changed partners? He nodded, a sly grin on his swarthy face. A sob caught in her throat. The one man she wanted was slipping away. Blake had become part of her life. Every morning she looked forward to seeing him, and every night her last thoughts were of him. She had memorized the details of his face, reflected on the words he had spoken, and had allowed intimacies that left her body flushed with satisfaction. Would she suffer another heartbreak? And would she recover from Blake as easily as she had from other men?

She forced her attention on Simon. "How is your new job?"

"Darius has given me a great deal of responsibility," Simon said. "He has the utmost confidence in me."

"You enjoy working for a profiteer? He confided he's hoarding wool."

"He says the war is an opportunity. You must seize the moment. It's his creed for business and personal life."

"*Carpe deum.*"

"I forgot you know Latin."

"Papa believed women should be educated."

"It's a waste of time for someone as beautiful as you, Colleen."

She ignored his innuendo. "It was nice of your future father-in-law to introduce you to people in Washington City."

"He was hoping Salmon Chase would attend, but Logan Pierce is his secretary. Sometimes an underling can yield an influence in delicate matters."

Underling? He didn't hesitate to insult someone behind his back. And what delicate matter required Mr. Chase's help? "Does Mr. Radcliff want a contract to buy cotton?"

"I forgot how quick you were at solving puzzles. Will you put in a good word for us?"

"Mr. Chase is an honorable man. He's careful about awarding contracts. Even a hint of impropriety can ignite a scandal."

"When have you worried about scandal? I heard how you *educated* the new teacher in Darrow Falls."

What lies had he heard? "The man wanted a teaching job to avoid the draft. He's a coward, and judging by your remark, a liar."

Blake and Valerie danced close. He nodded, but his gray eyes were dark and threatening to storm.

Simon pulled her close. "How do you know Blake Ellsworth?"

She struggled to put some distance between them. "Family friend."

"The Radcliffs and I stayed at his hotel in Albany. He was an excellent host. After a boring play, the ladies retired to their rooms, and the real entertainment began." He was baiting her, hinting at a lifestyle she had already turned down. But was Blake part of it? "We had a wild night on the town drinking, gambling, and whoring." He watched her. "Have I shocked you?"

"Was Blake with you?"

"He recommended a few places. Darius was familiar with most of them. He knows how to have a good time in any city." He gazed into her eyes. "You should have joined us."

"I thought the ladies retired to their rooms?"

"Delicate ladies miss much of life." He leaned close to her ear. "They don't have your exuberance for experiences."

"We've had this discussion before, Simon. I said no. I haven't changed my mind." She needed to change the subject. "Have you set a date for the wedding?"

Simon was admiring her décolletage. Some men were obsessed with a woman's breasts. Most had the good taste to avoid staring. "Did you say something?"

"Your wedding? Have you set a date?"

"In two weeks."

"The weather ought to be nice."

"It has nothing to do with the weather. The draft is in September."

"Margaret said you wanted to be an officer."

"For five minutes. Too many officers have been killed. I'm not foolish enough to risk my life. Darius has promised to pay someone else to serve my time," Simon said. "I would consider that money well spent."

"The army would agree with you."

He frowned. Had he understood her insult? "And what about you, Colleen? I almost wish I was going off to fight in the war to see how you would react. Would you cry a few tears for me?"

Only if you were dead. "I would shed tears for any local boy."

"I knew your feelings hadn't changed." He glanced around the room. "You want me as much as I want you."

Cole shook her head. How could he misinterpret her words?

Blake tapped Simon on the shoulder. "I believe this is my dance."

"We'll have to continue this conversation later," Simon said. He took Valerie into his arms and danced away.

Chapter Twenty-Four

Cole's wide skirt hid her foot swinging out to kick him in the butt. He was an idiot. Had the perks of the wealthy gone to his head? Did he think every woman would fall madly in love with him? "I don't think I will ever understand men."

"I was thinking the same thing about women," Blake said. "You're still in love with Simon."

Had she heard correctly? "What makes you think that?"

"The cat and mouse game I witnessed."

"I don't like being a mouse, especially to a pack of rats."

"You wanted to see Simon. Don't tell me you're disappointed?"

"I didn't know he would be here."

Blake studied her. "Then why did you come?"

She wasn't going to tell him she was jealous of Valerie Ferguson. "Logan promised a visit to Willard's." She shrugged. "It's not what I expected."

"I have to deal with some of these men," Blake said. "You will not find a more eloquently dressed band of liars, thieves, and cutthroats."

"Must make an interesting group to drink, gamble, and whore with."

"Watch your language, young lady." His voice was stern.

275

"Simon didn't think I was lady enough to censor his words. He said you were his host to an entertaining evening in Albany."

"It was Darius and Simon's idea."

"I was beginning to think you weren't like Simon. That you had a thread of decency in you, but I was wrong."

"I thought you knew me better. Have you ever seen me drunk or throwing my hard-earned money away at gambling tables? And the only woman I've shared intimacies with is you."

"Would your mistress agree?"

"My what?"

"Miss Ferguson."

Blake missed a step. "Valerie is not my mistress."

"Why don't you say that louder? Only half the room heard."

He lowered his voice. "What made you think she was my mistress?"

"I saw her arrive at the Mermaid's Mirth earlier today. She had her hands all over you, leaning against you, stroking your coat sleeve. You pay for her clothes. She's no mere acquaintance."

He grinned as if her words were amusing. "No. She's my stepsister."

Cole stumbled. Had she heard correctly? "What?"

"My father married her mother four years ago. I promised him I would take care of them, but they spend money as if I was printing it instead of Salmon Chase. My stepmother recently married, and I can relinquish my obligation. I agreed to be Valerie's escort tonight to maintain peace between us and end her dependence on me."

She studied Valerie flirting with her new partner. "She acts like she wants to be more than a stepsister."

"Valerie is utterly charming when she wants something. Unlike you, my dear canal brat, she doesn't believe in hard work. Not when others are willing to support her."

"What does she want from you?"

"The illusion of wealth." Blake nodded to Valerie and Simon. "She wants to ingratiate herself with the Radcliffs in order to snatch a rich husband."

"Isn't an ordinary man good enough for her?"

"She covets the lifestyle only a great deal of money can provide."

Simon promised wealth without marriage. "Is it a good idea to travel with the Radcliffs and Simon?"

"You think I should be worried?"

"You overheard Simon's outrageous proposal. What do you think?"

"I should have a talk with Valerie about the dangers of men who have no scruples."

"You should start with yourself."

"I haven't touched you without your permission, brat. Do you regret anything we've done?"

"Not that." Her face burned under the intensity of his gaze. What was he remembering? "I meant your night in Albany with…"

"My idea of entertainment isn't throwing money away on a crooked card game, watching two birds tear each other to shreds, or paying a frightened girl two dollars to satisfy a man's lust."

"What are you saying?"

"I used my injury as an excuse to leave the Mounting Stallion and went home."

"Does Simon know that?"

"He was already upstairs." He gripped her chin with his gloved fingertips. "You don't like sharing me with other women."

She jerked away. "It's not like you belong to me."

"I belong," he said. "Body, heart, and soul. Just like you belong to me." His gaze lowered and followed the line of her bodice. "Did your dressmaker run out of material?"

"I made this gown and purchased the silk with money I earned scrubbing uniforms and sheets. It may not be as fancy as some of their gowns." She waved her arm around the crowd. "But I like it."

"Your gown pales compared to the beauty of the woman wearing it."

"Do you think I'm going to gush about a fake flowery compliment?"

"I would be rude not to compliment you," Blake said. "After all, you wore it for me."

"Don't be conceited."

His chuckle drew everyone's attention. "You thought Valerie was my mistress, and you overheard we were coming to Willard's. You were jealous."

"I would have to be in love with you to be jealous, Mr. Ellsworth."

He frowned, his eyes caressing her. "Don't fall in love with me, brat. I'll be gone to fight soon, and I wouldn't want to break your heart."

"The last time I looked my heart was pretty strong."

A soft smile played on his lips. "You are over Simon."

"You sound surprised. I'm not a silly schoolgirl

who pines for a lost love. And I won't pine for you when you're gone."

His eyebrow shot up. Was he shocked? Or hurt?

He pulled her close, whispering in her ear, "I'll think of you every night we're apart."

Cole stopped dancing, tears gathering on her lower lids. "It appears Valerie is signaling you."

"It's my turn to dance with Margaret."

"Don't you like her?"

"A voice that high-pitched should only belong to a three-year-old." He offered his handkerchief, shrugged, and headed for his new partner.

Davy Cooke asked Cole to dance, but she asked him to escort her to the punch table instead. "What are you doing here?"

"I came to pass out business cards for Mr. Brady. He likes to photograph officers and politicians. Some day he may give me a wagon, and I'll photograph the battlefields. For now, I work at his shop and take portraits."

"Do you do wedding photographs?"

"Yes." He looked around the room. "Is someone getting married?"

Cole pointed at Margaret and Blake. "Miss Radcliff is the bride." She looked around for the groom. He was with Darius raising their glasses in a toast. It wasn't punch. After downing the drink, Simon had a coughing fit. Darius laughed, slapped him on the back, and filled his glass again. Had his future father-in-law been such a dominating influence he had transformed the small town boy into a drunkard and lecherous womanizer? Her imagination was running wild. Simon couldn't have changed that much. But he wasn't the prince in her fairytales. Poor Blake feigned interest in Margaret's endless dribble. He couldn't wait to join the army and be away from all these boring females.

****

Blake swirled Margaret around the dance floor, willing the music to end soon. Simon was drinking with Darius, and both men were staring at Cole in a way that made him want to thrash them. Margaret waved as she passed the two men. They didn't acknowledge her.

"Simon is making an impression tonight."

"Isn't he wonderful?" Margaret sighed.

Blake didn't know how to answer. "I'm sure he has many admirable qualities."

"He does!" she gushed. "He's so handsome and clever. My father says he could be president."

"President of your father's business?" Wasn't that why he was marrying her?

"Oh no, president of the United States."

A poor rail splitter from the backwoods becomes president, and everyone wants to throw his hat into the ring. "I didn't know he was so ambitious."

"He graduated nearly at the top of his class at college."

Nearly? "Where did he attend?"

"Western Reserve College in Ohio." She jerked her weak chin toward Cole. "Simon says the woman you were dancing with was one of his former acquaintances in Ohio."

"Miss Colleen Beecher." Canal brat extraordinary. "Logan Pierce is married to her sister."

Margaret pursed her lips in an unflattering expression. "Simon says Mr. Pierce is only a clerk."

"I believe he's Mr. Chase's secretary. It's an

important position."

Margaret waved her hand in dismissal. "Simon says Miss Beecher is the daughter of a poor country doctor and never attended finishing school. Poor woman. A true gentleman doesn't marry a woman who isn't refined."

"She taught school for a year." Until a draft dodger replaced her.

"Simon says women don't possess the intelligence or ability to do a man's job and shouldn't try to compete."

Was he playing a child's game? If she said Simon says one more time he might reveal what he knew about the future president of the United States. Was she blind to her father's sordid lifestyle? The same one Simon embraced?

"She also assisted her father with some of his patients." Like me.

"I hope she isn't a nurse." Margaret lowered her voice to a squeaky whisper. "Simon says the women bathe the men...and more."

"They give drink to the thirsty, feed the hungry, and bandage the wounds of men who are too tired, too beaten, and too near death to do more than be grateful."

"Simon says a woman shouldn't work when a man can do the job better." She giggled in short staccato bursts that assaulted his nerves. "I'm so glad I'll have him to take care of me."

And your money. "Congratulations on your good fortune."

Blake returned Margaret to her mother's care. Simon had found the perfect mate, but how long would she sing his praises when his indiscretions became more public? Valerie had finished dancing with Pete Burdett and joined them. She laid her hand on Blake's arm. "Would you mind fetching some punch? My throat is parched."

"Do you mind fetching me a glass, too?" Margaret added.

He readily agreed. Anything was better than maintaining an expression of interest as the women praised every minute detail of Simon's flawless character.

Chapter Twenty-Five

Davy Cooke was explaining how a twin-lens camera could capture two exact images which were developed on one glass plate. After processing the image, the two stereo images were placed on a viewing card which could be inserted into a viewer to create three dimensional images.

"When do you think you'll travel to the battlefield?" Jess asked.

"Alexander Gardner may take me on his next trip to help develop images, but it may be another year before I take my own photographs."

Jess was fascinated, but Cole looked around the reception hall. Her gaze found the man who made her forget everyone else. Blake strode toward her. His formal clothes were impeccable, the frock coat fit his wide shoulders and tapered to a narrow waist. His black vest and tie contrasted with his white shirt. Was this the same man who had worn a ragged coat and patched trousers aboard the *Irish Rose*? She introduced him to Davy.

"We've met," Davy said. "He bought several prints of your photograph, Miss Colleen."

Cole turned. Blake was running his fingers along his starched collar. "Did you?"

His smoky gaze burned through her. "It was cheaper than bidding against the soldiers. How do you feel being one of the most sought after trading cards?"

"You didn't buy a trading card."

"That expression! It's the one on the sign."

"I saw my photograph by your bed."

"Bed?" Jess looked worried.

"I was alone combing my hair for the sitting," she reminded her.

"I will be so happy when you are married and my days of chaperoning are over."

"What about Cassie and Jules?"

Jess groaned.

"So, Blake, what does my photograph by your bed mean?"

"You know what it means, brat." Blake poured several glasses of punch. "Now, if you'll excuse me, I have to quench the thirst of two gullible ladies."

"We're not done talking."

"I'd be happy to help," Davy offered, taking a fragile glass of punch in each hand. "Where are the recipients?"

"The two ladies in front of the dais."

Davy headed for Valerie and Margaret, a glass gripped in each hand.

Blake splashed a ladle of punch into a glass cup.

"Careful, you'll stain my new dress," Cole warned.

"I'm a bit clumsy with this thing." Blake returned the ladle and emptied the cup in one gulp.

"Men always say they're clumsy when they're nervous about answering a simple question. Why do you have my photograph..." Cole turned her attention from Blake and searched the room for Davy. He was highly strung, jittery, and carrying two glasses of strawberry punch. A dangerous combination. Davy was maneuvering his way through the crowd, the pair of punch glasses balanced precariously in each hand. "Oh, no."

Valerie and Margaret had their backs to Davy as he attempted to gain their attention. He moved both glasses of strawberry punch to one hand and tapped Valerie on her bare shoulder. Valerie spun, her outstretched arm knocking Davy's arm in an upward arc. The glasses emptied their contents into the air and splashed in a shower of droplets on Valerie's wide expanse of creamy bare skin above her ruffled and lace trimmed bodice. A high-pitched scream quieted every occupant in the room. The music stopped, and guests turned their attention to the dais.

Davy froze, the empty cups rattling in his hand.

"You clumsy oaf. You ruined my dress!" Valerie shrieked.

"I'm so sorry," Davy muttered. He searched his pocket for a handkerchief.

Jess turned to Cole, her face ashen. "They'll kill him."

Cole snatched the fabric of her wide skirt and ran across the floor, dodging bodies, frozen in mid-dance, waiting for the drama to unfold between Valerie and her hapless target.

Jess kept pace. "Do you have a plan?"

"When do I ever have a plan?" Logan and Jem were near the doorway. They had turned toward the commotion, but the distance and bodies in between blocked their view of the participants. "I'll take starboard of our clumsy friend. You take the other side," Cole said. "Once I distract Valerie, grab Davy and run for the door. Have Logan take you home." She skidded to a stop. "Don't wait for me. I'll find my own way home."

Margaret, whose gown appeared untouched, cowered in her mother's arms while Valerie poured out her wrath. "You stupid, ugly man." Her face was distorted with anger and revulsion. "What happened to your face?"

"The scars are from smallpox." Cole wrestled the empty glasses from Davy's tight grasp and handed them to a waiter who had a tray of filled glasses. "He didn't get immunized."

Valerie ignored her explanation. "What makes you think you should be allowed in the company of gentlemen and ladies?" Valerie dabbed at the colorful blotches with her lace-trimmed handkerchief. She waved the stained fabric in his face. "Not only have you ruined my dress, but look at my new kerchief." She glanced around at the statues of spectators. "Isn't anyone going to do anything?"

Simon grabbed Davy's coat and cocked his arm to hit him. Blake covered his fist with his hand. "This isn't the place for fisticuffs. Besides, you might bruise your knuckles against his face."

Valerie threw the soiled handkerchief at Davy. "You'll have to pay for a new dress."

He found his voice, shaky and apologetic. "How much does a dress cost?"

"My dressmaker charged me a hundred dollars for this gown."

Davy's eyes were wide, and he began to shake. "I don't have nearly that much money, miss."

"Then you'll go to jail."

"Calm down, Valerie," "Blake said. "It's only a

stupid gown."

"I won't calm down. Look at what that bungling oaf did!"

Cole nodded to Jess, who was on the opposite side of Davy. Cole took a glass of punch from the waiter, who hadn't moved, and dumped the contents on her dress. She gasped. The cold liquid dribbled into the crevice between her breasts, staining the new silk gown she had worked so long to make. A groan escaped her lips.

Valerie threw her arms into the air and screeched in a high pitch. "Are you insane?"

"What are you doing?" Simon demanded.

Cole spread her arms to expose her soiled attire. "If a socialite like Valerie covers her gown in punch, then it must be the latest in fashion."

Blake circled her as he laughed. "All young ladies will be wearing punch-splattered gowns this season."

Jess tugged Davy toward the door and safety. Cole twirled. "Now we're both the belles of the ball."

"I always liked strawberries." Simon's voice was husky, his eyes shadowed by something dark and sinister. He offered his handkerchief.

Valerie snatched it. "Is that clumsy oaf your friend?" She searched the room for Davy.

Cole shrugged. "I never saw him before."

"What am I going to do about my new gown? It's ruined." Valerie's face puckered as if she would burst into tears.

"Soak it in some water," Cole said. "It'll be fine." She hoped.

"For the rag you're wearing, but this is silk," Valerie shrieked.

"My gown is silk, too, and I labored more for the purchase and sewing of my gown than you did for yours." Cole spun on her heels, the sole sticking to the floor where a puddle of punch had pooled.

Blake took the empty punch glass from her grasp and handed it to the waiter. "You can't leave now." He signaled the conductor and took Cole into his arms for a dance.

"I can't dance. I'm covered in punch."

"Show them you don't care." It was a challenge she couldn't refuse. He led her in the waltz. Whether through fear of being stained by her gown or in awe of her bravado, the other dancers moved to the sidelines, watching as Blake twirled her around the dance floor. The gaslights blurred as he spun her in the fast steps to the three beat music. She clung to his shoulder. "I'm going to faint."

"You're not the type." He pulled her tighter against his chest.

"You'll stain your shirt."

"And everyone will know I was the man holding you in my arms."

The music ended, and the guests clapped. "You're truly the belle of the ball." Blake bowed at the waist.

She made a slight curtsy, acknowledging their praise, but when she rose, Margaret was glaring at her. "I think I've overstayed my welcome."

He escorted her toward the door. "Is Logan waiting for you?"

"If Jess followed directions, they all ran."

"You're a brave soldier to sacrifice your gown and dignity to save a poor assistant photographer." Blake made a sweeping bow. "I admire you."

"Don't be a ninny. If you want to help, escort me home."

"Let me retrieve my hat."

"I have a lace shawl." Cole searched in her reticule for the claim check. She handed him the cork circle with a number burned in it.

Cole paused near the reception door. The food had been eaten, the harder liquor consumed, and all that remained of the punch was a few strawberries floating in a puddle in the bottom.

Margaret, who had escaped any punch but a few flecks, was being comforted by her mother, who hadn't forgotten her manners and was bidding farewell to guests. Was Margaret sobbing because of some imagined damage to her gown or because no one was being attentive? Darius, her normally doting father, was absent along with Simon. Valerie was browbeating a maid who offered her a towel.

Cole searched for a maid, but a young male hotel employee approached her instead. "Do you have a towel?"

He handed her a key. "This room is at your disposal to remove your gown. A maid will have it cleaned and returned to you."

Cole examined the key with room 322 etched on the leather clasp. "Thank you, but all I need is a towel." Willard's Hotel knew how to treat its guests, even those not staying at the hotel. She searched for the young man to return the key, but he had disappeared.

Valerie snatched the key from her hand. "Did he say a maid would clean my dress?"

My dress. "I thought you had a room."

"Amelia has the key, and she blames me for

ruining Margaret's reception. They threatened not to take me to Europe." She displayed her skirt. "I was the victim." She swiped at a stain. "My whole future depends on remaining in their good graces."

"It was an accident," Cole said. "I'm sure the Radcliffs won't hold this little incident against you."

"You don't know the Radcliffs." Valerie jerked her head toward Margaret and her mother in the other room. "I'll have to listen to Margaret whine about how I ruined everything, and then I'll have to apologize."

"Do you want me to talk to her?"

"You? She thinks you're attempting to steal Simon from her."

"I was dancing with Blake."

"Only to make Simon jealous."

Cole handed her the key. "Margaret can have Simon, and you can have this room."

She looked past Cole's shoulder. "If the maid can't clean my dress, what will I do?" She burst into sobs.

Blake spoke from behind her. "Turn off the tears, Valerie, or I'll cut off your allowance immediately instead of in six months."

She lifted her head, her eyes dry. "Your pitiful allowance won't last six months if I have to replace gowns like this one."

"If you need more money, work for it." Blake draped Cole's shawl around her shoulders. "Other women do."

"The only work I enjoy is giving orders to the servants." Valerie clutched the key and ascended the staircase.

Blake stopped at the desk. "Do you know what room Valerie went to? If the maid can't clean the stains,

I'll pay for a new dress. That may stop her complaining for a few minutes."

"You act tough, but you have a tender heart." It was a good combination. "The key had room 322 on it."

"I hate that I let her take advantage of me. I'll be glad when some man takes her off my hands."

"No responsibilities." She wouldn't become one of them.

Blake wrote a message for Valerie. "Can you have this note delivered to room 322?"

The clerk took the note. "I'll see that Mr. Blackwater gets your message."

"Mr. Simon Blackwater?"

"He's in room 322."

Cole didn't need anyone to explain the implications. Simon must have paid the employee to give her his key. But for what mischief? "Valerie." Cole had to hurry to keep pace with Blake. Her corset didn't give her much room to breathe, and she labored for air by the time they reached the third floor. She paused as Blake pounded on the door.

A woman screamed inside the room.

Blake stepped back and turned his shoulder to the door.

"Wait!" Cole turned the knob. Valerie hadn't locked the door behind her. The gaslight from the hallway sconce cast a ribbon of light to reveal Valerie's discarded dress, petticoat and crinoline heaped on the floor. She was on the bed, hidden in shadows. Her white stockings and bloomers kicked up and down in a struggle. A naked man straddled her, his butt high in the air as he wrestled to control her.

Blake smacked the nearest body part, the sound

echoing in the darkness. "Get off, you bastard!"

Simon turned his head, a wild expression on his face as he panted, his arms holding Valerie down, his knee forcing her legs apart. "I'll give you a turn once I break her in."

"Are you insane? Leave her alone!" Cole grabbed a pitcher on the washstand and tossed water on him.

Simon bolted off the opposite side of the bed and stared at the intruders. "Colleen?" Simon studied the woman on the bed, his eyes widening when he recognized her. "What are you doing here, Valerie?"

Valerie pointed at Simon and screamed.

Cole wrapped the quilt from the bed around Valerie's trembling shoulders. The cold water hadn't abated Simon's arousal.

Blake tossed a pillow. "Cover up!"

Simon held the pillow to his groin and attempted to approach. "This isn't what it appears."

"Stay where you are." Blake turned to Valerie. "Tell us what happened."

Valerie sobbed, interrupted by quick, gulping gasps. "The maid unhooked my gown and went to fetch a robe. I entered the room, but the gaslight wouldn't work. I undressed and someone grabbed me." She turned to Simon. "How could you?"

"I didn't know it was you." Simon turned on the gaslight, his bare butt exposed to the others.

"You weren't his intended victim," Blake growled.

"Did you pay that boy to give me your room key?" Cole demanded. "You wanted to lure me here?"

Valerie turned to Colleen. "Why would he want to attack you?"

"He was courting me back home in Ohio until I

read about his engagement in the local paper."

"That doesn't explain this."

"Simon couldn't have her any other way," Blake said.

"It was a harmless joke." Simon looked at Cole. "I wasn't going to hurt you."

What if she had taken the key and come into room 322? She shuddered. "When does raping a woman not hurt?"

"Rape? I was going to make love to you. Every woman has a first time. You'd thank me afterwards."

"How can men believe that?"

Simon shrugged. "Don't women wait for their honeymoon for the same reason?"

"Most of them choose their husbands." Cole gathered Valerie's discarded clothes. "And what about your honeymoon? Have you forgotten you're engaged to Margaret Radcliff?"

Valerie gathered the quilt around her undergarments and hobbled to a screen in the corner. Cole handed her the crinoline, followed by the petticoat and gown. Blake tossed Simon his clothes. "Put these on."

Chapter Twenty-Six

Simon put on his shirt which was long enough to cover his private parts. He stepped into his trousers. "I haven't forgotten about Margaret, but you attended our reception. I thought you reconsidered my proposal."

Valerie poked her head out behind the side of the screen. "You asked her to marry you?"

"It wasn't an honorable proposal," Cole explained. "He wanted me to be his mistress."

"And she threw him out."

Simon confronted Blake. "How do you know?"

Blake rubbed his shoulder. "I was resting in the parlor reading a book and had fallen asleep when you met with Miss Colleen."

Simon buttoned his trousers. "You were the man who overhead everything?"

"I considered it rude to interrupt." He clenched his teeth. "At first." He turned to Cole. "Take Valerie out into the hall."

Cole glanced over her shoulder to see Blake hurl a fist into Simon's face. His shoulder was definitely healed. Through the door, she heard crashing and a few groans.

Blake joined them. His knuckles had blood on them, but he wiped them clean with a towel he had taken from the room. Simon would think twice before assaulting another woman. They made their way to the stairs. "Are you going to tell Margaret about her presidential candidate?"

Valerie paused, her face distorted in confusion. "Who?"

"You don't know about their ambitions to make Simon president of the United States?"

"Simon?" Valerie laughed, her snorting echoing in the stairway.

"Then you're going to tell Margaret what you know about Simon."

"Don't be stupid. Even if she believes me, she won't admit it. Pride will dictate she kick me out. I'll have to live with my mother and new stepfather."

"Would that be so awful?"

"How am I going to find a rich husband at my stepfather's church?"

"Not all the money in the world would make me want to marry a man like Simon," Cole said.

Valerie stopped at the door to the room she shared with Margaret and Amelia. "Sometimes you have to make sacrifices for security. After a couple of babies, a wife is glad to send her husband off to a mistress."

"What about love?"

"I hope I never succumb to its sickness." Valerie sighed. "I'll tell Amelia about Simon in the morning. She's not blinded by love for Simon, but she's loyal to her daughter. If they kick me out, it'll be easier to leave after a good night's rest." Valerie twittered. "Maybe Amelia will want me to stay around and help comfort Margaret after the honeymoon."

Cole hugged her, their punch covered gowns sticking in the release. "Are you sure you're all right?"

"Simon didn't do any damage," she confessed. "He

scared me more than anything."

Cole glanced at Blake. "I wonder how Simon will explain his face?"

"He'll think of a story by morning," Blake said. "His kind has an excuse for everything."

Valerie turned to Blake. "Why couldn't I make you fall in love with me?" Valerie shook her head, her fingers going to a loose tendril. She attempted to smooth it into place. "You always did the right thing, including taking care of my mother and me."

"You were family. Still are," he amended. "If you ever need anything, ask." He kissed her cheek.

Valerie took a deep breath and knocked on the door.

"Who is it?"

"It's Valerie. I don't have a key."

Amelia opened the door. "We wondered where you had gone. Margaret has already gone to bed." She looked at Cole and Blake. "I'm sure you understand why I can't invite you in."

They said their good-byes.

****

The night air was beginning to cool, and Cole wrapped her shawl about her bare shoulders. "I can't help but worry about Valerie. Do you think she'll be all right?"

"She's a graduate of Miss Wellington's School for Young Ladies. She'll survive," Blake said.

"Were you serious about them grooming Simon to become president?"

"It took every ounce of self-control not to laugh."

Cole shook her head, her curls bouncing with the gesture. "Let's hope the voters never sink so low to elect an egotistical moron for president."

"Sounds like you're no longer a fan of Simon."

"When you're not in love with a man, you can see his faults more clearly. Margaret may be willing to live with a lie, but I feel like I escaped a horrible future. What made Simon change so drastically, or was he always like this and I never noticed?"

"Darius wants a companion for his perverted pursuits, and Simon is more than willing to accompany him." Blake coughed. "About that night. I'd like to explain."

"You said you didn't go upstairs."

"I didn't."

"I believe you."

Blake stopped her. "You do?"

"When we first met I thought you were a cad because you invited me to share the bed on the *Irish Rose*. I thought you were like Simon."

"I was never like him."

"Then why were you so bold?"

Blake turned away. "What can I say? You dazzled me with your beauty." He faced her, his stormy eyes begging for understanding. "I've never invited a woman to share my bed before, but I threw caution to the wind."

Never? "What if I had said yes?"

Blake ran his fingers through his hair. "I don't know. I never thought that far ahead. I was afraid if I said nothing, I would regret it for the rest of my life. I don't blame you for being angry."

"I'd be angry if you didn't show an interest in me. I was upset about Simon and took it out on you. Besides, I wasn't dressed like a lady."

"You were barefoot and swaggered on the deck like you owned it."

"I don't swagger."

"Brat, you define the word."

"I thought you looked like a pirate with your scraggly beard." She touched his clean-shaven cheek. "I miss the whiskers."

"I'll grow them for you."

"I won't see you once you leave for the army."

"Officers can visit home."

"Where is your home, Blake?"

"Where ever you are." He meant it.

"I'm proud you're joining."

"Proud? After everything Jake and the Herbruck boys have told you? War is a miserable, cold, life-threatening experience. I'm an idiot for joining."

"If you believe that, then why not be like Simon? Sit back and make money during this war. Then gloat about your wise choices. How you outfoxed everyone."

"I can't do that," Blake said. "Men like Simon don't understand. Some values are worth fighting for. And dying for. And this is one of them. If the Confederacy wins, slavery continues. And no matter what anyone says, this fight is about slavery. How could I look at someone wearing shackles with their back striped with scars and say I didn't want to stop their suffering because I might have to march all day without food or water? I might have to fight in the heat of summer with bullets whizzing past my head. Slavery could have been solved by a signature on a piece of paper, but it's come to this. War is ugly and destructive, but it's necessary to force someone's hand when they refuse to do what's right."

He wasn't fighting for glory or fame. He was fighting for a cause he believed in. A cause she cherished. "When do you leave?"

"Not for a while. The paperwork is unbelievable. I may be drafted before I receive my commission."

She ran her fingertips along his sleeve. "You still want me to take care of your properties?"

His smoky gaze studied her. "You said you didn't want to. You wanted to be free to find a husband."

"I thought you had a mistress." She bit her bottom lip. "Can I change my mind?"

He pulled her into his arms. "I'm counting on it."

"Won't it look strange that you give me control of your wealth but not your name?"

"You want me to make you a wealthy widow?"

She hit his chest with her fist. "Sometimes you make me so angry."

He grabbed her before she could escape. "I've prided myself on keeping my distance, but tonight with Simon and that gown." His mouth lowered and claimed hers. His kiss was forceful, full of anger, but as she responded, he calmed, seeking mutual pleasure.

The crowd jostled them. Cole pulled away, looking around as people passed by. A man with a heavy bag hustled by, barely acknowledging them. Several others hurried past, clutching belongings. "It looks as if they're fleeing."

Blake called to a man on horseback. "What's happening?"

"Don't you see the flames in the southwest?"

Blake turned, searching past the roofs and treetops. The sky was lighter in the distance. "What is it?"

"Stonewall Jackson has flanked the Union army.

He's at Manassas Junction. He'll be here by dawn."

Cole didn't wait for further explanation. She hurried to Pierce House. The lights were on. Inside Logan, Jem, and Jess were standing in the parlor. They were still dressed in the formal clothes they had worn at Willard's. Deidre, who had been at the neighbor's house, was on the couch, asleep.

"Have you heard?" Logan asked.

Blake rested his hand on Cole's waist. "Something about Jackson taking Manassas."

"We heard rumors at Willard's, but it's true. Stonewall Jackson captured the Union pickets at Bristoe Station, derailed the railroad cars, and cut the telegraph lines," Logan said. "The fire is at Manassas Junction. Jackson and his men took what Union supplies they could carry and burned the rest."

Blake's jaw was set in a tight clench. "Where's Pope?"

"He was at the Rappahannock River when Jackson flanked him. Now he's heading for Manassas Junction."

"And what is between Manassas and Washington City?" Jem demanded. "A few regiments posted on Arlington Heights."

Logan put his arm around his wife.

"The boys were right," Cole said. "Our generals are always one step behind Jackson. He'll be in Washington City tomorrow having tea with the president and his cabinet."

"It would be best if you took your wife, her sisters, and Deidre north," Blake said.

"We wouldn't reach the outskirts of town with that mob in the way," Cole said. "We had to fight through it to reach Pierce House."

"We'll wait until morning," Logan said. "The telegraph lines will be working, and we'll know the situation."

"We're not going anywhere," Jem said. "This is our home."

"Jackson is a stone's throw away," Blake warned.

"The Ohio boys wouldn't let Jackson beat them," Cole said. "Not all the way back to Washington City."

"There's only a handful of them." Blake turned to Logan. "Where's McClellan? Can't he help?"

"McClellan is dawdling in the Peninsula, hoping Pope fails. He may get his wish. Only we may be the ones to pay."

"Do you think Lee will attack Washington City?" Blake demanded.

"He no longer fears McClellan attacking Richmond. It's the quickest way to end the war," Logan said.

Jem gasped. "With a Confederate victory?"

Logan hugged her. "We won't let them win, but move food and blankets to the cellar."

"The boys will make a stand, and we can't help hiding in a cellar," Cole said. "We better gather bandages and medicines. They'll evacuate the wounded to Alexandria."

Chapter Twenty-Seven

The wounded began arriving from Manassas, casualties from the Second Battle of Bull Run. Cole asked, but none of them had news of the Ohio boys. Blake was saving a few beds at the Mermaid's Mirth if any of them were among the wounded. They offered food and water to those arriving as soldiers were sorted. Officers were taken care of first and transported to the hospitals. Enlisted men were divided into three groups. Those who would survive, those who wouldn't, and those who had died during transportation.

The three-day battle had ended, but the wounded continued to flow into the city. The Union army had retreated to Fairfax Courthouse. If the Confederacy took it, Alexandria and the surrounding barricades would be the final defense line.

How could the Union lose the war? They had more men, more supplies, and they were fighting for a righteous cause. Lincoln had waited too long to draft more men. Cole put her bucket of water on the ground and handed a dipper to one of the men waiting for an ambulance.

She wiped her forehead with the end of the scarf covering her head. Suddenly, she was lifted off her feet and swirled around. She screamed. Blake, who had been loading an ambulance, nearly dropped his patient. Jess ran toward her.

"Jake Donovan!" Jess shouted when she recognized her cousin, his arms still around Cole.

Cole turned and smacked his chest. "I thought you were a Rebel who had broken through the lines." She choked on a cloud of smoky dust her hands had released from his soot-covered coat.

Ed had joined Jess, taking her hand in his. "You boys smell like smoke."

"We've been to a few barbecues," Jake said. "Been having a grand time at the rear of the army."

"We had our pick of the loot before sending it up in smoke," Ed added.

"We had a fine meal, new clothes, and each of us claimed a sword." Jake withdrew a sword from the scabbard strapped to his waist.

Sid tipped his hat when he joined them, revealing a white forehead above his blackened face. "Good to see you, ladies. Blake."

"No one had any news of you," Cole said. "We thought you were captured."

Blake examined Jake's sword. "Didn't you fight at Bull Run?"

"No, we were at the end of the Union line at Bristoe Station below Manassas during the fighting," Jake said. "They forgot all about us. Pope and the rest of the army headed north to Centreville and left us behind."

Cole looked from Jake to Sid. "Why would they do that?"

"We were ordered to burn nearly a hundred railroad cars of supplies." Jake pounded his chest, sending up a cloud of acrid smoke. "That's where we picked out our new clothes and a hearty meal." He patted his thick haversack.

"I have some nice cigars meant for the officers if you would like one." Sid offered Blake a smoke. He declined. "Fool officers gave us orders to torch the train cars from the wrong side of the tracks. We had to jump through the flames to reach the east side away from the Confederate army. To make it even more difficult, the ammunition started firing."

"We were ducking and dodging our own bullets." Jake hollered and raised his dusty hat into the air. "It was a wild adventure."

The Ohio boys had lost their minds. "Where were the Confederates?"

"Between us and the Union army," Sid said. "We had to head east and then north to get around them."

"On the banks of Bull Run we could see the smoldering remains of the battlefield," Jake said. "Must have been fierce. We all wanted to be in the fighting but knew we were lucky to have been spared."

"It was worse than the first time," Sid said. "At least I was familiar with the landscape. We were nearly to Centreville when they ordered us to head for Washington City."

"Heard Jackson had flanked Pope, again," Jake said. "Our general is an idiot."

Blake looked around. "You can say that and not be charged with insubordination?"

"No secret. Even the officers have been criticizing his command."

"When we arrived at Fairfax Station, we were ordered north to Chantilly Station where Jackson had picked a fight. Brigadier General Philip Kearny's division was marching parallel to ours and was ordered into the battle," Sid said. "Kearny was killed. He'll be missed."

"That was the strangest fight I ever experienced," Ed said. "The noise of battle was challenged by the thunder and lightning. It was as if God had joined the fight."

"We were in reserve and observed from beneath tarps," Jake said. "Jackson retreated at nightfall, and we marched through the rain to Fairfax Station."

"It'll give me nightmares until I die," Ed said. "The station was lit by lamps and the occasional flash of lightning. The surgeons had placed their operating tables on the platform end to end, and men were placed on them as the sawbones performed their gruesome work. After they were done cutting and sawing, the men were loaded on the train or ambulances and sent here."

Cole glanced around. "They've kept us busy."

"We would have been here sooner but were so exhausted, we lay down on the ground in the cold rain and slept," Jake said. "This morning we torched the Union supplies at Fairfax Station and marched here."

Jess grabbed Ed's arm. "Then Lee is attacking the city!"

"The general is too smart to attack our defenses," Jake said. "Lee will draw us out to meet him on his ground."

Sid slapped his hat against his pants. "Looks like they want us to head out."

"But you only arrived," Cole said.

"Walk with us," Jake suggested.

"I'll fetch the wagon and follow you," Blake said.

Cole and Jess walked beside the regiment as it

marched along the Potomac River to the shelter of Fort Albany, an earthwork bastion built to guard the approach to Long Bridge.

Jake dropped his haversack, canteen, and backpack. "Looks like we'll be spending the night here."

"We'll come by in the morning with food," Cole promised. "Unless you're stuffed from your feast."

"We're always hungry," Jake said. "How are you doing, cousin? You look worried."

"Not anymore. The sight of you has answered my prayers."

"Don't worry about me, Cole, darlin'. I'm having a grand time. Anybody here want to quit and return to your mamas?"

"I ain't complaining," Sid said, removing his cap. "But I sure would like to finish this war sooner than later."

Blake's wagon approached, and Jake waved. "Here's your ride. Ed offered his arm to Jess. "I'll walk with you for a spell."

Cole joined Blake by his wagon. Four men were loaded in the back. "I'm glad the Ohio boys weren't hurt, but I picked up a few who weren't as lucky."

Jake helped Cole board. "You better cross the bridge before darkness sets in."

He looked around. "Where's Jess?"

"She's saying good-bye to Ed."

****

The next day Cole and Jess gathered bread and medical supplies. Blake arrived at Pierce House with his wagon. "They're gone."

"What do you mean?"

"We promised to take them supplies," Jess argued. "They can't be gone."

"Broke camp this morning and headed to Maryland."

"But that's north." The battles were in the south.

Logan hurried down the street toward them. He had only left for work at the Treasury building an hour ago. He surveyed the group. "I take it you've heard."

Jess swiped at a tear. "The boys are heading to Maryland."

"Rumor is Lee is in Maryland." Blake looked at Logan. "The victory at Bull Run has gone to his head. He thinks he's going to win this war."

"I underestimated him," Logan said.

"And so did Pope," Blake added.

"Pope is out, and McClellan is in," Logan said. "The Ohio boys are in the Army of the Potomac in the Twelfth Corps with Brigadier General Geary in command of the division." He paused. "The war department thinks reorganization is the answer."

"Do they think changing the name of the army is going to win the war?" Cole asked. "McClellan couldn't win in the Peninsula campaign when he had the advantage. He's against Lee, Longstreet, and Jackson, and nobody knows the Shenandoah Valley better than Stonewall."

"The Ohio boys are familiar with the terrain," Blake reminded her.

"Remember what Sid said. Lee won't attack Washington City," Cole said. "He'll draw the Union army to a location of his choosing."

Blake looked at Logan. "I hope McClellan knows what he's doing."

"So do the men in blue."

****

Jem examined the boxes of medical supplies Cole and Jess were filling. "I think you can fit more bandages in this one."

Neither Jess nor Cole argued. They didn't mind Jem's supervision as long as she didn't do the work. Her morning sickness had passed, but the stress of a battle so close had everyone's nerves on edge. Work kept them too busy to think about the impending battle.

"Why do we need to pack everything so carefully?"

"Clara Barton is taking these supplies to the battlefield."

Cole shook her head. "That woman is insane."

"Why, I thought you admired her. The other day…" Cole elbowed Jess to silence her.

"She is brave, but it's awfully dangerous to go so close to the battle," Cole said.

"She's saving lives." Jem continued to examine the boxes. "The sooner the men receive care, the more likely they'll survive their wounds. Some men lie on the ground all day and night. And the longer they lie in the open without water or medical care, the more likely they die."

"By the time the wounded reach Alexandria, they're in bad shape," Cole agreed. "Does Miss Barton need help?"

"She's gathering a team to take with her."

"We could go," Jess volunteered.

"She's taking male nurses," Jem said. "I don't know about any women volunteers."

"Why is Miss Barton going to a battle site, but she

isn't taking any other women?" Cole asked.

"It's dangerous."

"I'm not afraid," Jess said.

"Haven't you been reading Ed's letters?" Cole argued. "A battlefield is a dangerous place."

Jem looked from Cole to Jess. "Dismiss any notions you might be entertaining. It's scary enough here."

Cole put her arm around Jess. "We like staying where it's safe."

"I might believe that if I didn't know you better."

****

Jess plucked a strand of Cole's hair from her braid and raised her scissors. "Are you sure?"

"Cut the top layer like yours."

"We're lucky we have thick hair." Jess cut Cole's hair, enough to frame her face and match her own shorter layers. They braided the remaining length in a single braid down the back. Each stared at the strange reflections in the mirror.

"Do you think we can pass for men?"

"You will. I'm going to need a little help." Cole loosened the lacings on her corset and raised it over her breasts. "Pull." The corset flattened her chest. She wadded a petticoat around her waist to thicken it, and Jess finished lacing the lower part of the corset to hold the padding in place. Cole arranged the lacings on the corset Jess wore to disguise any curves.

Their clothes were worn cast offs donated by civilians to clothe former slaves or for soldiers returning home. They wore their corset covers and bloomers under the linen shirts and wool trousers. They tucked their braids beneath the shirts. The suspenders kept the loose pants from falling, and the long wool jackets covered any hint of femininity. They added kerchiefs, gloves, and large brimmed, slouch hats to finish the disguise.

"How do you do, Cole Beecher," Jess said in her deepest voice.

"Fine day for a battle, Jess Beecher."

Cole opened the door and peered around. "Are you sure Jem left?"

"I don't hear anything."

"We'll find Miss Barton's wagons and slip inside one."

They had reached the foyer when a familiar voice stopped them. "Where do you think you're going dressed like that?"

Jem stood in the hallway, her hands on her hips.

Cole stared at her disapproving sister. "I thought you left."

She lifted the special basket she had taken on her journeys. "You'll need something to eat. You won't be able to help if you're ill from hunger."

"You're not going to talk us out of this?" Cole took the container of food. "You always said we were monsters for our antics."

"I think this is courageous. But be careful. I'm responsible for you, and I wouldn't want Papa and Mama to think I encouraged you." Jem fought tears. "If I wasn't expecting, I'd go with you." She pointed at the basket. "That helped me when I traveled to Manassas and Richmond. I hope it brings you the same luck."

They hugged Jem, who burst into tears. "Don't you dare get killed."

"Where do we find Miss Barton's wagons?"

"I took care of that while you were donning your disguises." Jem opened the door. Outside was Blake's team of draft horses hitched to his wagon, which was filled with water barrels, buckets, lanterns, and medical supplies.

Cole tugged on her gloves. "Blake is letting us borrow his wagon?"

"Not exactly."

Blake stepped out from behind the team. He was wearing a sack coat and wide brimmed hat. He strode to her, lifted her hat, and examined her hair. "What have you done?"

She grabbed her hat from his hands. "You're not talking us out of this."

He looked at Jem. "I thought you were the sensible one."

"I told Clara Barton my cousins would deliver the supplies, and they had medical training," Jem said. "She knows they're following her wagons."

Blake pointed to the bench seat. "Get aboard."

"You're not going to stop us?"

"I must be as insane as you are. I'm going with you."

Cole stood by the wagon, waiting for him to help her board. "Aren't you going to help?"

"You're not some helpless female. A young chap like you ought to be able to climb aboard a wagon."

"He's right," Jess agreed. "He can't treat us like women if we're going to fool anyone."

"He doesn't have to enjoy it." Cole waited for Jess to board and followed without any help from Blake.

He took the reins and headed north. They fell in line with Clara's wagons behind the army's supply teams. "This is a fool's journey."

Cole tugged on her boot. It was too big, but she had stuffed the toe. "You're one of the fools."

"I'm not letting you go to Maryland alone," Blake said. "Miss Jenny threatened to go if I didn't agree to escort you. She reminded me about how she traveled alone to Richmond. Does insanity run in your family?"

"You don't have to do this," Cole argued.

"Do you think I could sleep knowing you're in enemy territory?"

Logan had followed Jem into Southern territory because he was in love with her. Blake had never said the words, but his actions spoke volumes.

Jess looked around. "Where do you think Lee and Jackson are?"

"With our luck, he'll flank the army and sneak up behind us."

Jess and Cole looked behind them through the opening of the canvas covering the wagon. "Don't be funny."

"I'm not joking." He looked at the bed of the wagon. A couple of stretchers had been placed above the supplies. "You might want to sleep while you can."

Cole stopped Jess from moving from the seat. "How do we know you won't turn around and head back to Pierce House?"

"We've come this far. Seems a pity we miss the party."

Cole nodded to Jess. "We'll take turns. You sleep, and I'll make sure Blake doesn't get lost."

Chapter Twenty-Eight

The countryside was pretty in September. Red brick homes stood out against fields of yellow grain. Indian corn remained on the husk and would be harvested later to feed the cattle in the field when snow fell.

News filtered back through the lines. The Twelfth Corps, which included the Ohio boys, was leading the way with Geary's division in front.

"That's a new position for them," Cole joked. "They're usually in the rear."

It was Sunday, September 14 when they reached the Monocacy River where the Baltimore and Ohio railroad normally crossed.

"Isn't there a bridge?"

"Lee blew it up." Blake pointed to the remains of an iron railroad bridge. Soldiers were piling supplies from the train cars along the bank while others worked to repair the damage.

They had nearly reached Frederick the next morning when the familiar faces of Ed and the other men in the Twenty-ninth greeted them.

"Aren't you marching the wrong way?" Blake asked.

"We've been ordered back to the Monocacy River to guard the supplies at the railroad."

"They were piling them up when we passed."

313

Ed grinned. "They love sending us to the rear. That doesn't guarantee no fighting."

"Where's the Seventh?" Blake asked.

"We're on our own for this job."

"Why your regiment?"

"We're down to two officers." Ed shook his head. "Like we don't know how to fight." He raised his rifle and aimed at a tree. "Point at the enemy, and we can do the rest."

Jess relaxed next to Cole. "Then you won't face any fighting."

Ed stared. "Hey, you look familiar."

Jess lifted her hat. "Hello, Ed."

He turned on Blake. "What do you mean bringing them here?"

"Do you think I could have stopped them?" Blake tipped his hat back. "Lee and Jackson don't stand a chance against them."

It was a joke, but Blake's voice hinted at hidden pride. He of all people would understand why they were risking their lives for a cause. He planned to do the same.

Ed handed Jess his revolver. "I won't need it. You're the best shot I know. Use it if you have to."

Her face glowed. "Thank you, Ed."

Cole bumped Blake's side. "Why don't you give me gifts as nice as that?"

"I thought you preferred knives. Do you even know how to shoot?"

"I taught Jess."

"I thought she won the shooting contest."

"She did. I didn't compete."

"Why not?"

She crossed her arms. "My bosom had developed and was in the way."

He surveyed her coat. "Where are they now?"

"Beneath my corset. No peeking allowed."

He laughed. "If I survive this, I'm peeking."

****

The teamster wagons' convoy had fallen behind the Barton wagons, but the teamsters reclaimed the road and forced the medical wagons into the ditch. Instead of fighting for the narrow road, Clara Barton ordered everyone to remain beside the road and wait until the teamsters passed.

Blake napped in the wagon on one of the cots. Jess slept on the other while Cole remained seated on the bench, her kerchief covering her nose and mouth while the army teams stirred up dust in their passing. Cole took her turn sleeping and woke when it was dusk.

The driver in front of them informed them they were heading out. "Follow my lantern."

They drove through the night and arrived in the early hours of September 16, parking their wagons near the bank of Antietam Creek. Farms dotted the landscape with fields of tall corn forming a patchwork between them. The soldiers had arrived the day before, but McClellan in his usual hesitant manner, was taking his time to face Lee, who was entrenched along the roads outside Sharpsburg.

While Clara searched for Medical Director Doctor James Dunn, Blake and the girls searched for the Seventh Ohio. They were nearby on the northern end of the camp.

Sid was setting up a tent although others had chosen to sleep wrapped in blankets. Jake greeted Blake and stared at Jess and Cole. "What are you doing here?"

"Cole and Jess are helping Miss Barton," Blake said.

Sid overheard. "Miss Barton is here?"

"She's checking in with the doctor."

"Headquarters are at the Pry House," Sid said. "Major General George McClellan can't make a decision without debating it for several days."

"Then you won't fight tomorrow?"

"We'll go into battle," Jake said. "Wish they hadn't sent the Twenty-ninth away. We always fight side by side."

"We passed Ed on his way to the river," Jess said.

"I bet you fooled him with your flimsy disguises."

"I had to remove my hat," Jess said.

"I'll have a word with you," Jake said to Blake. They walked a distance to talk in private.

"What if Jake sends us home?" Jess asked.

"I'd like to see him try."

Jess pointed to a man who was giving Sid a flask, which he put in a pull-string sack. Another man gave him a deck of cards. "What is Sid doing?"

Cole motioned him near. "Hey, Sid, what's with the bag?"

"I'm gathering vices."

"What?"

He loosened the drawstring opening of the cloth ditty bag. Inside were playing cards, dice, tobacco, the flask, and a few photographs of scantily clad women. Blake had returned and peered inside. "No photographs of the fair Beecher sisters?"

"They're not a vice." Sid stared at Cole and Jess. "They're inspiration."

Cole didn't understand why the men were giving up their belongings. "Why are you gathering vices?"

Sid turned his attention to Blake. "The men like to rid themselves of anything that might hinder their way to a heavenly hereafter."

"They'll read their Bibles and say their prayers tonight," Jake said. "This is a big one."

"Let's hope Jackson stays at Harpers Ferry," Sid added.

"Jackson isn't with Lee?" Blake asked.

"Lee split his forces."

"Harpers Ferry is pretty far away," Blake said. "He couldn't make the battle in time if it's tomorrow."

"You ain't fought Jackson," Sid said. "His men travel light and fast. Let's hope McClellan doesn't wait until noon to fire the first shot."

Jake handed Cole his field glasses. "You keep a safe distance away and watch the battle through these."

When Blake and the girls returned to the wagons, Clara told them they had been ordered to remain on the east side of Antietam Creek. Jess slept on the bench seat while Cole and Blake each took a cot, but sleep didn't come easy.

"Do you think it's a vice for us to sleep side by side in the back of the wagon?" Cole asked from her cot.

"Not if you stay in yours and I stay in mine," Blake answered.

"Can I pretend you're holding me?"

"You scared, brat?"

"Terrified."

He took her hand and placed it on his heart. "So am I."

As dawn streamed across the dew covered stalks of corn, the first shots echoed in the distance. "It's begun." Blake stood at the back of the wagon, peering through Jake's field glasses.

Cole stepped over the supplies and joined Blake. "Where are the Ohio boys?"

"They crossed the river during the night."

Reports of the battle filtered to them in bits and pieces. The Second and Twelfth Corps had moved along the Hagerstown Turnpike to Dunker Church. Blake drew a crude map to follow the battle news. Hagerstown Turnpike ran north and south with a cluster of trees near Dunker Church. Smoketown Road angled from the church northeast through cornfields to another clump of trees. He used a round rock to mark the position of the Seventh Ohio.

Cole stood on the bench seat of the wagon, peering through the field glasses. "I see them going into the cornfields, but I don't see anybody coming out. The smoke from the cannons and muskets is too thick."

Blake tugged on her pant leg. "Hello, Miss Barton," he called out.

Cole sat down, hiding the field glasses behind her.

"Does your wagon have medical supplies?"

"Yes, ma'am."

"There's a field hospital on the farm northwest of here. I need you to deliver your supplies."

"I thought we were ordered to stay on this side of the river, ma'am."

"Am I wearing a uniform? Those orders are for military men."

Cole looked at the army supply wagons. "Why don't they order them to go?"

Clara's sarcasm was thinly veiled. "They are to remain safely behind lines to prevent capture by the Confederates."

Capture. Cole swallowed. Her throat was dry. "Should we return after delivering the supplies?"

"Only if you're not needed. I'm taking supplies to another field hospital. The wounded are already overwhelming the doctors."

Blake hitched Romulus and Remus. "Stay in the back, on your bellies," he ordered the girls. "I'll drive."

They squeezed between the supplies and didn't speak until they reached the farm. A barn had been transformed into a field hospital. Hundreds of men were on the ground in disorganized clusters, waiting for the surgeon to operate. Fresh from the battlefield, their skin was black from powder, uniforms torn and bloodied. Some had kerchiefs made from scrap material to stench the flow of blood while others pressed corn leaves against oozing wounds. Moaning and an occasional scream bore witness of their suffering. Others stared with vacant eyes, unwilling to admit they were dying.

Cole took a box from Jess. "How could there be so many victims of the battle so soon?"

A man wearing a blood-stained apron ran toward the wagon. "Do you have bandages?"

Cole opened the lid to the box she carried. Inside were neatly rolled cloths. He grabbed it and told her to find more. She took a box from Jess and followed. The surgeons had taken the barn doors and set them across sawhorses to form their surgical tables. The doctor grabbed a roll from her box, staining the white fabric red with his blood-covered hands. "I've been using corn leaves to stop the bleeding."

Cole removed the bandages, arranging them on a barrel lid. Blake carried in additional boxes. "Where's Jess?"

"I filled a couple of buckets. She's... I mean he's giving water to the wounded."

"The surgeon was in the middle of sawing the tibia bone on his patient. "Any of you have needles and thread?"

"I have some," Cole said. "I can sew a wound, too."

"Good. I can't grip a needle."

Blood coated his slippery fingers. She nodded and searched for the needles among the supplies.

Blake carried the last box inside. "Everything is in the barn. How can I help?"

"Take over for Jess and send...him in here. I can't keep up."

Blake looked at the torn body on the makeshift operating table and then met her gaze. "You all right?"

"I can't think or feel anything now. Maybe when it's over." Maybe never.

The battle ended in the late afternoon, but the battered men kept coming. Cole's fingers were numb from shoving needles through jagged flesh, linking edges that had been shredded apart. The doctor removed twisted and deformed lead balls, tossing them in a shallow pan used for holding milk for the barn cats, who had been scared off by the strangers. If the lead ball had shattered bones, the surgeon sighed, picked up his knife, and cut the skin, baring what remained of the bone and sawed off the rough edges. Cole tied off the arteries and stitched the flap of skin over the stump, allowing space for the wound to drain. The doctor tossed the amputated limb onto a growing pile.

When the light faded, they fetched the lanterns and continued to care for the wounded. Patients, who had waited while doctors cared for the more serious cases, were examined, stitched, and bandaged.

Blake tapped her on the shoulder. "You're done."

She looked around. "Where's Jess?"

"At the wagon. Sleeping."

She found a bucket of clean water used for rinsing the blood off the operating table and washed her face and hands. She removed the bloody apron she had worn all day and followed Blake outside. Moans and cries echoed from the butchered cornfield. "Are there more wounded?"

He didn't stop. "We can't help them."

"Why not?"

"No one has called a truce," Blake said. "If we go into the cornfield, we risk being shot. Let's sleep for a few hours, and help in the morning."

Jess was asleep in the bed of the wagon, a half-eaten sandwich in her hand. Cole grabbed it and took a bite. Her stomach convulsed. She hadn't eaten all day. Her throat was dry, and she gagged on the food. Blake searched the basket Jem had packed and handed her a jar of tea. She tipped her head back and drank. He grabbed a sandwich and gobbled it in three bites. He finished off her tea and hoisted a stretcher across the wagon walls.

"That has blood on it."

"All of them do." Blake climbed into the cot. "Good night."

Cole closed the basket and put her hat on top. She had worn it all day to maintain her disguise. Her hair was wet. She unbuttoned her coat but left it on. They had given away all their blankets. She settled on the floorboards of the wagon next to Jess and fell asleep.

Chapter Twenty-Nine

Cole stirred. Something was wrong. She had become so accustomed to the noise of the battle, the quiet was abnormal. She bolted.

Blake was standing at the end of the wagon, sipping coffee, the familiar aroma floating on the morning air. "The quiet woke me, too. It's unnerving after yesterday."

Jess stirred, and they ate some biscuits with honey and split an apple for breakfast. They could hear the moans and groans of men trapped in the cornfield. "We have to do something."

Blake pointed at a couple of soldiers carrying a stretcher. "Truce or no truce, they're bringing them out."

Jess and Cole couldn't carry a man, even on a stretcher. "What can we do?"

"Grab some buckets and dippers. I found a well on the farm."

They worked their way along the north edge of the cornfield. When they reached Hagerstown Pike, the traumatized men were lined up on each side waiting to be transported to a hospital. A constant stream of ambulances and wagons transported the wounded from the battlefield, leaving a bloody trail dripping between the spaces in the floorboards onto the road.

Dunker Church was a surgery site, and men lay

outside its white walls. Cole and Jess didn't need instructions. Soldiers with shattered limbs were placed closest to the church, waiting for their turn to have the mangled limb amputated. Those who had already suffered the surgeon's knife lay near the road, waiting to be transported. The men with head, chest, or abdominal wounds were grouped in the shade, given water and comfort as they waited for death.

If they were conscious or someone knew the wounded, Jess wrote his name, his regiment, and home state on a card and pinned it to his undershirt. No one wanted to die and be buried in an unmarked grave.

Blake wore a carrying yoke with a bucket of water on each side. Cole would offer a drink from a ladle and then wet the man's handkerchief if he had one to clean his blackened face. She carried what remained of her bandages in a bag over her shoulder with needles, thread, and a few of Jem's surgical instruments. She did what she could, but most of the medical care would have to wait.

She found a kepi on the road. A bugle with a seven marked the infantry regiment. She looked around. Sid was stretched upon the grass. Was he dead? "Sid!"

His eyes fluttered open. He raised his hand, blackened from gunpowder, to block the sun. "Miss Jenny?"

"No, Miss Colleen," she whispered as she knelt beside him. "But you better call me Cole." She held the ladle. He drank it dry. She poured water on his kerchief and wiped his face. Blood covered his boot and pant leg. A torn piece of blue cloth tied below his knee was soaked. "You were hit."

"Nearly every man in the regiment was hit."

Cole searched her boot for her knife. She cut along the seam and ripped the frayed fabric to the kerchief. She didn't dare remove his boot. His foot would probably come with it. Little remained to hold it to his shin. "You need a surgeon."

"I stopped the bleeding. I can wait a bit for the sawbones to do their work," Sid said. "I guess this is the end of the war for me."

Blake knelt beside Cole, removing his yoke and buckets. "What happened, Sid?"

His hands searched his eyes. "I lost my glasses."

"We'll try to find them," Blake reassured him.

He waved toward the broken cornstalks across the dirt road.

"Don't need them to see the men. We were in the cornfield. What fool thinks cornstalks can stop bullets? They fired before we had a chance to aim our guns. Men screamed like butchered animals. I never saw so many bodies in one place." He jerked at the sound of a gun. "Has the battle started again?"

"No. That was probably a mercy shot," Blake said. "A horse...or something."

Sid grabbed Blake's sleeve. "Did we win? Did Lee surrender?"

"Nobody won this fight." Blake choked back a sob.

"McClellan waited too long. He didn't think Jackson could make it from Harpers Ferry. But we knew better." Sid coughed.

Cole offered him another drink.

"Jackson moves his men like lightning in a storm. And we've fought them enough not to underestimate them." Sid leaned against the slope behind him. "They don't run from a fight unless Jackson orders them to run. And when they charge with that Rebel yell, you start praying."

Cole glanced around. "What do you think Lee will do now?"

"I wish I knew. He's coming off victories at the Seven Days Battle and Bull Run. He can smell victory. We have to stop him from marching to Washington City."

"I think you did," Blake reassured him.

"I don't see how." Sid swiped at a stray tear. "We have arrogant fools for generals."

"What do you mean?"

"After you left camp, we were ordered to march north to a farm on the other side of Antietam Creek. We spent the night there and formed our columns about eight a.m. beyond the woods along Smoketown Road."

Cole bandaged what remained of his leg. The makeshift tourniquet had cut off the blood flow to the lower part. The flesh below it had turned black.

"The Seventh Ohio was in Brigadier General George Greene's Division under the Twelfth Army Corps commanded by Major General Joseph Mansfield," Sid explained. "Only he didn't last long. Inexperienced fool was shot before we were even in position."

"Mansfield was listed among the dead," Blake agreed. "The list is long."

"We remained in reserve for the First and Sixth Corps. The worst fighting I've ever seen happened between Brigadier General John Gibbons Wisconsin boys and Brigadier General John Hoods Texas troops. The Wisconsin boys lay down on the ground at the edge of the cornfield and waited until they could see the

Texas boys among the stalks. I don't think there was a Texan standing, and the shooting didn't last longer than half an hour. We had to march over those Texas boys. They were lined up on the ground like they were in formation."

Sid pointed toward the church. "We drove Jackson's men back from Smoketown Road across Hagerstown Pike to the woods near Dunker Church. We took position behind the ridge opposite the church and filled our ammunition pouches. The batteries kept Jackson's boys pinned down, and we stuffed our ears to keep from going deaf from the cannon noise."

Sid wiped his brow. "Around ten-thirty we crossed Hagerstown Turnpike and entered the woods near the church. We waited there until noon before retiring to the woods where we had started. Bloody circle." Sid shook his head.

"Was the fighting over for you?"

"Hardly. The generals don't attack all at once. No, they send in small groups to be slaughtered. Then they send in the reserves to fight. When we entered the cornfield, we stepped over the bodies of the First and Sixth Corps. Mr. Miller can forget harvesting that corn."

Cole stared at the corn. Most of it was broken, sheared off by lead balls, the rest trampled by soldiers' feet. The ground was stained with blood, the smell of rotting corpses attracting crows and other scavengers.

"Sumner's Second Corps attacked Lee's flank across the cornfield and into the woods past the church. That was a mistake. They had no way out, and the Rebels opened fire on them. More than two thousand wounded or dead in under half an hour. Revenge for the

Texans, I guess. I was hit in the cornfield." He looked across the street. "Jake was farther down the line."

Cole looked around. "Where is Jake?"

"Someone dragged me out this morning." He looked around. "Jake ought to be here."

Blake stood. "Stay with Sid."

He headed for the cornfield. Cole ignored Blake's order, grabbed her bag, and followed. She gagged from the smell of rotting flesh, bodies black and bloated from the hot sun. Black powder coated everything on the battlefield, its acrid smell stirred into the air by their footsteps. Blake covered his lower face with a kerchief. Cole did the same. They walked along the rows of dead, searching for the men in the Seventh Ohio.

Red hair, matching her own, beckoned for a closer look. It was Jake. Bits of cornstalk stuck to his blue jacket and light blue trousers.

Cole knelt beside his body. She dampened a kerchief with water from a canteen she had confiscated and gently wiped his face clean, removing the gunpowder from his lips where he had bitten the tops off his cartridges to load his gun. She washed his hands. He had big hands, strong from working the canal, calloused from the ropes he wrapped around the snubbing posts to halt the *Irish Rose* in the locks. His jacket was torn in the shoulder. She discovered a hole in the jacket, and blood stained his white shirt beneath. Another hole was lower. One shot had not been enough to kill Jake Donovan. Her tears splattered on his coat, scattering the dusts and leaving marks of purity on the war ravished surface.

Cole looked at Blake, kneeling on the other side. He swiped his hand across his eyes, tears blinding him to her scrutiny. He had loved Jake, too. In the short time they had known each other, they had bonded like real brothers.

"I want to send his body home."

Blake choked on his words. "I'll fetch a stretcher."

Cole stayed with Jake. He couldn't be dead. Jake was full of life. His future had yet to be written. It included a wife and children. "I love you, Jake Donovan." She kissed her fingertips and placed them on his lips for a final farewell.

****

Lee took what remained of his troops to Virginia, and the North gave a long sigh of relief. As the dead and wounded were tallied, correspondents were calling Antietam the bloodiest day of the war with more than twelve thousand victims of the carnage estimated on each side.

Blake found a coffin for Jake's body. One of the doctors drained his blood and replaced it with formaldehyde to preserve him for the journey home. General Greene signed the paperwork to ship the coffin by train.

Most of the wounded were transported to Frederick. Cole, Jess, and Blake took Sid there after the surgeon amputated his foot. Cole had stitched the flap, and Jess had bandaged the stump. Some victims were taken to the Steiner Building at Church and Market streets. The women in town ministered to the injured. Those who could travel were sent to Washington City.

The Twenty-ninth Ohio was stationed at Frederick after the railroad bridge was repaired. The reunion was somber with the news of Jake's death and Sid's injury. After searching through the unclaimed haversacks piled before the battle, Cole had found Sid's spare spectacles. She handed him his bag and clutched Jake's. Inside was a letter he had begun.

"Dearest Colleen, Blake and I have talked hours about his joining the army. He is determined to carry on the fight. He loves you enough to spare you any pain, but happiness is never guaranteed. We must grab the bits and pieces life offers. Live every day as if it were your last. No regrets. No grudges. No words left unspoken. I know you have the courage to love him."

****

The journey to Washington City was silent, mostly because of utter exhaustion. They had worked non-stop for three days tending the wounded. Some of the women in Frederick had packed their basket with food for the journey home. Jem had been right about it being special.

They followed the well-worn path of the ambulances and supply wagons along the fifteen miles to the capital.

Cole rode beside Blake while Jess slept in the back. He turned south on the route along Lee's plantation to Long Bridge. It was Saturday, September 20, and the bridge was crowded with soldiers and civilians heading into town for a night of enjoyment.

Life had gone on while they had seen thousands die. They had been wearing the same clothes for nearly a week. Clothes stained with blood, and the smell of gunpowder, sweat, and death lingered in the fabric.

Blake stopped at the Mermaid's Mirth. Cole, who had been resting against his side, stretched, and looked around. "Don't you want to take us on to Pierce House first?" She longed for a hot bath to soak the grime and dirt of war from her body. The memories of what she had seen would never disappear.

Blake surveyed the dark hotel. "Something is wrong." He jumped to the ground and handed her the reins. "Stay here. I won't be long."

The sun was low in the sky behind them and cast long shadows across the lawn. Cole removed her hat and ran her fingers through her damp, dirty hair. She moved the horses forward to a stone trough along the road and let them drink. She tapped her foot on the floor boards.

Jess stirred and leaned over the back of the driver's seat. "Where are we?"

"Mermaid's Mirth. I don't know what is taking Blake so long. I should tell him we'll walk home."

"I wouldn't mind getting out of this wagon." Jess stretched and climbed over the bench seat and jumped to the ground. "What happened to your sign?"

The Mermaid's Mirth sign was broken, the splintered parts scattered below the post. It wasn't the only item disturbed. The barn doors were open, and a chair was overturned on the porch. No one, not even Blake, had lit any lamps in the front of the hotel. "Something *is* wrong." She grabbed the haversack from the wagon bed behind her and retrieved Jake's revolver. "Did you return Ed's gun?"

"He told me to keep it."

"Loaded?"

"I need to add percussion caps."

Cole added the caps to the cylinder of her gun, and Jess did the same.

"Who would want to cause trouble here?" Jess whispered.

"I don't know, but Blake should have been out by now. Let's peek in the window."

Jess and Cole creeped across the yard, heading for the dark side of the hotel, away from the setting sun. The parlor windows were long and narrow with sheer draperies, allowing the fading light to illuminate the interior. She raised her palm to Jess, a signal to stop they had learned from the boys. The place had been torn apart. Furniture was overturned. The sofa cushions were cut and stuffing tossed aside. Dirt, tobacco juice, and food scraps stained the rugs and wooden floors.

"Where's Blake?" Cole tiptoed to the next window. Blake's meticulously organized office had been ransacked. The drawers had been emptied from his desk and turned upside down or broken apart. Piles of discarded papers littered the floor.

A light glowed in the hallway, and a man entered the office. Cole pressed against the building away from the window, her fist stuck in her mouth to silence a scream. She had recognized the scarred face of Clyde Cassell. Had he seen her? She signaled to Jess to stay close to the building. The light faded, and she dared a look. He was gone.

Jess crawled below the window and joined Cole. "Who was it?"

"Clyde Cassell." Cole released her breath. "Buck must be here, too. They always travel together."

"I know the Cassell brothers are short on brains, but what are they doing in Washington City?"

"They followed Blake to Ohio for his gold. Washington City is a short trip from Southern territory."

"I thought he spent his money on the inn in Ohio."

"The Cassell brothers don't know that."

"Where do they have Blake?"

Cole shook her head and moved to the back of the hotel. A light glowed from inside through the windows, spreading a yellow pattern of squares on the lawn.

"If we look in the window, they might see us."

Cole pointed to the outhouse. They stayed in the shadows and hid behind it. From the distance they viewed the drama in the kitchen. Clyde entered the door from the hallway. Blake was tied to a chair, and Buck screamed in his face, "Where's the gold, Ellsworth?"

"Gone. I spent it."

Buck smacked Blake in the face, and blood spurted from his mouth.

Cole cringed. "We need to save him."

"Do you have a plan?"

"I never have a plan. Why should this time be any different from before?"

Jess looked toward the road. "I could fetch help."

"They could kill Blake by then."

"We could shoot them from here."

"If we miss, Blake is dead." Cole stared at the three figures gathered around the kitchen table. "We need a distraction. Something to separate them from Blake." Cole pinched her nose. The stench from the outhouse was strong, triggering a memory. "Remember the old man who kicked your dog, Blue?"

"I remember. We put a sack of Blue's dung on his porch and lit it on fire. He stomped on the flames and dirtied his big bad boots."

"There's plenty of manure in the street if Romulus and Remus haven't provided any fresh stuff."

"I saw a burlap sack in the back of the wagon."

Cole handed her a tin of wooden matches. "Light it, knock on the door, and join me here."

Chapter Thirty

Cole watched and waited for Jess to create the distraction. Every blow Buck delivered tested her patience. She inched closer to the kitchen and heard Jess pound on the front door.

"I'll git rid of 'em," Buck growled as he left the room.

Jess joined her, and they pressed their bodies against the wall of the hotel. "I told a man on the street to fetch the police."

"We can't wait," Cole whispered.

Clyde had stayed with Blake, but Buck's curses at the front door drew him away. "What's wrong, brother?"

Cole bolted through the kitchen door and cut the ropes holding Blake prisoner. Jess stood by the hall doorway, watching for the Cassell brothers to return. "Hurry."

Cole removed the final ropes, but Blake was unconscious. She called his name, but he didn't respond. His eye was swollen, and blood dribbled from his lip. She grabbed his arms to carry him, but he fell with a thud against the floor. Jess joined her, and they dragged him a few feet, but he was too heavy for them to carry to safety. Jess tiptoed to the far side of the opening to the hall. "They're returning," she whispered.

Cole joined Jess on the other side of the doorway.

Voices filtered from the front of the hotel.

"It had to be some brats playin' a prank," Clyde said.

"I got shit all over my boot," Buck replied. "I'll kill those dirty ruffians if I catch them."

"We got to git out of town," Clyde said. "Once it's dark, the sentries will start shootin'."

"Not without our gold," Buck said.

"You better hope he wakes up soon," Clyde said. "You shouldn't have hit him so hard."

"He's a tough one to kill. Lucky we found out he was alive and livin' here."

"Maybe he's tellin' the truth about spendin' it all," Clyde said. "We didn't find no gold here."

"He's a lyin' Yankee. He's got money hid somewhere." The heavy thud of their boots stopped.

Clyde's voice was a hoarse whisper. "What's wrong, brother?"

"He ain't sittin' at the table no more."

"But he was out cold." Clyde raised his voice. "Ellsworth, you in there?" The click of a revolver echoed in the hallway. Cole and Jess cocked their guns.

"He didn't have no gun," Buck said. Shots rang out, shattering the glass in the window behind them. Both girls fired blindly into the hallway, staying behind the thick log wall that separated the kitchen from the main building.

The Cassell brothers crashed into Blake's office. "I've been hit, brother."

Cole glanced into the empty hallway and examined her gun. "Two left."

Jess nodded. "I have three shots left."

"Throw your guns and knives toward the kitchen

and surrender!" Cole shouted in her deepest voice.

"You'll have to kill us first," Buck replied. Glass shattered from their hideout.

"They're trying to escape." Cole ran out the door and shot through the office window. From inside, the Cassell brothers cursed.

From the road, a shrill whistle disturbed the calm of dusk. The gunfight had attracted the authorities. "The police are here," Cole shouted across the yard. "Surrender!" She hid her gun in her jacket pocket and waved at the two policemen responding to the gunshots. "Two Confederate spies took Mr. Ellsworth prisoner," she told them. "They're pinned down in that room."

The older policeman ordered the younger one to watch the window while he followed Cole to the kitchen.

Blake had regained consciousness and was seated on the floor.

"I'm Sergeant Horace Van Dyke. What's going on?"

Blake touched the back of his head and winced. "The Cassell brothers clobbered me as soon as I stepped inside."

Van Dyke looked at Cole. "You said they were Southern spies?"

"Deserters," Blake added. "Bad men no matter what you call them."

"This is the police," Van Dyke shouted down the hallway. "Raise your hands over your head and walk toward me."

"We've been shot," Buck argued.

"Then crawl!" Blake shouted. "Like the snakes you are."

Buck appeared in the hall. "Don't shoot." He limped toward them, his arms bent over his shoulders, his hands hidden behind his back.

"Where's Clyde?" Cole demanded, withdrawing Jake's revolver from her pocket.

"He's hurt bad," Buck said. "He ain't goin' to make it."

"They're beat." Van Dye pointed at Cole's gun. "You won't need that."

"You can't trust them, sir."

Van Dyke moved into the hallway opening. "You're limping. Do you need help?"

"Yah." Buck staggered.

Cole looked at Jess on the opposite side of the doorway. "I don't like this."

Jess nodded. "That old limp is from me back in June."

Buck paused, turned his head, and shouted, "Git!"

It was a signal to Clyde. Glass and wood broke as Clyde jumped through the damaged window. The other police officer outside shouted, "He's escaping!" and fired two shots.

Van Dyke pointed his revolver at Buck. "Surrender."

Buck flung his arm forward and threw his Bowie knife. Van Dyke stumbled back into the kitchen, the hilt protruding from his chest. His gun fell to the floor. Cole fired the remaining shot in her gun while Jess emptied hers.

Outside police were shouting and firing their guns. Van Dyke was leaning against the table, his hand on the hilt of Buck's knife.

"Don't remove it." Cole helped him to sit in a

chair. She grabbed a towel and pressed it next to the blade. "Yell."

"What?" He hollered when she withdrew the knife and slapped the towel over the wound.

"Hold that in place."

Jess kept her empty gun pointed at Buck, who was seated on the floor, his back against the blood splattered wall. He reached for the pistol in his holster.

Cole grabbed Van Dyke's revolver and clicked the hammer. "Give it up, Buck."

"It's empty." His hand slumped to the floor, his breathing strained with exertion. He blinked his eyes. "How do you know me?"

Dressed as men, he hadn't recognized them as the Beecher sisters. "Everyone knows the Cassell brothers," Cole lied. "You're famous."

He grinned, revealing several empty spaces among black gums. He spat some tobacco juice across the hall, decorating the wall with brown slime. "Damn straight."

The young policeman entered the kitchen. He stared at Van Dyke. "What happened?"

"Flesh wound. Better fetch an ambulance for this one." He pointed toward Buck.

"No need." Buck removed his hand from his belly. It was covered in blood, and his coat was soaked. "Gut shot is a death sentence." He banged his head against the wall. "What happened to my brother?"

"Wounded, but he got away."

Buck laughed. "Run, brother, run!" His head fell to his chest and a final breath escaped his parted lips. The young policeman rushed to Buck before anyone could warn him to be careful, but Buck was dead.

"Gather some men and find the one that escaped,"

Van Dyke ordered. "Send a physician here."

"Yes, sir." The young policeman left. Cole changed Van Dyke's towel. The bleeding had slowed. Buck's blade had missed any vital organs.

"Do you know what you're doing?" he asked.

"We came from Antietam. I'm no doctor, but you'll live."

"Antietam? That explains the blood on your clothes."

She didn't bother to hide the bitterness in her voice. "We waded in it."

He raised his hand to his brow. "I'm a little lightheaded."

Blake stood on unsteady legs. "I'll ask Thomas to prepare a bed for you."

"Thomas!" Cole pushed Blake into a chair. "We'll find him."

Cole and Jess lit several lanterns and opened every door, searching for the manager of the Mermaid's Mist.

Cole opened the door to the closet beneath the stairs. A gagged and tied Thomas fell to the floor. "He's here!"

Jess cut the ropes while Cole untied the gag. His face was badly bruised. They helped him to the kitchen. He paused at the body of Buck. "That was one of the men who beat me."

Cole made him sit next to the other two injured men. She fetched water in a pitcher and dampened a towel for Thomas and another for Blake.

Thomas asked for a drink of water. "They asked when you'd be returning, Mr. Ellsworth. I told them you were due any time. Then they told the remaining guests they had to leave to make room for the wounded arriving from the battlefield. I sent Amber and her girls home, and then they beat me. They wanted to know where your gold was hid. I told them I didn't know about any gold. They made me open the safe, and then they tied me up in the closet."

"When was this?"

"About noon. I could hear them throwing furniture and shouting obscenities."

"They did a lot of damage in a few hours but nothing that can't be repaired. I hope you don't quit because of the Cassell brothers."

"I won't let vermin like them scare me off."

A string of curse words could be heard from the front door.

Cole looked at Jess. "I hope that isn't the doctor."

A loud knock echoed down the hall. "The police said a doctor was needed here. It better not be a hoax."

"What is he so mad about?" Blake stood.

"I can go," Cole volunteered.

"I'm finding my bearings." Blake kicked Buck's boot as he passed. "Just to be sure," he explained.

Blake opened the front door where the doctor was wiping his shoes in the stiff brush for guests to clean their footwear. "What's that smell?"

"A horse left a fresh pile of manure in front of your door," the doctor said. "Are you the patient?"

"No, a policeman in the back. Careful you don't slip on the blood in the hall."

Blake grabbed the back of Cole's coat as she turned to follow the doctor and yanked her back to the doorway. He pointed to the porch. "What are horse droppings doing on my porch?"

"Jess lit a sack of it on fire to lure Clyde and Buck

away from the kitchen so we could rescue you," Cole said.

"Don't you girls ever think about acting scared and defenseless?"

"Why?"

He poked his finger through a bullet hole in her coat. "Here's one reason."

****

Blake halted the team in front of Pierce House. He helped them down, handed over the bags and basket, and followed them inside.

"You're back!" Jem hugged each of them before she realized they were filthy. "You look like you've been…"

"Through a war," Cole finished.

"I'll fix something to eat."

"We have to tell you something first." Cole didn't know how to soften the news. "Jake is dead."

Jem froze in her path to the kitchen. Logan caught her before she collapsed to the floor. He helped her to a dining room chair. She ran her fingers along the table's smooth surface. "He was seated at this table a couple months ago, eating pie and laughing about the baseball game."

"Sid lost his foot," Cole added. "But he's alive."

"Sid has been such a dear friend." She grabbed Logan's hand.

"I'll see about having him transferred to the Mermaid's Mirth," Blake said. "After I clean the place."

"What's wrong with it?"

"Trouble with Buck and Clyde Cassell," Blake said before Cole could stop him.

"Buck was killed but Clyde escaped," she added. "He's hurting. The policemen found a blood trail."

"I'll check the doors and window," Logan said, leaving them.

Jem reached her hand toward Jess. "What about Ed?"

"The Twenty-ninth Ohio wasn't in the battle. They were guarding the supplies."

"At least Ed was spared," Jem said.

"We sent Jake's body home."

"Then we'll need to return home for the funeral."

"We'll all go," Blake said.

Chapter Thirty-One

The First Congregational Church stood on the north side of Darrow Falls square. The whitewashed wooden building had double oak doors. The bell tower was nearly four stories high, the tallest structure in town. Blake studied the church architecture, glancing toward the lone figure in the cemetery next door.

Jake Donovan's funeral had been two days ago in this church. So many people had attended, the doors had been left open, and the crowd overflowed to the square. The family had sat in the front pews. Cole had taken his hand and asked him to sit beside her. She had been quiet, calm in public, going through the motions of serving food, nodding when someone mentioned how much Jake would be missed, and receiving condolences with a tear-stained handkerchief.

Her grandfather had held an Irish wake with guests telling stories about Jake, recalling his daring deeds, humorous pranks, and tender memories that eased the ache of his death. Cole had stolen away from the family to visit Jake's grave. Blake had allowed her some privacy, but she glanced toward him and signaled him to join her. The dead leaves crunched beneath his boots. Dead flowers decorated the dirt covering the grave, and a headstone had been added with the inscription, *Jacob Michael Donovan, born 1841, died 1862*. Cole's ginger hair was a stark contrast to her black mourning clothes.

She had added fresh flowers to the others covering the grave.

Her face was tear-streaked, her handkerchief crushed in her fist. He stood beside her, and she leaned into his strength, her head resting against his broad shoulder. "I miss him."

"So do I." Blake had maintained his composure through the funeral service, but Jake's grave was a stark reminder of their loss. A sob caught in his throat.

"You loved him, too."

"Jake gathered friends with open arms. Everyone liked him. But more, they admired him and wanted to be like him. He was more than a soldier. He was an example of life. I can't believe he's gone."

"I know soldiers talk about fate, and there's no rhyme or reason for why one man survives and another perishes," Cole said. "I keep reading the words Jake wrote before the battle. He said I should live life to its fullest. No regrets."

"I agree." Blake offered his arm and escorted her to the lone buggy on the square. He helped her board and took the reins.

On the seat was the local newspaper. "Have you read the Emancipation Proclamation?"

"Everyone has been talking about it." She placed the folded paper in her lap. "It's a nice sentiment, but it only sets slaves free in states belonging to the Confederacy. Maryland, Delaware, Missouri, and Kentucky can keep their slaves."

"I talked at length about it with your father and brothers-in-law. West Virginia has the same dilemma. If slaves are set free in the border states, the Confederacy would invade to retrieve their runaways."

Blake headed down River Road to the Beecher farm. "Tyler has the papers for you to manage my properties. He'll handle any legal issues. Thomas Hill will help you with the Mermaid's Mirth, and Vincent Grey has been running the Dutchman since I was a boy. Most of your work will be at the Pirate's Cove in Ohio."

"When did you receive your commission?"

He had kept the news secret to spare her further anguish, but she was a clever girl. "It was in the mail scattered on the floor by the Cassell brothers." He took her hand. "I didn't want to burden you so soon after Jake's death."

"When do you report?"

"In three weeks." He turned to her. "I want you to know my reasons."

"The adventure, comradery, challenge," she listed.

"Those were a boy's reasons. I didn't want to miss out on the war."

"But you've seen the misery, the wounded, and the dead. How can you want to fight?"

"I can't lie and say I'm not scared, but this war is important." He pointed to the newspaper. "The Emancipation Proclamation gives me the best reason for fighting."

"How?"

"Every state in the Confederacy we invade, every victory from now on will free the slaves. The goal isn't to kill the enemy, it's to force a retreat and remove the shackles from his property."

"I feel ashamed for being an abolitionist and not encouraging you," Cole said. "Will the freed slaves recognize the sacrifice so many men are making to right a wrong our forefathers ignored for too long?"

"Free blacks want to fight. They know freedom, equality, and democracy can't be given to someone like a gift. You have to want it enough to sacrifice everything you hold dear."

"I know you've always wanted to be part of the fight. No responsibilities." Cole bowed her head but a sob escaped her lips.

"I never realized how lonely no responsibilities would be." He stopped the buggy and lifted her chin with his fingertips. "I want someone to write, worry, and wait for my return. And if necessary, cry over my grave."

She stared at him, tears visible on her cheeks. "And you have to hope enough for life to take chances. Do you love me?"

"More than anything."

"Then marry me."

He turned away. "What if I'm killed? Or maimed? I don't want you to have to play nurse to me for the rest of my life."

"How dare you insult me!" She hit his arm. "Should I only marry a man who is wealthy and promises to live a long life? Am I so shallow I would abandon you if disfigured? I'll turn the Mermaid's Mirth into a home for veterans if necessary."

"You're young and beautiful. Why not wait until the end of the war?" He took her hands in his. "I don't want you to regret your decision."

"I'm not afraid." Her voice didn't waver. "I survived Jake's death. I survived Antietam. I'm no weeping maiden who crumbles at bad news. If you die, I'll weep, but I won't be destroyed. Haven't I proven that by now?"

"You're the strongest woman I know and the bravest." He pulled her into his arms. "You're right. I have three weeks, and I don't want to waste them afraid something could happen."

Cole put her hand against his chest. "You have to say it to make it real."

It took him a minute to figure out what she wanted. "I love you." His mouth crushed hers. He could taste the hunger on her lips as she nipped and plundered, matching his desire, building until they gasped for breath. "Will you marry me?"

****

Blake Loren Ellsworth married Colleen Josephine Beecher in the First Congregational Church in Darrow Falls. They had spent the afternoon accepting congratulations at her parents' home and had dined with family and close friends. Then he had driven her to CJ's Inn in Peninsula where they would spend their first night together.

Blake paced the parlor floor, glancing at the ceiling. He had given his bride an hour to prepare for their wedding night, so why did he hesitate? How much did she expect of him? One advantage of marrying a virgin was her ignorance of the pleasure she was entitled to from lovemaking. Yet, he didn't want to disappoint her. Would he have enough self-control to meet her needs? He would soon find out. He bolted up the steps and knocked on her bedroom door. No answer. He turned the knob and entered. Her wedding dress and veil were draped over a chair. He turned to the bed. It was empty. Where was his bride?

A note was on the bed. He read it with trembling

fingers. Had she changed her mind and jilted him? Was this revenge for all the men who had hurt her?

Come to the Irish Rose.

He brushed the window curtains aside. From the second floor he could see the *Irish Rose* docked below, a light on its stern cabin deck as the sun cast its final rays on the still waters of the canal. He hurried to his destination, his mind racing to make sense of her words.

The *Irish Rose* was docked apart from the other boats and appeared abandoned. He climbed aboard and opened the stern door. A voice greeted him as he descended to the cabin.

"I was beginning to think you had left to join your men and forgotten you had a wife." She ran her fingers along the blue fabric of the officer's coat she had made him. "First Lieutenant Blake Ellsworth."

He barely noticed the uniform. Cole wore a nightgown and nothing more, apparent by the sheerness of the fabric. Her hair was undone, cascading in a fiery wave down her back with a thick lock draped over one breast like a familiar mermaid. The only jewelry she wore was the gold band he had placed on her left hand when he vowed to love her as his wife.

The captain's bunk had new bedding and a quilt. "You didn't like the room at your grandmother's inn?"

"When we first met, you asked me to join you in this bed." She patted the coverlet. "I wasn't nice, and I want to make amends." Her voice was silky and seductive.

Blake grabbed the ladder for support. If he made it through the night, there wouldn't be much left for the army to claim. "I've seen that look on your face before.

Tobias painted it, but I don't know what it means."

"I found my portrait beside your bed, and I knew no matter how much you denied it, you loved me. That look is a woman in love."

"You fell in love with me because I bought your portrait?"

"No." A soft smile played upon her lips. "My heart softened when you told the soldiers Jess and I could play baseball."

Her words stopped his advance. "What? That wasn't romantic, brat."

She moved around him, a dream in white, just out of arms' reach. "It was chivalrous. You defended our right to play against the wishes of the men. Even Jake didn't do that." She laid her hand on his chest, his heart pounding beneath her fingertips. "You respected me."

"I hope you feel the same way when Tobias makes a new sign for the Mermaid's Mirth."

She frowned. "Does it have a seashell?"

"Painted on." His hand caressed the curve of her hip, paused at her waist, and cupped her breast, his thumb brushing against a stiff peak. "From now on I'm the only man who's going to know what's behind the shell."

Her blue-green eyes danced with mischief. "Is that all you want to know?"

He laughed, pulling her close against his chest. His hands roamed her body over the flimsy garment. It provided minimal modesty for her innocence. So many curves to explore. Where did he begin? He didn't want to rush his lovemaking, but her near nakedness was testing his self-control.

She rubbed against him, her hands unfastening the

buttons on his coat. "Are you going to take your clothes off?" She tugged on the sleeve of his coat.

"All my attention is on you for now and forever." He kissed her and her response was urgent, matching his own.

She pulled his coat free and began to unbutton his vest. "I want to see you naked."

He discarded the vest and slipped off the suspenders. "I thought you peeked."

She laughed with a coyness that rushed his blood to his lower regions. "I did, but it was dark."

He chuckled and tossed his shirt on top of the pile cluttering the bottom bunk. His trousers hung low on his hips. "I may have a surprise for you."

Cole traced the ribbon of black hair on his chest, pausing above the waistband of his pants. His hand covered her. "We should slow down. After all, you've never been with a man."

"My sisters prepared me." She slid the top button through the opening of his fly. "They even made drawings, but I want to see the real thing."

Drawings? "What did they tell you?"

She paused in her task, her fingertips resting in the opening above his throbbing flesh. Was she oblivious to the torture she caused him? "Everything I need to know to make this the best three weeks of your life. You're going to regret leaving me."

Should he tell her tonight or wait until morning? "Who said I'm leaving you?"

"You're in the army. You have to report for duty."

"And you're an officer's wife."

She struggled with the second button. "Why does that make a difference?"

351

"I'll be spending the winter in Frederick, Maryland. Do you want me to be cold and lonely?"

She paused. "You're taking me with you?"

"I'll send for you once I have a place for you and Jess."

"Jess?"

"I can't break up a team. Besides, she'll want to visit Ed, and you can be her chaperone for a change."

"You are the most wonderful husband in all the world." She kissed his face, leaving a trail from ear to lips, where she lingered. "I can't wait to tell Jess everything I learn tonight."

He lifted her in his arms and kicked off his trousers. "Brat, there are secrets between a husband and wife they don't share."

She wrapped her arms around his neck. "Is there something my sisters didn't tell me about?"

He lowered her to the bed and slipped in beside her. "Let's find out."

A word about the author...

Laura Freeman has been a reporter for the past eleven years and covers the historic town of Hudson, Ohio. She has won the Press Club of Cleveland's Ohio Excellence in Journalism award twice and the Ohio Newspaper Association award several times. Her novel *Impending Love and Lies* is the sequel to *Impending Love and Death* and *Impending Love and War* and takes place in the fictional towns of Darrow Falls and Washington City during 1862, where the Beecher sisters help the local Ohio boys fighting in the war. She lives in Ohio, where she is working on her next book, *Impending Love and Capture*.